The troub... that she ... he removed the cloak she'd given him, his hand brushed against hers. Her lips parted and he wanted to kneel at her feet, goddess as she was.

Callum didn't want her pity. Though his body and voice might be broken, he wouldn't allow her to believe that he was less than a man. His hands threaded with hers, cold skin merging with warm.

He brought her fingers to his ragged cheeks, absorbing the warmth. A few strands of her golden hair slipped from her veil, resting against her throat. And when he brought her hand to his lips she inhaled a gasp.

He released her instantly, expecting her to pull back in disgust. Instead, her eyes were shining with unshed tears, her fingers remaining upon his face.

"I won't forget you," she vowed, pulling her cloak around her shoulders. Then she picked up her skirts and disappeared into the night.

In the shadows, Callum caught a movement and turned his head. The earl was standing there, watching.

And fury burned within his eyes.

* * *

Tempted by the Highland Warrior
Harlequin® Historical #1098—July 2012

Author Note

When I wrote the first book in my MacKinloch Clan series—
Claimed by the Highland Warrior—I was intrigued by the
characters Callum and Marguerite. Their situation reminded
me of the classic tale of Romeo and Juliet. As a broken hero
who cannot speak, Callum worships Marguerite…and yet
he believes he can never win the heart of a duke's daughter.
Marguerite is deeply sympathetic to Callum's plight, but as
she loses her heart to him she has the challenge of standing
up to her father and casting off the duties that bind her.

This book was quite difficult to write, especially since the
hero cannot speak. It presented unique dialogue scenes, but I
tried to give a strong sense of the emotions and words Callum
wanted to convey. I hope you'll enjoy this third book in the
MacKinloch Clan series—if this is the first book you've tried
there are several other connected stories.

Claimed by the Highland Warrior is the first book, which
tells the reunion story of escaped prisoner-of-war Bram and
his childhood sweetheart, Nairna. *Seduced by Her Highland
Warrior* is about the estranged marriage between clan chief
Alex and his wife, Laren, a stained-glass artist. Finally,
Craving the Highlander's Touch is a novella that gives
Lady Alys of Harkirk her own chance at happiness with
Finian MacLachor, a man seeking redemption.

Will Dougal MacKinloch ever get a story of his own? Time
will tell.…

You're welcome to visit my website at
www.michellewillingham.com for excerpts and behind-the-
scenes details about my books. I love to hear from readers,
and you may e-mail me at michelle@michellewillingham.com
or write via P.O. Box 2242, Poquoson, VA 23662, USA.

MICHELLE WILLINGHAM

Tempted *by the* Highland Warrior

HARLEQUIN®
entertain, enrich, inspire™

Recycling programs
for this product may
not exist in your area.

ISBN-13: 978-0-373-29698-9

TEMPTED BY THE HIGHLAND WARRIOR

*Available from Harlequin® Historical and
MICHELLE WILLINGHAM*

Her Irish Warrior #850
The Warrior's Touch #866
Her Warrior King #882
Her Warrior Slave #922
Taming Her Irish Warrior #966
**The Accidental Countess* #981
**The Accidental Princess* #985
Surrender to an Irish Warrior #1010
†*Claimed by the Highland Warrior* #1042
†*Seduced by Her Highland Warrior* #1054
†*Tempted by the Highland Warrior* #1098

Available in Harlequin Historical *Undone!* ebooks

The Viking's Forbidden Love-Slave
The Warrior's Forbidden Virgin
***An Accidental Seduction*
Innocent in the Harem
Pleasured by the Viking
†*Craving the Highlander's Touch*

*The MacEgan Brothers
†The MacKinloch Clan
**Linked by character

**Did you know that these novels are also
available as ebooks? Visit www.Harlequin.com.**

In memory of Rafiq Salim Soufan, with special thoughts for his wife, Fatin, and their children.

Chapter One

Scotland—1305

The sound of a man screaming awakened her from sleep.

Marguerite de Montpierre jerked upright, clutching the coverlet as she stared at her maid Trinette. 'What was that?'

Trinette shook her head, her eyes wide with fear. 'I don't know. But we should stay here, where it's safe.'

Marguerite moved to the tower window, staring outside at the darkened moonlit sky. The man's screams had fallen into silence now. Already, she sensed what that meant.

Stay here, her mind ordered. *Don't interfere.* What could she do, after all? She was only a maid of eight and ten. Both her father and Lord Cairnross would be furious if she went out alone.

But if someone needed help, what right did she have to remain in her chamber? Fear shouldn't overshadow the need for mercy.

'I'm going to find out what it was,' she informed her maid. 'You can stay here if you want.'

'My lady, *non.* Your father would not allow this.'

No, he wouldn't. In her mind, she could imagine her father's commanding voice, ordering her to remain in her bed. She took a breath, feeling torn by indecision. If she remained behind, she would be safe and no one would be angry with her.

And someone could also die. This wasn't about obedience; it was about trying to save a life.

'You're right. The Duc would not allow me to leave. But he's not here, is he?' Marguerite murmured. She prayed her father would return as soon as possible, for with each day he was gone, her life became more of a nightmare.

Guy de Montpierre, the Duc D'Avignois, didn't know what was happening here, for her betrothed husband had behaved with the greatest courtesy toward their family. The Duc was a man who valued wealth and status, and Gilbert de Bouche, the Earl of Cairnross, would provide a strong English alliance. A youngest daughter couldn't hope for a better marriage.

But although the earl had treated her with respect and honour, his cruelty horrified her. He was a man who firmly believed the Scots belonged in servitude. He'd captured several prisoners of war, and she'd observed them building walls of stone for hours on end.

Trinette shivered, looking down at the coverlet. 'I don't think you wish to anger Lord Cairnross by leaving this chamber.'

Marguerite didn't disagree. But the prisoner's cry haunted her, digging into her conscience. She'd seen Cairnross's slaves and the men were so very thin, with hopelessness carved into their faces. Two had already died since her arrival. And she suspected, from the screaming, that another man lay dying.

'I can't stand by and do nothing,' she murmured. Otherwise it made her no better than the earl.

She pulled on a closely-fitted cote with long sleeves, a rose-coloured surcoat, then a dark cloak. Her maid gave a resigned sigh and helped her finish dressing before she donned her own clothing.

It was past midnight, and soldiers were sleeping along the hallways and in the larger chamber of the main wooden tower. Marguerite kept her back to the wall, her heart trembling as she stepped her way past the men. Her father had left half-a-dozen soldiers of his own as her guards; no doubt they would stop her if they awakened.

She left the wooden tower and moved towards the inner bailey. There, she saw the cause of the screaming. A man, perhaps a year older than herself, was lying prostrate upon the ground. Blood covered his back and his ankles were chained together. Long dark hair obscured his face, but she saw his shoulders move. He was still alive…for now.

Marguerite whispered to her maid. 'Bring me water and soft linen cloths. Hurry.' Though she didn't know who the man was, she wouldn't turn her back on his suffering. He needed help, if he was to live through the night.

Trinette obeyed, and after the girl disappeared, Marguerite took tentative steps toward the man. When she reached the man's side, she saw him shudder, as if he were cold. She didn't want to startle him, but whispered quietly in English, 'Would you allow me to tend your wounds?'

The man tensed, his palms pressing into the ground. Slowly, he turned his head and his battered face was swollen and bruised. But the man's dark brown eyes were empty, as if he felt nothing. She knelt down beside him and saw his blood staining the ground.

'I am Marguerite de Montpierre,' she said, switching to Gaelic in the hopes he would understand her. Though she was good with languages and had been learning the language of the Scots for the past year, she worried about her speech. 'What is your name?'

The man studied her, but didn't speak. Pain darkened his expression and he eyed her with disbelief, as though he couldn't understand why she would show pity. A lock of hair hung down over his eyes and she reached for it, moving out of his face.

It was meant to help him see better, but the moment she touched him, his hand captured hers. Though his palm was cold, he held her hand as though it were a delicate butterfly.

The gentle touch startled her. Marguerite's first instinct was to pull her hand back, but something held her in place. When she looked past his injuries, the planes of his face were strong, with the resilience of a man who had visited hell and survived it.

She waited again for him to speak, but he held his silence and released her palm. It made her wonder if Lord Cairnross had ordered the prisoner's tongue cut out. She lowered her gaze, afraid to ask.

When Trinette brought the wooden bowl of water and linen, Marguerite saw the man's shoulders tighten with distrust. 'Stay back,' she whispered to her maid, 'and call out if anyone approaches.'

Marguerite dipped the first cloth into the water and wrung it out. Gently, she laid it upon the prisoner's bloody back and he expelled a gasp when she touched it. 'Forgive me. I've no wish to harm you.'

Though his mouth clenched at her touch, he made no move to push her away. Marguerite tried to wipe away the blood and dirt, hoping the cool water would soothe him. She'd never tended wounds such as these, for her father did not allow her near the soldiers when they were injured.

The sight of his blood bothered her, but she forced away her anxiety. This man needed her. As she cleaned his wounds, she kept her touch light, knowing how it must hurt. The whip lash had gouged his skin, leaving harsh ridges that would form scars.

'Why did he do this to you?' she asked, soaking the cloth again. She moistened his cheek with the cool cloth and he touched his mouth and throat, shaking his head as if to tell her he couldn't speak.

'It was you who cried out in pain earlier, wasn't it?'

The man shook his head. Then he stretched out his arm and pointed into the darkness.

And Marguerite saw the motionless body of a prisoner with sightless eyes.

Every bone in Callum MacKinloch's body ached, his limbs raging with pain. He couldn't move if he'd wanted to. The English soldiers had beaten him bloody, then continued with twenty more lashes.

They hadn't killed him yet, but they would. It had become a test of endurance. Although his body was weak and broken, his mind had transformed into an iron band of strength. He hadn't cried out in pain, for he'd lost the ability to speak, almost a year ago. After all the nightmares he'd witnessed, he supposed it wasn't surprising.

Another wet cloth covered the lash wounds and he shuddered. This woman had offered him compassion when no one else would. Why? She was betrothed to the earl, a noblewoman who shouldn't have left the sanctuary of the keep. From his peripheral vision, he caught glimpses of her. Her rose gown accentuated her slim form, and, as she leaned forward, long strands of golden hair hung from beneath her veil.

Callum didn't deserve her sympathy. He'd been locked away for the past seven years, ever since he was a boy. His father had died in the raid and he'd been taken captive, along with his older brother Bram.

He lowered his face to the ground, wondering if Bram had escaped after all. It had been a while since he'd left and though his brother had sworn he would return to free him, Callum didn't believe it. How could he?

No one would save him. It wasn't possible. He was going to die, likely tortured to death.

Callum closed his eyes, wincing when Lady Marguerite sponged at one of the deeper wounds. The feminine scent of her skin cut through the fetid air, like a breath of mercy. He held on to it, inhaling deeply, as if he could absorb the memory of her.

When she'd finished, she lifted the cloths from his back and tried to ease him to sit. Callum glimpsed her face and wondered if he had died after all. Her clear skin and heart-shaped face were fragile, with soft lips and blue eyes that would haunt him for ever. He'd never seen a more beautiful creature in all his life.

'You're cold,' she whispered and removed her cloak, settling it around his shoulders. Her scent clung to it, along with her body heat. He smelled exotic flowers and a hint of citrus, like perfumes from a distant land. As he stared at her, he took in the signs of her wealth—not only the expensive silk gown, but also the softness of her hands and her pale skin.

How could she marry someone like the Earl of Cairnross? The idea of such a man possessing this innocent maiden made Callum's hands clench into fists.

You couldn't stop him even if you tried, came the voice of reason. The whipping had nearly killed him. He still wasn't certain why the soldiers had stopped. They'd left him here, no doubt believing the exposure to the cold air would finish his life.

Instead, Lady Marguerite had intervened. Though he wished above all else that she could help him to escape, tonight it would be a futile effort. A dozen guards patrolled the gate and he lacked the strength. He could hardly stand, much less run away from Cairnross.

Callum struggled to rise, but his knees seemed to fold beneath his weight. Lady Marguerite reached out and helped him balance himself. Though her face flushed at having to touch him, she offered, 'Let me help you.'

He shook his head in refusal, steadying himself against a stone wall. He'd rather crawl on his knees like a dog than make her lower herself in such a way. She'd tended his wounds and given him her cloak for warmth. He couldn't understand why she would want to help a stranger and a Scot at that.

Closing his eyes, he heard her murmur words of comfort in her own language. He heard the softness of her French accent, the soothing tones sliding over him like silk.

When he tried to take a step forward, his legs gave way and he nearly stumbled from his chained ankles. Lady Marguerite moved to his side, bringing her arm around his waist for support. He wanted to tell her no, for he was filthy and bloodstained. She shouldn't have to endure contamination from him.

But she walked at his side, guiding him across the fortress. 'You're going to be all right,' she whispered. 'I'll come to you and bring food. Perhaps when you're stronger, I'll petition the earl for your release.'

He sent her a questioning look. *Why? Why would she spare a moment for someone like him?*

The troubled look in her eyes suggested that she didn't know the answer. When he removed the cloak she'd given him, his hand brushed against hers. Her lips parted and he wanted to kneel at her feet like the goddess she was.

Callum didn't want her pity. Though his body and voice might be broken, he wouldn't allow her to believe that he was less than a man. His hands threaded with hers, the cold skin merging with warm.

He brought her fingers to his ragged cheeks, absorbing the warmth. A few strands of her golden hair slipped from her veil, resting against her throat. And when he brought her hand to his lips, she inhaled a gasp.

He released her instantly, expecting her to pull back in disgust. Instead, her eyes were shining with unshed tears, her fingers remaining upon his face.

'I won't forget you,' she vowed, pulling her cloak

around her shoulders. Then she picked up her skirts and disappeared into the night.

In the shadows, Callum caught a movement and turned his head. The Earl of Cairnross was standing there, watching.

And fury burned within his eyes.

'I saw you with him last night,' Lord Cairnross began, when Marguerite joined him in breaking their fast. 'The prisoner who was punished.'

Marguerite kept her eyes averted to the floor, showing no reaction at all. If she appeared dismayed, no doubt the earl would have the prisoner killed.

'I heard a man suffering,' she murmured. 'It awakened me from sleep.' She kept her tone even, as if she were speaking of a wounded animal.

'You are so young, Lady Marguerite,' the earl chided. 'These are not noblemen, as you are accustomed to,' he explained, making her feel like a small child. 'They are ignorant Scots who dared to rise up against the King. They should be grateful that I've given them the chance to atone for their sins.'

Sins? She forced herself to stare at her hands, wondering what he was talking about. Although some of the men were, no doubt, rebellious toward the English, the prisoner was only a year or so older than herself. From the look of him, he'd been imprisoned for years.

A shiver crossed over her skin, for the look in the man's eyes had been deliberate. She didn't doubt that he could kill his master without a trace of regret.

'Do not punish the prisoner for my ignorance, my lord,' she murmured. 'I saw him bleeding and meant only to tend his wounds.'

The earl took her hand in his. 'Lady Marguerite, Callum MacKinloch dared to touch you. And that I cannot forgive.'

A coldness threaded through her as she stared at Lord Cairnross. In his eyes, she saw a man who believed in his own supremacy, who cared for no one but himself.

'Did you take his life?' she asked. Her voice held a quaver that she despised, but she tried to keep her tone calm. *If he did, then it's my fault.*

'I should have. But the MacKinloch clan is not far from here. They have remained resistant to the English troops and I have decided to keep him as a hostage. But not at a risk to you, my bride.' His gaze turned possessive upon her, as if he'd guessed the uncertain feelings she held towards the man she'd saved. 'I sent him south, where he won't trouble you again.'

Marguerite feigned acquiescence, though inwardly she felt the cold anger filling her up. 'You are a man of great mercy, my lord,' she lied, and his arrogant smile sickened her as he raised her palm to his lips.

Whether or not he was telling the truth, at least she knew the name of the man who had touched her that night: Callum MacKinloch.

She didn't know what it was about Callum that entranced her. He was hardly more than a wild man, with an unkempt appearance that should have repelled her.

Yet the touch of his mouth against her palm had conjured up a trembling fire within her. She'd thought of nothing else since she'd seen him.

He was a fighter who'd resisted his enemy, surviving amidst insurmountable odds. When he'd stared at her, it was as if he saw something more than others saw. A woman of strength, instead of a woman who blindly obeyed.

Were she in his place, she'd have broken apart. It was not in her nature to defy anyone. She obeyed her father, did as she was told. As his youngest daughter, she'd prided herself on obedience.

Or was it cowardice? She'd let her father select a husband for her, without even knowing the man. She'd journeyed to Scotland with the Duc, to the northern lands where hardly anyone spoke her language. Though she told herself that her father wanted only what was best for her, she questioned his judgement with the betrothal to Lord Cairnross. The marriage was meant to strengthen the alliance with England, after the recent war had ended.

Yet, Marguerite couldn't imagine wedding Lord Cairnross after what he'd done to the prisoners. He enjoyed watching the men suffer and she loathed everything about the man.

She thought of Callum and the way he'd stared at the gates of Cairnross, as though he'd do anything to escape. They were alike, in so many ways. Both of them imprisoned, though her invisible chains were of her father's making.

Somehow, she would find a way to free herself from this marriage.

Two days later

Callum dreamed of Marguerite as he slept upon the frozen ground. The bodies of other prisoners huddled near, for it was the only way to survive the freezing cold. They had been brought to Lord Harkirk's stronghold to die and already he'd witnessed some of the weaker men succumbing to Death's quiet invitation.

In his memory, he recalled her beautiful face, the gentle innocence of her touch. He couldn't say why she had tended his wounds or why she hadn't run away from him. Callum knew what he was—a battered horror of a man.

But he wasn't weak. Over the years, he'd kept his arms strong, lifting stones to build the walls. He'd learned, in the early years, how to steal an extra portion of food when the guards weren't looking, to keep himself from starving. When his brother had been imprisoned with him, Bram had warned him to keep up his strength. There would come a time when they could escape together, his brother had promised.

But Bram had left him behind, seizing his own freedom, even when the soldiers had held a blade to Callum's throat.

Callum squeezed his eyes shut, trying to push away his resentment. They hadn't killed him that day, though he'd expected to die. Bram had called their bluff and it had worked.

Although a part of him knew that his brother hadn't abandoned him, he wished he could have left this place. Seven years of his life had faded away. And so had his voice.

Days ago, when the guards had picked him up, forcing him into the back of a wagon with four other men, Callum had tried again to speak. They might have had a chance at escaping, if the others would join him in resisting the soldiers. But no matter how hard he tried, not a word would break forth. It was as if someone had locked away his words, keeping him trapped in silence.

Worse, the others treated him as if he lacked intelligence. Several of the men talked about him, as if he couldn't hear their words.

But when one tried to shove him back upon their arrival, Callum seized the man's arm and stared hard at him. The startled look turned to an apology and Callum released his arm with a silent warning. Rubbing his forearm, the prisoner glanced at the others, who now viewed Callum with new eyes.

I may not speak. But I understand every word.

And from that moment, they'd held their distance.

As the days passed at Lord Harkirk's fortress, whatever hope he'd had of being rescued began to fade. Callum didn't know any of the prisoners and, without a familiar face, he started to slip into the madness that had plagued so many. Visions collided in his mind and he tried to focus the memories upon Lady Marguerite. If he concentrated hard enough, he could almost imagine the scent of her skin, the softness of her hands.

She'd been real. In his hands he grasped a crushed ribbon that he'd stolen from her blonde hair. It was a lighter blue than her eyes, but it confirmed that he hadn't imagined her. She had tended his broken flesh, treating him like a man instead of a slave.

She was the sort of woman he would die to protect. Innocent and pure, she deserved to be with a man who would love her, who would set a kingdom at her feet. The way he never could.

He stared at the wooden walls surrounding the fortress. Lord Harkirk had begun converting them into stone, using the labour of Scottish prisoners like himself. Callum fingered the silken ribbon, imagining it was the curve of Marguerite's cheek.

He would never stop trying to escape. Even if it was only for the chance to see her, one last time.

One week later

The fortress was on fire. Smoke billowed into the night sky and, outside, she heard the battle cries of men fighting. Marguerite's hands shook as she reached for her cloak, silently murmuring prayers that somehow they would make it out alive.

Though it should have been safer to remain hidden within her chamber, the fire might spread to the main tower. Dying by the sword was at least swifter than being burned alive.

Her maid Trinette was openly weeping as she packed their belongings into a bundle. Marguerite went to the window and stared at the chaos below. Swords rang out against shields, the roar of the prisoners breaking the stillness. The earl shouted orders, unsheathing his own weapon while smoke tainted the air.

This was their best chance to escape, while the men were caught up in the fighting. She seized the bundle from Trinette. 'We have to leave. Now.'

When her maid looked hesitant, too afraid to move, she gave her a slight push. 'Go!' she ordered, and Trinette hurried down the spiral stone stairs. Marguerite held on to the bundle in one arm while following her maid. The smoke created a dense fog within the main gathering space and in the darkness she couldn't see the doorway.

Her heartbeat raced as she struggled to see, her throat

raw in the smoky haze. She dropped low to the ground, trying to discover where Trinette had gone. She crawled upon the earthen floor until, at last, she spied the flare of a torch outside.

There. With a burst of energy, Marguerite fought her way towards the entrance, keeping her head down.

Outside, the cold air burned her lungs and she coughed again, trying to clear the smoke. The prisoners were escaping. She could see them pouring from their crude shelter, fighting hard, despite their chains. Another Scottish clan had attacked and half of the men created a diversion, while the others worked to free the slaves. Vengeance lined their faces while they struck hard against the Cairnross soldiers.

It was a welcome sight, watching the men go free. The only disappointment was knowing that if he'd been here, Callum MacKinloch would have been among them. Because of her interference, he was still a prisoner.

It simply wasn't fair.

Marguerite huddled against one of the outer stone walls, tears clouding the back of her throat. She didn't know what to do or where to go and dropped the bundle of her belongings upon the ground. She closed her eyes, wishing she could silence the sounds of death and fighting. Fear locked her feet in place.

'Are you a hostage?' a man shouted at her in English.

Marguerite turned her head slightly and saw a tall, dark-haired man standing before her. She gripped her arms, too afraid to move. He could kill her with a single blow if he chose to do so. But the look in his eyes held no threat and she saw a resemblance to Callum in the man's features. She remained motionless when he reached out and lowered her hood, revealing her veiled hair.

'If you want to leave this place, my brother can grant you sanctuary,' he offered. 'My wife will look after you and I promise you'll face no harm.'

Marguerite closed her eyes, wondering what to do. Her first instinct was to refuse. It made no sense at all to leave Cairnross, fleeing a burning fortress with the strangers who had attacked it.

Yet the only choice was to remain here with a man she despised. She stood, trying to make a decision, when, in the distance, she spied her maid. Trinette had started to panic and screamed, running towards the earl, as if he could protect her from the brutal fighting that surrounded them.

Lord Cairnross was caught up in his own fight, too busy to pay Trinette any heed. When she ran too close, Cairnross reached out with his dagger and sliced it across the woman's throat. Trinette dropped to the ground, her sightless eyes staring back at him.

Marguerite doubled over in horror, sickened by what she'd just witnessed. *Dear God have mercy.* Had she not seen it with her own eyes, she wouldn't have believed it. The earl *knew* Trinette was her maid yet he'd murdered her, simply because she'd been in the way.

Panic flooded through her lungs and Marguerite fought for breath. The truth was staring her in the face—she had to leave Cairnross or else be entrapped by a monster.

'Please,' she begged, searching for the right Gaelic words, 'help me get to my father.' She reached down and picked up the fallen bundle of clothing, trying not to think about Trinette. The maid had been her only companion from France and it broke her heart to imagine how alone she was now.

The Scottish warrior caught her hand and drew her outside the fortress, away from the fighting. Marguerite followed him, hoping she hadn't made a mistake in this decision. But what else could she do?

This was her only choice, no matter how terrifying it was. The man led her to a group of waiting horses where she secured her bundle. She moved with numb motions, letting her mind fall into nothingness. If she tried to think of anything beyond the simple task before her, she'd start to weep.

Behind her, the fortress blazed with fire, the scent of destruction darkening the air. She rested her hands upon a brown mare, trying not to think of what would happen to her now.

Then another Scot strode towards them. His dark hair hung to his shoulders and a long claymore was strapped to his back. Fury and disbelief raged in his eyes. 'Bram, what in God's name have you done? She's not coming with us.'

He spoke Gaelic, likely to keep her from understanding his words. Marguerite shrank back and stared at her hands, pretending she wasn't eavesdropping. Her fingers shook, but she waited for the men to make their own decision.

'We can't leave her there,' Bram argued. Her rescuer stared back into the face of the other man in open defiance.

'She's one of them,' the first snapped. 'And if you bring her, Cairnross's men will follow her to Glen Arrin.'

She could see the doubts forming in her rescuer's eyes. If she didn't say something, he might leave her here.

'No,' Marguerite interrupted, using Gaelic to reveal that she'd understood every word. She had to leave, at all costs. Searching for a way to convince the other man, she offered, 'If you send word to my father, he'll come for me and you will be rewarded.'

'And just who is your father?' he demanded.

Marguerite sent him a cool stare. 'Guy de Montpierre, the Duc D'Avignois.'

Although she'd never before evoked the power of her father's rank, she saw that it indeed made a difference with the first man. His face grew intrigued, as if to wonder how he could use her.

She didn't care. As long as he helped her escape from Cairnross and summoned her father, she would ensure that he was rewarded for his assistance.

'I am Marguerite de Montpierre,' she continued, sending him a regal nod. 'I was betrothed to Lord Cairnross.' Distaste filled her mouth at his very name.

'You may have our protection until your father arrives,' the first man agreed. 'But you'd best pray that Cairnross doesn't find you.'

She didn't doubt that at all. If the earl learned that she'd conspired with the enemy to escape, she might share in Trinette's fate. Silently, Marguerite uttered a prayer for the woman's soul.

Bram boosted her onto the saddle, and she arranged her skirts around the bundle of clothes she'd brought. Her hands shook as she gripped the saddle, wondering if she was making a mistake to go off with strangers.

She didn't know these men at all, nor was there any reason to trust them.

But thus far they'd behaved honourably. Their leader hadn't been pleased with the idea of bringing her with them, but he'd agreed to protect her, at a risk to his own people. It was the only hope she had left.

The fighting between the freed prisoners and Cairnross's men continued in the distance, as the men led her away. Flames consumed the garrison, filling the air with smoke. 'I'm glad to see it destroyed,' she murmured. The earl deserved to lose his stronghold after everything he'd done.

'How long were you there?' Bram asked, as he climbed up behind her, urging the horse faster.

'Just over a sennight. But the prisoners…' She shuddered at the memory of all those who had suffered. Most had been freed this night, except those who had died fighting.

'Did you ever see a man called Callum MacKinloch?' Bram asked. 'Younger than me, one of our brothers?'

She glanced back at him and realised she'd been right about the strong resemblance. It made her feel better about leaving with them, though she couldn't say why. 'He was sent away a few days ago,' she admitted. '*Oui*, I saw him.'

'Where?'

She shook her head, keeping her gaze fixed forward. 'To the South. That's all I know.'

'But he was alive and unharmed?'

'Alive, yes.' At least, that's what she wanted to believe. Her hands dug into the folds of her gown as she prayed it was still true. 'Will you try to find him?' she whispered, as they took her deeper into the hills.

'He's our brother. We'll bring him home,' Bram vowed.

The intensity of the promise gave her hope that he would keep his word. She didn't understand why she felt the need to ensure that Callum was safe. She'd only met him the one night. There was nothing at all between them, not even friendship. But when he'd brought her hand to his cheek, it was as if an invisible bond had drawn her to him. He'd dared to touch her, and though she couldn't say why he'd evoked these feelings, it was as if he'd been searching for her all his life.

As if he'd been waiting for her to come.

Deep inside, she wished she could see him again—if only to convince herself that she hadn't imagined the interest in his eyes.

Chapter Two

Callum refused to remain a prisoner. After seven years of misery, waiting on his brother to make the decisions about how and when to escape, damned if he'd wait another day. Even if he died in the effort, he'd be no man's slave.

Each day, he defied the soldiers, fighting to escape Lord Harkirk's fortress. The baron was no better than Cairnross, for he killed men each day as an example to others. Callum didn't doubt that he would one day be the next victim, his head mounted upon a pike.

Strangely, his rebellion appeared to entertain the soldiers. Each time he attempted to run away, they collected wagers from one another, depending on how far he'd managed to go. And once they captured him again, they took turns punishing him. Sometimes they withheld food, or other times he felt the pain of the lash upon his shoulders.

But everything had changed when he'd stolen a bow several nights ago. They'd whipped him afterwards, taking it back until one soldier had decided to test Callum's skills. A guard stood behind him, holding a dagger to his throat while the others set up a wooden shield as a target.

'Do you know how to shoot, MacKinloch?' the guard had taunted, pricking him with the blade. 'Show us what you can do. Hit the shield and you won't feel the lash upon your shoulders any more this night. If you miss, you'll have another dozen strokes.'

Already his limbs were leaden, blood pooling down his back. Callum's vision blurred from dizziness and he knew they wouldn't release him until they saw him shoot. It had been years since he'd used a bow, but he'd gone hunting often with his father and brothers. He'd always had a good eye and spent hours practising until he could hit anything.

The bow felt comfortable in his hand, like a lost friend. Although the soldiers expected him to miss, he knew the skill was there, buried through the years. He closed his eyes, feeling the weight of the weapon.

Without an arrow, he pulled back the bowstring, testing the tension. It wasn't as taut as the bows he'd used as a child. Eyeing the distance of the target, he knew he'd have to use his arm strength to increase the speed of the arrow.

'One shot,' the soldier said, handing him an arrow. 'If you try to shoot one of us, you die.' The men gathered behind him to watch, keeping away from the target.

The cold blade rested against his neck, but Callum ignored it. He focused all of his concentration upon the shield, ignoring the fierce pain within his muscles. Pulling back the bowstring, he adjusted his aim. In his mind, he heard the memory of his father's voice.

'See your target not only with your eyes,' Tavin

MacKinloch had instructed him. *'See it with your arm, your stance. Let it fly only when you know you'll strike true.'*

His arm was shaking now, the arrow pulled tight. A bead of sweat rolled down his cheek and he ignored the jeers of the soldiers. He envisioned the arrow embedding deep within the shield. Then, at last, he released the bowstring, letting the arrow fly.

It struck the centre of the shield, just as he'd imagined.

The roar of the soldiers was deafening. They took the weapon from him, dragging him away. As promised, they hadn't whipped him that night, but afterwards, they made him shoot every day, wagering upon him. It was an unexpected gift, allowing him to rebuild the lost skill.

He didn't hit all of their selected targets and had been punished when he missed. But he hardly felt the blows any more. His silence intimidated the other prisoners, making them believe he possessed an unearthly tolerance for pain. They'd come to fear him and it heightened the sense of isolation. It didn't matter. Soon he would find a way to make his escape from the fortress, leaving all of them behind.

One night, he thought he'd spied a weakness in the walls, only to be distracted by the sight of Lady Harkirk standing at the entrance of the tower. In her eyes, he saw the bleakness that echoed his own emotions. Her marriage to Lord Harkirk made him think of Marguerite, betrothed to a man who would eventually destroy her.

Callum's hand paused on the wooden palisade wall. Instead of seeing Lady Harkirk's brown hair and slim form, he saw Marguerite's lighter hair and deep blue eyes. The young woman's face was burned into his memory, though he didn't understand why. Perhaps it was because he'd never imagined that a beautiful woman like her would ever bother with a man like him. The vision held strong in his mind, binding him to her.

Had Marguerite suffered any punishment for granting him mercy? The earl was infatuated with her, eager to have her as his wife. The idea of such a man touching her, forcing himself upon her slender body, brought out a violent edge to Callum's temper. He wished he were at Cairnross, if only to grant her the shadow of his protection.

'Behind you!' he heard Lady Harkirk cry out. Her warning broke through his vision and Callum spun, finding three armed soldiers in chainmail armour. He ran hard, but the chains at his ankles hindered his stride, making it impossible to gain any speed. The men closed in on him and another stepped in to trip him with a quarterstaff.

Callum crashed into the ground, their laughter ringing in his ears. He tasted dirt and blood in his mouth and, when he raised his head, saw the silent sympathy of Lady Harkirk.

The soldiers dragged him back to the centre of the fortress. He saw where they were taking him and ceased his struggle.

'Beg for mercy, MacKinloch, and we won't put you inside,' one taunted. They knew he couldn't speak, much less beg for anything. Callum stared back in defiance.

They lifted the trapdoor leading to the underground pit and threw him inside. All light extinguished when they closed the ceiling lid, weighing it down with a heavy stone. Though he tried to push against it, the stone wouldn't budge.

Suffocating darkness overwhelmed him and he wondered how long they would leave him in here. The small space was akin to a grave, and he forced himself to breathe slowly. They wanted him to be afraid, to lose his last grasp of sanity. Instead, he closed his eyes and sat down, reaching inside his tunic for the crumpled ribbon. He held it to his nose, absorbing all thoughts of Marguerite.

As the minutes drifted into hours, he remembered the gentle touch of her hands, the soft music of her voice. If there were such a thing as a living angel, it was she.

And hours later, when they dragged him out, he kept the ribbon gripped in his palm as the whip struck him down.

'You should set the MacKinloch slave free,' Lady Alys Fitzroy of Harkirk remarked to her husband. 'He's half-dead and no good to you any more.'

Last night, she'd been too late to stop the brutal beating. The prisoner, Callum MacKinloch, hadn't uttered a single scream. And she'd found him lying among the other slaves, huddled with his knees drawn up, trembling violently. One of the other Scots had put a tunic upon him and the fabric was stained dark with blood.

Harkirk's gaze narrowed. 'You saw his family approaching.'

Alys shrugged, as if it were no matter. 'Aye. The sentry reported that they've brought a purse to ransom him.' She prayed her husband would accept the bribe, for Lord Harkirk valued silver far more than a man's life.

'Why would I let him go? If I release him, it will weaken my authority. Better to let him die for his insolence.'

'He might die anyway. And you'd still have the bribe.'

Though it bothered her deeply, Alys lowered herself to kneel beside his chair. Robert preferred her subservience and she saw the moment his eyes gleamed with interest.

He reached out to rest his palm upon her head. 'You found him handsome, didn't you?'

'My loyalty belongs to you, my lord,' she answered quietly. 'If you wish to keep the slave, then that is your right.'

'It is.' His hand dug into her hair in a silent reminder of possession. Thick fingers moved over her face, down to her shoulder. 'I will consider your request.' When his fingers slid beneath the neckline of her gown, touching her bare skin, she flushed with embarrassment. 'And I'll share your bed tonight, wife. For that is also my right.'

Alys said nothing, keeping her head bowed in obedience. An icy shield kept her courage from shattering apart. Just as the Scots were imprisoned in servitude, so too, was she a captive in this marriage.

She couldn't free herself…but she could help them. It was her own form of silent rebellion. Although most of the prisoners were men, there had also been a few women. And recently a young girl, hardly more than ten years old.

Only a monster would imprison a child. Above all others, Alys would fight for the life of the girl.

She only wished Harkirk were dead, so she could free them all.

A restlessness brewed within Marguerite. Though Bram and Alex MacKinloch had gone on a rescue mission to free Callum, nearly a sennight ago, she couldn't stop herself from pacing. Bram's wife Nairna had given her a few tasks to occupy herself while they were gone, but household duties had done little to ease her preoccupation. She wished for a needle and thread, for sewing often helped her to calm herself.

'They'll be back,' the chief's wife Laren reassured her. 'And soon your father will come for you.'

'Perhaps.' Marguerite wasn't entirely certain that her well-being was more important than political alliances. Though the Duc had been good to her and her sisters, his primary interest was in using their marriages to support his own position. No doubt he would be furious when he learned she'd run away from the earl.

Ever since she'd come to live with the MacKinlochs, the immense freedom had been overwhelming. There was no one to tell her what to wear, where to go, or what her duties were each day. Although Marguerite tried to offer her help, she was unaccustomed to living this way. She felt awkward, trying to settle into a pattern that wasn't her own.

A commotion outside caught their attention and Laren hurried to see what it was. Marguerite followed and saw the men returning on horseback. Callum was with them, but he stared off into the distance as if he were blind. In his broken posture, she glimpsed a man who had suffered years' worth of torment in only a few weeks.

An aching regret squeezed her heart. *It's my fault*, she thought to herself. If Callum spied her, he might be angry with her for what had happened. A strange rise of nerves gathered inside her like a windstorm of leaves. She wanted to see him again, but it was possible he didn't remember her.

She disappeared within the fortress and gave orders for a hot bath to be prepared for Callum. It shamed her to realise that she was hiding from them. From her vantage point in the far corner, she saw the men gathering. Nairna's face was pale as she followed behind her husband and the others.

When Bram tried to touch the ragged tunic, Callum exploded into a fight. He was like an animal, raging at his brother, attacking with his fists. He didn't seem to recognise his own family any more or realise that they were trying to help him.

It was awful seeing him like this. It was as if the man she'd saved was no longer there, lost in a world of his own madness.

Alex and Bram tried to subdue him, but Callum kept fighting, his blows striking hard.

'Help us bring him above stairs,' Alex said to Ross, one of their kinsmen. The older man had greying hair and a full beard, but there was no denying the brawny strength of his forearms.

'He needs food,' Ross said and Nairna hurried to fetch it. When the men half-dragged Callum up the winding stairs, Marguerite moved behind them. They brought him into Alex's chamber and she remained on the stairs, watching from a distance. When they tried to remove his bloodstained tunic, Callum fought harder. Bram expelled a curse as a fist caught him in the eye.

Men and women came and left the chamber, but Marguerite remained in the shadows, feeling like a coward. Several of the MacKinlochs had brought in hot water, but she didn't know if Callum would avail himself of the bath.

After a time, Nairna found her and the woman's face was lined with worry. 'You said you helped Callum on the night he was wounded. Would you be willing to go to him now?'

'I don't know if I could do anything,' Marguerite admitted. 'He might not remember me.' Or if he did, he might resent her for being sent away.

'Will you try?' Nairna took her by the hand, drawing her into the hall. 'You're the last hope we have.' Her face grew upset, but she revealed, 'The tunic on his back has stuck to the wounds. He won't let us take it off. It will grow poisoned if we leave it.'

Marguerite closed her eyes, suppressing a shudder. Callum would die a long-suffering death, if he didn't allow anyone to assist him. She took a deep breath and nodded. 'I'll do what I can.'

She followed Nairna into the room, worrying that she would be unable to help. Inside, she saw Bram seated across from his brother, an untouched cup of mead resting upon a table beside him. Callum stared at the wall, as if he weren't aware of his brother's presence. His knuckles were bloody, matching his brother's swollen face.

Nairna spoke quietly to her husband, while Marguerite tried to summon her courage. *Why would you think you could help him*? her mind demanded. *He won't even remember you.*

But the moment she stepped forward, Callum turned to face her. There was disbelief in his expression, as if he couldn't understand how she had come to be here. His brown eyes stared into hers, and though she saw the pain within them, there was something else. Almost…a longing.

Her throat grew swollen, her eyes blinking back tears, but Marguerite didn't turn her gaze away from him. He was drinking in the sight of her, as if her presence brought him comfort. Seeing his wounds made her heart bleed, knowing what he'd endured.

You have to help him, came a voice within her. *He needs you.*

As if approaching a wounded wolf, she continued moving towards Callum. One foot before the other, moving closer, until she took Bram's place across from him. She gripped the folds of her sapphire silk gown, trying to think of what to say.

Nairna took her husband's hand. 'We'll wait just beyond the door if you need us.' They retreated, leaving the door open by only an inch or two.

When they had gone, Marguerite forced herself to look back at Callum. He hadn't taken his eyes off her and she grew nervous beneath his stare. 'I never meant for this to happen,' she murmured in French, knowing he wouldn't comprehend her words. 'I had hoped to save you. Not to make you suffer.'

He reached out, his palm covering hers. The rough skin contrasted against her own, but she understood his silent forgiveness. With each second that passed, she grew more sensitised to his touch. Not just his hand, but the warmth of his knee pressed against hers as they sat across from one another. The heat of his eyes burned into her, speaking more than any words could say.

Her cheeks flushed at his attention, but she turned her palm over to clasp his. She stroked her thumb across his skin, as if to soothe him. Although she was seated a slight distance away, it felt almost like an embrace. If she leaned forward, she could rest her head against his chest.

Callum brought her hand to touch the pulse at his throat. She could feel the rapid thrum beneath his skin, as if he were telling her the effect she had upon him. Her lips parted and she wondered what it would be like to kiss him. Would he be fierce and demanding? Or quiet and arousing?

His nearness flustered her, so Marguerite rose to her feet, reaching for a length of linen that Nairna had left. She soaked the cloth in the warmed water of the tub and brought it to his bearded face. Though he had only minor wounds upon his cheeks and chin, she wanted him to trust her, to understand that she wouldn't hurt him.

Callum endured the cleansing, breathing slowly as he allowed her to tend him. Then, he caught her hand and pressed something into it. She opened her palm and saw one of her ribbons, wrinkled and faded. There was a faint bloodstain upon the edge of it, as if he'd gripped it hard.

'Where did you get this?' she asked, in his language.

Callum reached up to her hair, removing the veil. Marguerite felt the touch of his warm hand, threading into her hair. His thumb caressed the edge of her temple, as if to apologise for what he'd done.

He must have taken it from her, the last night she'd seen him. She'd never noticed it was gone.

He'd kept it, all this time. In her mind, all she could imagine was him gripping the ribbon while the soldiers scourged him. A guilty tear spilled over, as she thought of what had happened to this man.

Marguerite pressed the ribbon back into his hand before resting her hands on his shoulders. 'It was my fault you were sent away.'

He shook his head, denying it.

'I'm so sorry for it,' she whispered. 'Your brother came for you, a few days after I saw you last. He brought me here, after Cairnross was burned.'

His gaze turned stony, but he gave a nod to show he'd heard her.

'He would have freed you,' she said softly. 'They never stopped looking for you.'

Callum didn't seem to believe her words, from the dark look in his eyes. She turned her attention to his back and the sight of the bloodstained tunic made her stomach turn. She knew what she had to do, but it didn't make it any less horrifying.

'I want to help you,' she said quietly. 'The tunic should come off so I can treat your wounds.'

Tension knotted his face, but he seemed to understand her. He turned around and gripped the edge of a table, as if to brace himself for the worst.

'I'll try not to hurt you,' she offered. The garment had stuck to his skin; no doubt removing it would re-open many of his wounds.

Marguerite loosened the ties and brought her hands to the hem of the tunic, lifting it slowly. The underside wasn't so bad, but when she reached the middle of his back, it was stuck fast. Callum's knuckles whitened on the table and she had to force herself to continue.

She closed her eyes, as she felt his skin tearing away from the cloth. Revulsion formed in her stomach and she heard a rushing sound in her ears as she pulled the tunic over his head. It wasn't until the edges of her vision started to blacken that she realised she was about to faint.

Don't, she ordered herself. She bit hard against her lip, taking deep breaths with her head lowered. And when she'd regained control of herself, she opened her eyes and saw his bleeding wounds.

Mon Dieu, he was suffering so badly. Marguerite soaked another cloth in the bathwater and touched Callum's face again before she wet it once more and laid it upon his bare back.

He lifted his head to look at her, and though she'd caused him pain, there was also relief in his eyes.

'You're safe now,' she whispered. 'It will be all right.'

But the way he was looking at her made her feel vulnerable. She didn't understand the needs hidden behind his eyes, or what he was thinking.

'I'll leave you to bathe,' she whispered. 'If you want, I can send Bram back to help you.'

He shook his head, returning to the bench. Though he said not a word, he rested his forearms upon his legs, lowering his head. Exhaustion weighted him down and she didn't like the look of the wounds upon his back. He was thin, his ribs revealed in the torchlight. But his arms held a wiry strength, his muscles well defined.

'Or would you rather I stayed to help you?' she blurted out.

Heaven only knew what provoked her to make the

offer. Although she'd assisted her father's guests with their baths in the past, there had always been several servants in attendance. It was an expected duty and she'd thought little of it.

But the prospect of seeing this man naked made her feel breathless, almost anticipating something that would never happen.

Callum stood up and raised questioning eyes to her. Marguerite held still, trying to feign a calmness she didn't feel. Her mind was ordering her to leave, for to stay meant far more than tending his wounds. She was a maiden, untouched and innocent.

'It's all right,' she whispered. 'If you need me, I'll stay.'

When he turned his back, reaching to untie his trews, she quickly averted her gaze.

The water had grown cooler, but it was like sharp blades cutting into his back. Callum sat in the wooden tub with his knees drawn up, wincing at the burning sensation.

He should have sent Marguerite away. Letting her see him like this wasn't right. But the past few weeks had changed him, making him care less about what was expected and falling into the instinctive urges that bordered on wildness.

He wanted her with an urgency that consumed him. When she dipped a cloth into the water, washing the dirt from the wounds on his back, he was grateful for the pain. It kept the urges under control, for her very presence had aroused him.

As she moved her hands to wash his shoulders, his skin erupted with shivers. His treacherous mind envisioned her hands moving over his chest, down to the part of him that was growing harder.

Callum slowed his breathing, trying not to get distracted. He'd never been with a woman before, and right now her touch upon his skin was firing up his imagination.

He remembered one night at Cairnross when a prisoner's wife had visited her husband, trying to free him. She hadn't succeeded, but they'd spent an hour in each other's arms. She'd lifted her skirts and rode him, impaling herself upon his arousal.

Every man had been unable to tear his eyes away when her head had fallen back in passion, her rhythmic cries making each of them wish that he could experience such a pleasure.

When Marguerite's hands moved to his hair, Callum let out a gasp. Though no sound broke from his mouth, his fingers dug into the wood as he struggled to keep from touching her.

'I'm sorry,' she said. 'I didn't realise that would hurt you.'

It wasn't that. God above, he wanted to reach out and pull her into a kiss. He imagined tearing her gown apart, baring the softness of her body before he laid her down upon the bed, tasting every part of her until she knew the same torment he did.

He nodded for her to continue and she washed his hair, her fingers massaging his scalp. It felt so good that he closed his eyes to immerse himself in her touch. When her hands moved to the base of his neck, he started to lose his edge of control.

To distract himself, Callum held his breath and dipped his head beneath the water. *She doesn't want you*, he reminded himself. This was a duke's daughter, a woman who ranked the same as a princess. She shouldn't have to lower herself, bathing him.

When he emerged for air, water droplets rolled down his bearded face. He opened his eyes and saw her staring at him. Beckoning to her, he touched his beard and pointed to the blade at her waist.

Her eyes furrowed a moment. 'You want me to help you shave?'

He nodded. The heaviness of the beard bothered him, for it seemed that the dirt of the prison was caught within it.

'Would you rather do it yourself?' she asked.

If he tried, no doubt he'd slit his own throat without meaning to. He'd been imprisoned since he was a young boy and when the first signs of a beard had come a few years ago, he'd simply let it grow. Never before had he shaved and he didn't know how.

But he wanted the touch of her hands upon him, no matter what the reason.

'All right,' she agreed, 'but I'll need a sharper blade. Wait here.'

While she was gone, he soaped his face, trying to wash the dirt from it. It seemed that no amount of scrubbing would rid him of the wretched years he'd spent in chains.

When Marguerite returned, she knelt before the tub and touched his chin. First, she trimmed away the beard with shears, then reached for the soap again. When her hands washed his roughened cheeks, he remained motionless. Right now, he wanted to close his eyes and revel in the feeling of her hands upon him. He imagined her hands moving lower, to his shoulders, and while she shaved him with the blade, his desire for her intensified. Her face was so near to his, her blue eyes concentrating on the task.

He was hungry for a taste of her lips, but he forced himself not to move. Instead, he drank in the sight of her, memorising every feature. When she finished shaving him, she ran her fingertips over his cheeks.

'I don't think I missed any places,' she said, but before she could move away, he captured her face in his hands. Gently, he drew his wet thumbs over her temples, down to her cheeks. Her lips parted in surprise and he drew closer, watching. Wondering if she would let him steal the kiss he wanted so badly.

Her face flamed, and she stood up. 'Y-you can do the rest while I get your clothes.' Handing him the soap, she moved far away from him, leaving him to wonder if he'd only imagined the answering interest in her eyes.

Callum washed his legs and the rest of his body, hiding himself from her. Upon the floor, he spied a drying cloth and picked it up. He emerged from the tub, drying himself off and wrapping the cloth around his hips. Marguerite turned around, her gaze furtive. He waited for her to approach, not wanting to frighten her. Beneath the cloth, he was still heavily aroused; if she dared to look, she would see it.

She walked slowly and he noticed the way the blue silk clung to her body, outlining the curve of her breasts and her slim figure. Her veiled hair hung below her waist, a few of the golden strands damp from the water. When she held out the clothing to him, he didn't take it.

No words would come from his throat, no sound to tell her how grateful he was for her presence. There was no means of telling her the thoughts imprisoned deep inside. He couldn't speak.

But he could touch.

With his hands, Callum traced the curve that skimmed from her shoulders to her throat. His fingers moved up her jaw line, watching to see if she would pull away. Her blue eyes held a myriad of emotions: regret and sympathy, along with hesitation. She didn't know him at all, nor would she understand what her kindness meant to him.

Death was easy. So was madness. But something about this woman drew him nearer. In all the darkness he'd known, she'd become the single shard of light that gave him a reason to survive.

She uttered a soft breath when he drew his hands down the back of her neck. Beneath his palms, her delicate skin prickled. He could feel the tension within her, but as he massaged the tightness, she closed her eyes.

'I shouldn't let you do this, I know,' she whispered.

He touched a finger to her lips, bidding her to be silent. Then he went down on one knee before her.

'What is it?' she asked, frowning at his position. But Callum took her hand and set it upon his head, needing her to understand what he couldn't say.

Her hand moved against his wet hair and she sighed. 'I know you're not going to hurt me.'

Slowly, he stood and took her hands. He struggled to speak, trying to force the words out. *I never thought I'd see you again.* The desperate need for words tormented him, but nothing came forth. Marguerite saw his failure, but instead of offering sympathy, she stood on tiptoe, resting her cheek against his.

God above, he'd never expected this. Her arms came around his neck, offering solace. And danger.

The scent of her skin, and the fluid lines of her body made him fully aware of all the ways he wanted to worship her. Never taking his eyes from her, he lifted her hand and placed it over his racing heart. The touch of skin on skin enslaved him. She was a woman he could never have, so far beyond his reach as the sunlight in the sky.

But for this moment, he would take what he wanted.

He rested his mouth above hers, waiting for her to pull away. Her blue eyes held confusion and the flushed warmth of her cheeks revealed her embarrassment. At any time, she could pull back and he wouldn't stop her.

Slowly, he lowered his mouth to hers.

Chapter Three

Marguerite couldn't breathe when Callum kissed her. His mouth was warm, coaxing her to let go of her shyness. Although it wasn't her first kiss, this one slipped beneath her skin with a slow burning fire, transforming her inhibitions into ashes.

The connection went deeper than that between a woman and a man she'd rescued and tended. He treated her as though no one else on the earth existed. As if he needed her more than the air he breathed.

It was something she wasn't used to. At home, she was the youngest of four daughters, largely overlooked. Her older sisters were mischievous and outspoken, accustomed to having suitors vie for their hand. Marguerite was quiet and usually remained in the background, unnoticed.

But she suspected that Callum MacKinloch would always notice her.

He was half-naked before her, his body pressed against her own. There were no thoughts spinning through her mind, only the need to bring him closer. Her arms wound around his neck but when she felt the evidence of his arousal, it didn't frighten her as she'd thought it would. Instead, it awakened her own response, with an answering need between her legs.

The kiss turned deeper and Marguerite let out a shuddering gasp as Callum conquered her mouth, bringing her back against the wall. With his kiss he broke down her defences, until she was trembling beneath the onslaught.

At last, he let her go, resting both hands upon the wall. His dark eyes were heated with desire, his mouth looking as if he wanted to do more, kiss her in other secret places.

She didn't know what to do or what to say now. Confused, she fumbled for words—anything to distract herself from the turmoil of ragged feelings. 'Y-you should get dressed,' she told him quietly.

He studied her, his eyes discerning. Then he touched her cheek, a question hidden within his expression—almost as if he were asking if he'd overstepped his bounds.

She didn't know what to say. Colour flooded her face at what she'd done, for she could give no reason why she'd allowed him to kiss her. Only that she'd wanted him to.

Taking his hand, she led him over to the pile of clothing. 'Nairna brought these for you.' Then she went to the far side of the room, turning her back. Inside, she trembled from the kiss. He'd shaken her deeply, making her crave his touch.

From behind her, she heard the light rustle as he picked up the clothes. Heaven only knew what possessed her to do it, but she turned over her shoulder to steal a look at him.

Callum's shoulders and back held stripes of both healed and unhealed lash marks, scars that he would carry for the rest of his life. His waist was lean, but, despite his thin frame, he had the body of a fighter. He had tight, muscular buttocks and powerful thighs.

And, oh God, he'd caught her looking at him.

A slow, wicked smile curved over his mouth, as if daring her to look further.

Marguerite whirled around, wondering why she'd done such a thing. But he hadn't been angry. In fact, she'd caught a glimpse of amusement in Callum's eyes, as if he'd wanted her to look.

He was undeniably handsome, despite the harsh conditions he'd endured. His dark eyes held secrets and an intensity that weakened her senses. Long dark hair flowed past his shoulders and she imagined what it would be like cut short. His clean-shaven face revealed a strong jaw and a determined confidence in his demeanour.

She didn't know why she was attracted to a man who'd been held prisoner for so long. It might be compassion, but more likely it was her own curiosity. Callum had made no secret of his interest, and she could not have chosen someone more different from herself.

She'd been raised in a castle, surrounded by servants. And although it wasn't her nature to demand material goods, she'd had everything she ever wanted. Callum was the third-born son, with hardly more than the clothes on his back. He could give her nothing at all.

Perhaps that was what drew her to him. He saw *her*, while the other men saw only her father's wealth and power.

When Marguerite risked another look back at him,

Callum was sitting on the bed, fully dressed. His wrists rested upon his knees, his head bowed. He looked tired, yet unable to sleep. She took a step forward, and the sound of her motion prompted him to lift his head. He let out a slow breath, his face masked. Then he touched the place beside him in a silent request for her to sit.

She remained still, unsure of herself or what he wanted from her. Time hung suspended while she debated whether or not to stay a little longer. He appeared calmer, more in command of himself.

'You can't kiss me again,' she warned.

He didn't tease her with a smile, but gave a single nod as his silent promise. In his hands, she saw the faded blue ribbon.

She took a breath and moved a slight distance beside him. 'It's all right to sleep, you know. No one will harm you.' Though she was tired herself, she intended to return to her own room, once he had found a peaceful rest.

Callum reached out and pulled her to sit beside him. Then he laid his head upon her lap.

The gesture should have made her uneasy. Instead, as she stroked his long hair back and watched him close his eyes, heavy tears pricked at her. He'd suffered for so long, chained in the dark. Was it any wonder that he yearned for human comfort?

Although the weight of her own exhaustion burdened her, Marguerite didn't move. Callum clasped her other hand in his while he slept. She let him rest against her, though her back ached. In time, she succumbed to the need for sleep, lying back against his pillow.

The raucous cries of a raven haunted him. The birds were known for circling the camp, awaiting the moment when a prisoner died. Callum hated them, for they fed upon the flesh of the dead. Just the sight of the birds sickened him, and he'd chased dozens of them away from the corpses.

Though most of the other prisoners were nameless companions, they didn't deserve to be dishonoured, their flesh picked away by black-winged predators.

And so he'd begun collecting their feathers. He couldn't say why, but when the guards watched him making more arrows, he'd glued their dark tips to the shaft. It was as if he could honour the memory of the fallen.

One day, he would avenge them. He'd grown to hate Lord Harkirk as much as his former master. While Cairnross had believed himself superior to the Scots, punishing them for imagined crimes, Harkirk cared nothing for men's lives. Men were killed for no reason at all, simply as entertainment.

But Harkirk would die one day. And, God willing, he'd be struck down by a black-feathered arrow, one of his own.

Callum's eyes opened as the remnants of sleep slid away. Against his cheek, he felt the softness of Marguerite's hair and their bodies were tangled together. Her delicate scent surrounded him, his arms cradled her body close. He savoured the moment of holding her, wishing to God he could make it last.

It wasn't yet dawn and in the faint light, he saw the golden outline of her hair. For a moment, he listened to her breathe, watching her sleep.

He'd never dreamed she would let him kiss her. It hadn't been his intention, but when she'd put her arms around him, resting her cheek upon his, he'd lost sight of the world. Her lips had tasted sweet, but beneath her innocence, he'd tasted the promise of more. She'd tempted him, until he could do nothing except savour the moments that wouldn't last. She was a duke's daughter and despite the fierce desire to be her protector, he knew he'd never be a part of her life.

A sound from outside caught his attention. Callum reluctantly got out of bed, listening to the sounds of night. In the corner, he saw Bram sleeping and he wondered why his brother had allowed him to sleep with Marguerite. Silently, he moved to open the shuttered window. In the darkness, he spied faint pinpricks of light moving towards them. He didn't know what it was, but within seconds the light vanished. Instinct warned him that whatever the source of the light was, he had to warn his brother.

Before he could say a word, he heard Marguerite moan in her sleep. She clenched the sheets, murmuring words in French that he didn't understand. And when he tried to awaken her by touching her cheek, her eyes flew open.

She sat up and gripped him hard, still shaking from the nightmare. Callum held her tight, stroking her hair to soothe her.

It's all right. I'm here.

'I'm sorry,' she whispered. 'I was dreaming about the tower and the fire that night. I dreamed I couldn't get out.' Her face rested against his neck and he kissed her hair, moving his mouth lower to console her in the only way he knew how.

She drew back, closing her eyes and lifting her mouth to his. Before he could taste her lips, the door swung open and Alex entered. His brother's face darkened with misunderstanding, as if he thought Callum was trying to dishonour Marguerite.

'Get away from her, Callum,' Alex warned.

At the sudden sound, Bram woke up from his place on the floor and stood. 'Leave them,' he said, stretching. 'She calms him.'

'Did he hurt you?' Alex asked Lady Marguerite. She shook her head, her face turning dark red.

'I should go,' she murmured. 'I never meant to fall asleep.' Embarrassed, she fled the room.

Callum stared at his brothers, needing to tell them what he'd seen. He pointed toward the window, trying to signal to them, but they didn't understand.

He saw in their eyes that they believed he'd gone mad, as if he weren't aware of what was going on.

'Did he sleep at all last night?' Alex asked Bram.

'He kept waking up, but Marguerite stopped him from lashing out.'

'We should keep her close, then, if she's able to get through to him.'

Callum's temper exploded. He moved between the men, grabbing each of his brothers by the shoulder.

Look at me. I hear your words. I understand them.

But not a single sound came, despite his mouth moving. Frustration clawed at him that he was unable to communicate anything at all. He grabbed Bram's tunic and hauled him towards the window, pointing outside once again.

'There's nothing out there,' Bram said. 'You're safe now.'

He didn't believe it. And they were fools if they did.

Alex poured a cup of wine into a goblet and handed it

to him. 'Have something to drink. Whatever it is, we'll look in the morning.'

He drank the wine and, too late, tasted the bitter herbs within it. Staring at his brother's betrayal, he wondered what they'd done to him.

'It will help you sleep,' Alex said. 'You need rest, to regain your strength.'

Despite his efforts to fight them, the heavy narcotic effects of the herbs pulled him under. As he slipped into the dark dream, he inhaled the scent of Marguerite upon the sheets.

Callum awakened with his mouth dry and the aftertaste of the herbal brew lingered. His back still hurt from the lash marks, and he struggled to open his eyes. He overheard Bram's wife Nairna talking to her husband and caught the last few words of his brother's conversation.

'I don't know if he's even aware of where he is.'

Callum gritted his teeth. He knew exactly where he was, yet no one trusted him. He struggled to rise from the bed, thankful that Alex and Bram were focused upon Nairna instead of himself.

'When I was out walking this morning, I saw a torch light in the hills,' the young woman said. 'Do you think any of Lord Harkirk's men might have followed us?'

No doubt of it. From the flickering torches he'd seen, it was impossible to tell how many men there were.

'I'll inform the men,' Alex replied. 'If it is an attack, send a runner to Locharr and alert the Baron that we may need his help.' He turned to Nairna. 'Tell Laren—'

'She's already gathering the women and children.'

'Good.' Alex turned back and Callum met his gaze

steadily. His brother's face held a magnitude of worry for all the people they had to protect. There weren't enough men and if they were invaded, many would die.

In an instant, his older brother assessed him, as if to decide whether or not he was dangerous. Callum stared back, meeting the silent question with a determined look of his own. He had no doubt of his ability to defend them, especially with a bow.

'I'll need your help guarding the women and children,' Alex said at last, unsheathing his sword. 'Even Lady Marguerite.' He held out the weapon, hilt first, and Callum inclined his head in answer.

Though he couldn't stop his hands from trembling, he managed to grasp the sword. Alex had offered him the chance to fight and he wouldn't fail his brother, though a sword wasn't his first choice. From the corner of his eye, he caught Bram's wife Nairna eyeing him with uncertainty.

I can fight, he wanted to tell her. Especially if it meant protecting Marguerite. Upon the floor, he spied the faded blue ribbon and reached for it, tucking it away for safekeeping.

Callum followed them down the stairs, still feeling the effects of the potion from the night before. He settled his mind to the task ahead, though he didn't know if it was a small raid or a larger force.

Nairna led them outside to the place where she'd seen the torches. Though it was now dawn, the faint light wasn't enough to determine how many men threatened Glen Arrin. While his brothers and Nairna climbed up to the top of the gatehouse, Callum stayed below, beside the gate. He studied the opposite side, wondering what had happened to the lights on the far end of the fortress.

Then the sun gleamed over the hills, revealing the glint of chainmail armour. They were outnumbered, perhaps three to one. Callum didn't doubt that both Cairnross and Harkirk were allied in this attack.

The only question was how many of his clan would survive it.

Marguerite followed Laren to warn the rest of the clan. The chief's wife looked terrified, but she explained what was happening. One by one, they gathered the women and children, leading them back to the tower.

'We'll bring them underground,' Laren explained. 'We've taken shelter there before.'

Marguerite picked up Laren's youngest daughter Adaira and started towards the keep. When she glanced behind to be sure that no women or children were left, she saw Callum approaching.

He walked slowly. In his eyes, she saw the grim look of a man who was about to fight. Seeing his ruthless determination made her heartbeat quicken, for he wouldn't hesitate to shed enemy blood to protect them. Marguerite set the child down, then hung back from the others, waiting for him.

Callum stopped walking a moment, his eyes passing over her. From the top of her veil, over her face and down her body, it was as if he needed to assure himself that she was all right.

'Did you sleep at all?' she asked, feeling self-conscious from the look in his eyes. He gave a slight nod, then sent her a questioning look as if to ask the same.

She shrugged. 'A little. I was worried about you.'

Callum took her hand and led her behind one of the small homes. She didn't understand what he wanted, but

Laren and Nairna were guiding the rest of the women and children inside the keep.

Her pulse beat against her throat as he slowly pressed her back against the wall. With his hands, he touched her veil, moving down the sides of her face as if he were trying to memorise her features. Marguerite saw the promise in his eyes, of a man who would lay down his life for hers. An aching fear clenched within her, for she didn't know what lay ahead.

Though he was strong, he'd been badly wounded and shouldn't be fighting so soon after his rescue. Yet, in his eyes she saw the steady resolve. Callum wasn't a man who would stand aside while his family was in danger.

'Will you be all right?' she whispered, touching his shoulders.

His answer was to lean in, stealing a kiss. It was as if he drew strength from her, needing this one last touch. His mouth was gentle upon hers, unravelling the edges of her heart. There was no reason to kiss this man, nor give him any reason to think that they could stay together. Once her father came for her, she would have to go with the Duc and marry a man of his choosing.

But as she surrendered to Callum's kiss, answering his need with her own, she refused to feel any guilt for it. He had endured so much, remaining strong in the face of suffering. Knowing that he wanted her, and that she felt the same answering desire, was enough for now. Either of them could die today.

When he pulled her into an embrace, she felt the quiet assurance of his protection. He wouldn't leave her, no matter how dire the circumstances. Marguerite took a deep breath. 'We should join the other women and children. They'll need you to help guard them.'

He took her hand and led her forward, his gaze searching the perimeter for any threat. When they caught up to the others, Marguerite went with him into the underground passageway beneath the fortress. For now, they would hide from the invaders. And if the worst happened, she knew he would use every last breath to defend them.

Callum worked with Nairna to find the secret tunnel that led outside the fortress. The damp smell of earth permeated the space and he could sense the fear of the women and children behind him. Though most men would be afraid of the impending battle, inwardly he felt a sense of calm. Once he found a bow, he could strike down any man who dared to attack the women. In this, he would not fail. And if he died this day, at least he would keep Marguerite safe.

The taste of her lips lingered upon his mouth. He still couldn't believe that she'd allowed him to touch her again. She'd welcomed him into her arms, until his thoughts went well beyond a kiss. He could imagine her creamy naked skin, the flush of arousal rising on her face. God above, what he wouldn't give to spend a night pleasuring her. This woman, who had given him a path out of darkness, made him want to live.

The acrid scent of smoke caught his attention only seconds before his brother's wife Nairna sensed it. The invaders had set fire to the keep and it was only a matter of time before it spread below. 'We can't stay here,' she insisted, staring at him with horror. 'We have to evacuate the others.'

Callum moved to examine the underground chamber, knowing that his older brother would have more weapons hidden somewhere. Behind him, he heard Alex's wife speaking with Nairna, both arguing about whether to stay or go. He kept searching until, at last, he found the weapons. There were two longbows with arrows and a crossbow, as well as a few dull knives and one sword.

He claimed one of the bows for himself, along with a quiver of arrows. Though he still had the sword Alex had given him, he preferred to fight from a distance, since he lacked stamina.

His younger brother Dougal, who was only four and ten, looked uneasy at the prospect of fighting, but he'd agreed to help defend the women and children. Callum emerged from the darkness, holding out a bow for Dougal and more arrows. When Nairna tried to take his weapon, Callum shook his head, keeping his grip tight upon the bow.

In her eyes, he saw the lack of trust. 'Can you defend us?'

He stared back at her and gave a single nod, hoping she would understand that this battle was his to face, not hers. Nairna stepped back, as if she were still wary of him. He gave no reaction, for she would see his skills soon enough.

Marguerite gathered the women together while Dougal cleared the exit to the outside. Callum reached for her hand and felt the cold soft skin of her palm.

He held it for a time, watching her, trying to let her know the words trapped inside of him. *I'll do everything in my power to keep you safe.*

A blush transformed her face as she nodded. 'I know.' She remained at his side as they moved towards the exit. The sunlight reflected the rainwater within the ditch. They would have to cross through the water and up the opposite hillside to reach the sanctuary of the trees and the dwellings hidden in the forest.

When Nairna started to move forward, Marguerite stopped her. 'I know the way to your house, Nairna. I'll go first and lead them, if you'll help Laren gather the others. I don't know them as well as you do.'

Callum slung his quiver of arrows over one shoulder. Though he understood Marguerite's desire to help, he wouldn't let her go anywhere without him. He chose a single arrow from the quiver, while Nairna returned to the store of weapons, choosing a crossbow. The young woman's face was pale with fear, but Callum admired her willingness to fight.

The smoke grew worse, and when the children began coughing, Laren picked up her own daughters, one over each hip, as the women gathered together. Marguerite moved to the front of the passageway, but Callum kept at her side, nocking the arrow to his bow.

Her blue eyes held terror and she cast a last look at him.

It will be all right, he wanted to tell her. *No one will harm you.*

But without the words to reassure her, he reached out and stroked the side of her face with one hand. She held his fingers to her cheek and sent him a nod of trust.

And it was what he needed to face the danger ahead.

Callum left the shelter of the tunnel, studying their surroundings. There were no soldiers on this side of the fortress, nor any sign of them in the forest ahead. Satisfied, he signalled Dougal to cross the bank and take a position on the opposite side of the ditch. With both of them armed, they could protect the others from all sides.

His younger brother obeyed, but Callum didn't miss the apprehension in his eyes. The lad was afraid, and whether or not he could shoot with accuracy was anyone's guess.

While Nairna climbed down into the water with Marguerite, Callum kept his bow taut, searching for any threat. From his peripheral vision, he watched the women making their way through the water. Nairna's dog dove in behind them, paddling across the water. The animal appeared unconcerned by the exodus and Callum took it as a good sign that the enemy had not yet reached this side of the fortress. Bram and Alex must have kept them occupied with fighting in the main fortress.

'Go and take cover in the trees,' Nairna told Marguerite, setting her crossbow on the ground. 'I'll stay with Dougal and help the women out of the ditch.'

Callum watched over her and Marguerite sent him one last look. He locked the image into his mind, afraid it was the last time he would see her. Her long golden hair gleamed against the sun and her blue eyes filled with worry. Despite the danger, he didn't regret the moments he'd spent with her. If he died today, at least he'd glimpsed Heaven.

You're unworthy of her, his conscience reminded him. *All you can offer is your protection.*

While more women evacuated with their children, Callum could only hold his position until Marguerite disappeared into the forest. He resumed his place on the bank beside the fortress, the arrow poised to shoot. And yet, he couldn't stop his hands from shaking. It wasn't fear—only the raw anticipation coursing through him.

Nairna's dog began barking and Callum spun, taking aim at the emerging soldiers. He stretched the bowstring taut, adjusting his aim. Slowly, he waited for the soldier to draw near and when he loosed the arrow, it struck the man's face.

Too high.

He followed up with a second shot to the heart, dropping the man where he'd stood.

A slight motion caught his attention and, while Callum readied another arrow, he saw Marguerite watching from the trees. Whether it was her thanks or a quiet farewell, he met her gaze with the promise to defend her.

His brother Dougal cried out a warning and Callum seized another arrow. When more men crossed to the opposite side, the boy panicked and fired too soon. The arrow struck the ground, but before his brother could run, Callum sent a steady stream of his own missiles into the charging soldiers, one after the other, each arrow striking its intended target.

He dulled his mind to the fighting and death around him, focusing only on bringing down the threat. For the first time in years, he could defend his clan. With his bow, he was no longer less than a man, but equal to his brothers. It didn't matter that he couldn't speak, only that he could wield a weapon.

In this, he had a purpose. And soon enough, the women and children would be within the forest, away from the worst of the fighting.

Behind him, Callum heard the groaning of the keep's tower, while Nairna brought the last of the women out of the water. He kept his gaze focused on his surroundings and saw his brothers Bram and Alex approaching at a full run.

Bram crossed through the water, helping his wife up the hillside before he pulled her into his embrace.

At the sight of them, a tightness expanded through Callum's chest. Nairna gripped her husband as if she never wanted to let go. He envied them, for he wanted to be with Marguerite, to reassure himself that she was all right. Letting her go while he stayed behind was the only choice, but he didn't like it.

A shower of fire sparks drifted in front of him and a prickle of awareness caught him. Behind him, a cracking noise resounded, just as his brother roared, 'Callum, dive!'

He threw himself into the ditch, just as the tower collapsed. The icy water numbed him, but Callum swam to the opposite side, dragging himself out. His bow and arrows were soaked, and he rested on his knees, catching his breath.

Nairna was pushing Marguerite back inside the forest. 'He'll be all right. Take the women up to the ridge and I'll send him soon.'

Callum's gaze snapped to hers. She was holding on to Nairna, as if she didn't want to leave. It seemed that she'd started to lead the women away, only to return when the tower had fallen.

As if she cared about him, despite the danger to herself.

If he could have, he'd have abandoned all else, taking her away from the chaos of battle. But that wasn't a choice. He was bound to defend his family and the only home he'd ever had.

As if to remind him of that, Bram extended a hand

and helped him up. And for a moment, he saw the gratefulness on his brother's face. 'Thank you for defending them,' he said below his breath, so that only Callum would hear. 'And I'm sorry for every day you spent in captivity. I blame myself for it.'

Though he could make no reply, he squeezed Bram's hand in forgiveness. After what they'd been through, he knew his brother had done everything possible to free him. Nairna sent him a smile of gratefulness, still standing by her husband.

Before his brother Dougal could join the women and children, Callum offered his sword. The lad needed a weapon of his own, now that he'd spent all of his arrows. After taking it, Dougal disappeared into the forest, just as more enemy soldiers emerged, surrounding them on all sides.

Though Callum wanted to reassure himself that Marguerite had escaped with his youngest brother, he forced himself not to look, for fear of drawing the soldiers' attention there.

Too late.

One of the archers fired several arrows towards the forest before he could bring the man down. Not all of the women had made it to the top of the ridge, and Callum worried that one of them could have been struck. The thought of Marguerite lying prone, her life ended by an arrow, sent a dark rage pulsing through him.

Bram and Alex split off on either side to meet the men, their shields and weapons ready. Callum kept firing at the enemy archers, dropping as many as he could, until he had only a single arrow left. Alex handed him a shield, but he refused it, needing both hands to wield the bow. They were completely outnumbered by the enemy and he saw no way out.

Nairna held fast to Bram while their enemy awaited the order to kill. Callum held his bow steady, hoping he could take out Cairnross or Harkirk with his last arrow.

Even if he did, there was one unavoidable truth. Today he was going to die.

Marguerite clenched her hands together, her heart racing. Though she'd made it into the forest, away from the battle, she couldn't stop herself from returning to watch. She chose an isolated place near the edge of the trees, her heart numb with fear as Lord Cairnross and Lord Harkirk closed in.

Through a haze of tears, she sat, wondering if she could plead with Cairnross for their lives. Was it possible that he might spare them, on her behalf?

No. She'd fled with the MacKinlochs, betraying their betrothal. Though the earl might still want her for his wife, she didn't trust him to free the others. Especially Callum.

She stood, resting her hand against a tree, her heart sick with terror. Because of her, Cairnross had come. If she'd remained behind, none of these men would have died.

Marguerite took a step towards Callum, but before she could emerge from the trees, she saw Bram explode in fury. His claymore flashed as he brought down man after man and Alex stood at his back to defend him.

They fought for their lives and in the midst of the battle, Callum seized a quiver of arrows from a dead archer. As he released the arrows, one after the other, he moved into the forest, moving straight towards her.

Marguerite didn't move, not understanding why he was leaving his brothers behind. When he reached her side, he pulled her veil free and dropped it, pulling her to higher ground. She suddenly realised that the white colour had made her visible from below. And she was still in range of their arrows, where she'd been standing.

'You can't leave them behind,' she pleaded, looking back at Bram, Alex and Nairna. 'They need you.'

Callum's face hardened and he climbed atop a large boulder, drawing back his bow. He released another stream of arrows toward the enemy, bringing down one man after another.

Shame reddened her cheeks when Marguerite realised she'd accused him of cowardice. That wasn't it at all. He'd been moving into a position where he could better defend them.

'I misunderstood,' she apologised. 'I'm sorry for what I said.' By leaving his brothers and hiding within the trees, he'd gained a more strategic position, fighting where the enemy couldn't see him.

Callum pointed to the top of the ridge, in a wordless order for her to join the other women. She understood, but hesitated, not wanting to leave him behind. 'Thank you for protecting me,' she whispered.

He lowered his bow for a moment. His brown eyes held a steady reassurance, as if he would never allow anyone to harm her. The look on his face was of a man prepared to die.

Marguerite reached down to the fallen veil and brought it to him, binding it slowly around his left forearm. 'Take this,' she said. 'It will protect your arm from the bowstring.'

It was all she could give him. Callum remained

motionless while she tied it off, then he covered her hand with his. The warmth of his palm reassured her, and he squeezed her hand in silent farewell. She didn't know what would happen to either of them now, but she squeezed it back.

The rumble of horsemen approaching caught Marguerite's attention. She saw two armies of men and, at the sight of the tall man leading the group, her heart soared. The Duc D'Avignois had come at last.

She started to move downhill, but Callum caught her by the arm. 'It's my father,' she explained. 'I have to see him.' If she could reach the Duc in time, she might convince him to save the MacKinlochs.

She started to pull free, when something made her stop and turn around. Callum held his bow over one shoulder, his gaze shielded. He gave her a signal to leave, that he wouldn't stop her. But she realised the truth of what was happening.

The moment she reached her father's side, everything would return to the way it had been. She would be safe with her family, and likely she wouldn't see Callum again.

Regret pulled at her, even though she'd known the moments between them were never going to last. They would fade into bittersweet memories.

'I'll never forget you,' she whispered, touching his cheek in farewell.

Callum drew his bow as soon as Marguerite left the trees, intending to shoot any man who came near her. Two of her father's guards escorted her to safety and she spoke to them, gesturing toward the MacKinlochs as if to intervene.

He kept low, crouching with his bow as he watched the men. Harkirk was still alive, but the body of Cairnross lay upon the ground, slaughtered by his brother Bram.

He should have been relieved that Marguerite would never marry the earl. Instead, angry resentment filled him up, that Bram had wrought justice instead of himself. He'd wanted to be the one to set her free.

More, he wanted to take the earl's place as Marguerite's husband. He touched the veil she'd bound around his arm as a makeshift guard and the softness reminded him of her.

I'll never forget you.

He didn't believe that. As soon as she returned to France, her father would arrange another marriage to a nobleman. She would wed the man, bear him children and forge a different life for herself. One that didn't include him.

Callum watched as they brought a horse for her. He saw his brothers negotiating a truce while Harkirk's men withdrew and Nairna spoke to the Duc. And just as he'd expected, Lady Marguerite rode away with her father. The evening sunset glinted upon her hair like a fading band of gold.

And he knew he would never see her again.

Chapter Four

Summer—1306

The blue ribbon was so faded it had turned to grey, the edges frayed with time.

'*You're hurting by being apart from Marguerite, aren't you?*' his brother's wife Laren had said to him, only months ago. '*Surely, she would find it romantic if you were to steal her away, taking her back with you.*'

Romantic? Callum didn't know where she'd come up with that idea, but he had nothing to offer a duke's daughter. The Duc would murder him where he stood. To prove his point, he nodded to Laren and drew a line across his throat.

'*Aye, her father might kill you.*' She smiled and ventured, '*But you'd die a happy man.*'

Without warning, a laugh broke forth from him. The unexpected sound shocked him and he touched his throat in disbelief.

'*You'll speak again,*' Laren predicted. '*And I think you'll have a stronger reason to, if you find her.*'

* * *

The past few months had been frustrating, for he'd not regained his speech, regardless of the time he'd had to heal and train. He'd done everything he could, but the harder he tried, the more the words remained trapped within him. Worse, the other clan members avoided him, treating him as if he were somehow malformed.

And so he was. Aye, he'd been tortured and brought to the brink of death time and again, but by now the nightmares should have stopped. Instead, they'd grown worse, until he could hardly bring himself to close his eyes at night.

His mind was splintering apart and the more he fought the memories, the greater his anger festered inside. He hated his life and the way he lacked purpose. Captivity had ruled his days for so long, he didn't know what to do with his freedom or how he would ever adapt to a life with no way to speak.

With every day that passed, he isolated himself more from his family, for he couldn't communicate with them. The anger seethed inside him, the frustration dominating every second of the day.

Nairna took it upon herself to confront him. Cool-headed and firm, she'd taken him aside. 'Vengeance hasn't given you peace, has it?'

He stared back at her and she reached for an arrow from his quiver. 'You've fought at our side over the past few months. You helped save Laren's daughter when she was taken. But I see the anger in you. It's growing stronger every day.'

Pity filled up her green eyes and she softened her voice. 'You miss Marguerite, don't you?'

The words were like a spear thrust into his heart.

Marguerite was the one person who had never treated him as if he were weak-minded or less than whole. In her eyes, he had been the warrior he wanted to be.

But she'd returned to the life she had known before him. The life she deserved.

'Marguerite worried about you all the time you were held captive,' Nairna continued, never ceasing her assault. 'If you're too blind to see the way she felt about you, and you won't fight to win her heart, then you deserve to lose her.'

She handed him the arrow and ordered, 'Either go after her or stop sulking.' A smile warmed her expression, a blend of sisterly love and her own frustration.

She was right. He'd stood back and let Marguerite go, without raising a single protest. It was the mark of a coward, and God knew he wasn't that.

But how would he ever convince a duke's daughter to come away with him? It was like trying to bring down the moon.

Laren's earlier suggestion, that he steal her away, resonated as a definite possibility. But would Marguerite want to leave her family and the vast wealth she had known all her life? He couldn't imagine it.

Yet, Nairna's suggestion gave him a purpose. He could stop pacing around Glen Arrin, feeling caged by his lack of speech. No matter how impossible a task, the thought of seeing Marguerite again eased the anger within him.

And so he'd begun the quest.

Callum shielded his eyes from the sunlight, staring down at the forest below. It stretched for miles, curling around Duncraig Castle, which lay tucked within the hills.

He'd never travelled to this part of Scotland before, but he'd heard from other clansmen that these lands belonged to the Duc D'Avignois, inherited from Norman ancestors. Tall square towers stood atop the hill, the imposing battlements ridged with machicolations.

At the sight of the duke's holdings, a cold emptiness cast its shadow over him. He didn't belong here and the fist of doubt squeezed at his courage.

It had taken weeks of sending Dougal to ask questions of the neighbouring clans, but thankfully it wasn't too difficult to track a French duke with over a hundred retainers.

Callum led his horse Goliath down into the woods, planning to set up his camp within the forest where no one would find him. Thus far, he had no idea how long he would stay. It depended on whether or not Marguerite was here and if she wanted to see him.

The darker part of his soul wanted to abduct her now, taking her away from her father's wealth and claiming her as his own. As tempting as it was, he owed her the right to choose. The time they'd spent apart might have changed everything.

Callum studied the pathway, skirting the main stretch so as to avoid the castle inhabitants. The trees were thicker now, making it more difficult for the horse to get through. As the shadows lengthened and sunlight gleamed from the west, he found a small stream to water the horse and set up camp for the night.

Uneasiness gnawed upon him as he delayed going to see her. His presence might not be welcome here. It might be best to spend a day watching over her, observing the castle to ensure that she was safe and happy. Besides, even if he did approach her, he couldn't speak or give any explanation for his presence. She wouldn't understand, that for the past few months, she'd haunted his mind, tormenting him with memories.

At nightfall, he moved to the outer edges of the trees, studying the castle and its defences. A moat encircled the structure and thick stone walls stood taller than the height of a man. Two square towers stood on each side with both gates were heavily guarded. He listened and heard the sound of…was it music?

Callum hadn't heard music in so long, the sound seemed to wend its way through the forest, drawing him closer. He kept low to the ground, hiding within the darkness, until he reached a place in the wall with a crevice small enough to see through. Inside the castle, men and women celebrated with tankards of ale, laughing amid the lilting song. Callum rested his cheek against the cool stone, taking in the sight.

It had been years since he'd had anything at all to celebrate. Watching the people with their smiling faces made him yearn to be a part of it.

Especially when he spied the familiar figure he'd been searching for the past few weeks.

Marguerite's long golden hair was veiled, but it spun out as she whirled in a dance with the others. Callum saw the men watching her and a possessive air came over him.

Seeing her again after so many months was like a balm to his broken spirits. He needed to go inside, to satisfy the need that had tormented him since the last time he'd watched her walk away.

Fate intervened when a group of men and women approached the drawbridge. Callum moved from his hiding place by the wall and drew his hood over his head. Disguised among the villagers, he entered the gates.

Marguerite danced with the other women, but her movements held less energy, as though she didn't want to be there. He drank in the sight of her, memorising her beautiful face and the way she moved.

The music shifted again, to a softer, more plaintive tone. Marguerite stepped away from the dancing, her face flushed. As the others gathered around the musicians, she leaned back against the wall.

Callum never took his eyes from her as he moved through the crowd, keeping out of the torchlights. And when he was an arm's length from her, the sweetness of her scent pressed a dark aching through his chest. If he could stand in her shadow for the rest of his life, it would be enough.

She turned toward him, her eyes narrowed. He saw the moment she realised she wasn't alone. Though he could have lowered his hood, revealing himself, he spied the Duc watching over her.

She clutched her waist, taking a step back towards the people. His opportunity was disappearing and Callum could say nothing to stop her. But he needed to tell her that he was here.

When the sound of laughter resonated from the crowd, Marguerite's attention flickered for a moment. It was all he needed.

As he left the castle, he pressed a single, frayed ribbon into the palm of her hand.

He was here. He'd come back to see her.
All night long, Marguerite had held on to the ribbon,

like a faded memory. She didn't know why Callum had travelled to Duncraig, but the unexpected surge of anticipation broke through her disconsolate mood.

Ever since she'd left Glen Arrin, she'd been unable to forget Callum MacKinloch. The fierce, silent Scot had invaded her dreams, leaving her with memories of his kiss. At night, she imagined his mouth moving down her jaw, down to her throat. She remembered the hardened lines of his body, the taut warm skin that had invited her to touch.

'Marguerite.' Her father interrupted her idle thoughts the next morning, setting his silver cup upon the table beside her. 'I am leaving for England on the morrow. I'll be escorting the Earl of Penrith here for your wedding.'

She nodded her head, trying not to betray the disappointment inside. Even so, her father noticed her unhappiness. 'I know these past few months have been difficult for you. But be assured, this will be a better marriage for you, *ma petite*,' he continued. 'The earl has estates here, as well as in England and Ireland. He is favoured by the English king, and I have it in good faith that he is a nobleman worthy of being your husband. You should be well pleased with him.'

But what if I'm not pleased? she wanted to ask. *What if he's as terrible as Lord Cairnross?* Although she'd known her father would arrange another match, the shadow of restlessness haunted her.

Months ago, the idea of questioning her father's orders had never occurred to her. As the head of the family, it was the Duc's responsibility to choose her husband, selecting a nobleman who would best provide for her. None of her personal desires mattered. Yet now it seemed that the invisible bands of obedience stretched over her, strangling her into submission.

'How long will you be gone?'

'A fortnight or so.' He reached out and took her hand. His heavy gold ring pressed against her fingers as he squeezed his reassurance. 'There are plenty of my men to keep you safe. And soon enough, you'll live in England as lady of your own castle.' He sent her a warm smile, believing that was all she'd ever wanted.

He had no reason to think otherwise. Only months ago, she'd wanted to rule over her own demesne, with a strong husband at her side. She had planned to be his obedient wife, creating a comfortable home for him and bearing children.

But everything had changed since she'd spent time with the MacKinlochs. Despite the danger and the terrifying battle, she'd shattered the glass of her protected life. Another woman lived inside her skin, someone with courage. A woman who had seized her own escape from Cairnross.

When her father had brought her to Duncraig, she'd expected to resume her old life, like a familiar shadow. Instead, the past haunted her, making her dream of a silent warrior who had torn apart her defences, awakening her.

And now he'd come back.

She knew little of Callum MacKinloch, nor could she guess what he thought of her. Yet the need to see him again overwhelmed her, filling her mind with impossible thoughts.

'We'll hunt this morning,' her father said. A warm smile crinkled the edges of his eyes. 'I want a little more time with my youngest daughter before she leaves me as a wedded woman.' He summoned a servant and ordered their horses to be readied. 'While I'm away, you are not to leave these grounds. Is that understood?'

You are not to think for yourself or make any decisions that contradict mine, she thought bitterly. But she gave the expected response, *'Oui, mon père.'*

'You will also spend your time sewing or in prayer,' he added. 'Do not trouble yourself with the needs of the household. I have appointed Lady Beatrice to oversee the servants and to guide you in my absence.'

Marguerite suppressed a groan. Though outwardly kind, her mother's sister Beatrice had a thin air of superiority that didn't sit well with her. The next fortnight would, no doubt, be an exercise in patience.

'Obey her, Marguerite,' he insisted.

In spite of her nineteen years, he still treated her as if she were only seven years old. Marguerite veiled her frustration and rose from the table, ignoring the rest of her food. At his enquiring look, she gave the expected response, 'If that is your will, Papa.'

Approval settled into his expression and he dismissed her with a hand. 'Go now, and we'll ride out together in an hour.'

She found her father waiting for her near the stables. He sent her a welcoming smile while she mounted her horse. 'The others are not yet ready to join us on the hunt. If you're willing, we'll go out for a short ride together.'

It meant that he wanted to speak with her in private, she guessed. With a nod, she followed him outside the gates.

Within her bodice, she'd tucked the frail ribbon Callum had given her last eve. Her skin tightened with the desire to see him again. Why had he come back? Knowing that he was here had opened up the Pandora's box of her forbidden wishes. Marguerite stared at the trees around them, wondering if he was nearby.

The Duc led her along the perimeter of the forest, toward the open fields. When she drew her mare alongside his, he suggested, 'Shall we race? I'll grant you a small lead.'

She suspected that he intended to let her win, as he'd done when she was a young girl. Though she returned his smile, she guessed that he had other news to impart that she would not like.

'I don't need an advantage,' she countered, adjusting her skirts. 'I can win without it.'

The challenge brought a smile to her father's face. 'What shall we wager? A length of silk or a golden chain with a jewel to match your eyes? Perhaps a fur-lined cloak to keep you warm in winter?'

She shook her head. There was no need for luxuries, not when he'd granted all of that in the past. 'A favour to be granted at a time of my choosing.' With the reins in her hand, she added, 'What do you want, if you win?'

His face softened. 'A visit, from time to time. Your sisters hardly ever come to see me any more.' For a fleeting moment, she spied the loneliness in his expression. He'd lost her mother years ago and had not remarried, though she was not naïve enough to believe he'd been without female companionship in that time.

'All right,' she agreed. 'Say the word and we'll ride.'

'To the edge of the shore,' he said, pointing to the coastline in the distance. The Duc lifted his hand, eyeing her to ensure she was ready. Then, when he lowered his palm, they both rode hard across the countryside. Marguerite leaned into the wind, watching as her father kept his horse in check, giving her the lead. Though he loved to ride as much as she, he'd always been indulgent, wanting her to win.

Just as he'd given her everything she'd ever desired, whether it was a silk gown or a purse filled with gold. She'd adored him as a young girl, believing that it was her purpose in life to comply with his every dictate. But the past few months had unsettled her, regarding the decisions he'd made. No longer was he the benevolent ruler whom she obeyed without question.

Suddenly she felt the urge to defy his intentions again. At the last moment, just before she won the race, Marguerite pulled her horse to a hard stop, letting her father ride past.

The Duc turned the horse and sent her a surprised look. 'You cheated.'

'*Oui*, I did.' She sent a mischievous smile, adding, 'Don't deny you were about to do the same.'

He shrugged and came to join at her side. 'A father is allowed to grant favours to a beloved daughter, is he not?'

She reached out and took his hand. 'I suppose I'll have to come and visit you in France, after I wed.'

'I'll hold you to that vow.' But in his face she could see the shadow of concern.

'What is it you haven't told me?' Marguerite asked him. 'You're hiding something.'

He let out a sigh and guided her back toward the castle to join the others. 'Nothing of any import, I suppose. The Earl of Penrith is a good friend of the king's. I am certain he will grant every wish you could have.' But his smile lacked sincerity, setting her mood on edge.

She followed her father back to join the hunting party awaiting them, her mind distracted. What wasn't he telling her? As they rode out into the forest in search of game, she fought the anxiety that edged her spirits.

The woods blurred in a golden haze of sunlight filtering through the trees. Though she continued with the others, her mind was distracted and not at all interested in the hunt.

'A boar!' one of the men shouted, pointing toward the forest. The riders quickened their pace and Marguerite held back, letting her father take the lead. Although she didn't doubt that the hunters would prevail, she wasn't about to get in the way of a boar. The aggressive beasts had vicious tusks and more than a few men had been gored by them.

Along with her father, a dozen men and women rode past, while Marguerite remained on the outskirts. The others were so intent, no one seemed to notice her absence.

Then she heard a scuffling sound. Marguerite turned her horse around, only to see a second boar racing towards her.

Mon Dieu. She urged the horse faster, trying to get away from the animal. No one else noticed and she turned her mare deeper into the woods, trying to escape. Her horse reared up and she struggled to hold her seat.

Arrows sliced through the air, embedding within the boar. Marguerite stared at them, her heart racing when she saw the black feathers. Then, suddenly, someone dropped from the tree behind her, landing on her horse. The man's arms came around her, and he forced the horse into a gallop, leading her away from the others. The instinct to scream died down in her throat, for she knew, without a doubt, the identity of the hooded silent man.

When the woods grew so thick her horse could no longer make it through, he dismounted and lifted her down. Beneath the shadowed hood, she saw the dark eyes of the man she'd dreamed of over the past few months.

'Callum,' she whispered, unable to believe it was he.

He said nothing, but took her hand, guiding her through the woods for what seemed like a mile. Marguerite didn't care that the others might miss her presence. She could think of nothing but the man who was with her now.

When at last he stopped, she spied the remains of a camp site and the ashes of a fire. Before Callum could stoop to rekindle it, Marguerite threw her arms around him. He gripped her hard, his face buried in her hair. She melted against the planes of his body, unable to believe he was here at last.

'It's been so long,' she breathed. 'Are you well? How is your family?'

His eyes stared into hers, but gave no reply. She understood, then, that his speech had not returned.

But he had his own way of speaking, in a manner that captivated her.

Callum removed her veil, sliding his hands into her hair. She caught her breath as he moved his palms down to her shoulders, resting them upon her hips. The warmth of his touch sent a shiver of longing through her.

'Why have you come?' she whispered.

He didn't have to answer for her to know. Despite the months that had been lost between them, it was as if nothing had changed. She touched his smooth cheek, marvelling at the difference in him. No longer did he have the starving look about him; his face had filled out. There was no doubting the strength in his arms or the quiet assurance he exuded. He'd kept his hair long and the dark strands grew past his shoulders, like the wild Scot that he was.

The stirrings of interest caught at her, forbidden thoughts of the time they'd spent together months ago. She remembered his mouth upon hers and the shocking desires he'd evoked.

Feeling suddenly shy, she stepped back and he took a moment to rebuild the fire. Though she couldn't stay with him for too long, she would steal whatever moments she could.

When the fire burned brighter, she sat down on a fallen log and told him of the months they'd travelled from northern Scotland down to the Southwest.

'My father has arranged a new marriage,' she admitted. 'I'm to wed the Earl of Penrith.'

She needed him to know it, to be fully honest with him about the way her life had shifted in the past few months. At her confession, Callum's expression tensed. He picked up a dry piece of wood and tossed it on the fire. Marguerite didn't know what else to say, but she offered, 'I'm glad you came. I—I thought of you often.'

His silence only intensified the awkwardness between them. Without a voice, he could tell her nothing of the past or what he was thinking now.

She tried to think of something else, but could only ask, 'Has your back healed?'

Callum sent her a curious look, but set down his quiver beside the bow and removed his tunic.

When he turned his back, she saw that the scars still held a red tint, but they had fully healed. She reached out to touch the skin and he flinched.

'Did I hurt you?'

He shook his head, lifting her hand to touch him again. The warm skin was rough from the scarred gouges, but the lines of suffering had only strengthened him. When she traced his flesh with her fingertips, he leaned into the touch, as if her palms were healing him.

She moved her fingers over his shoulders, down to his ribs. A sudden deep laugh escaped him, as if he were ticklish. Shocked, Marguerite murmured, 'I didn't know you could make any sounds at all.' It made her wonder if he would one day speak again. And if he did, what he would say.

Callum took her hand and brought it to his throat, his eyes watching her. The intimate touch of her fingers upon his skin made her feel awkward and she sensed that he wanted something from her.

Abruptly, his expression grew stoic and he put his tunic on again, reaching into a pouch of his belongings. He retrieved a silver chain holding a pendant of sapphire-coloured glass. Marguerite held it in her palm, captivated by the shifting colours in the blue necklace. He lifted it over her neck and the pendant settled upon her bosom.

'It's beautiful.' She ventured, 'Laren made this glass, didn't she?' At his nod, she offered, 'Thank you.'

She touched the pendant, not knowing what else to say. A sinking sensation pulled at her gut and she dared to ask again, 'Callum, why have you come?'

Dark brown eyes fastened upon her, with the intensity of a man who wanted more than she could give. He took her hand in his, holding it gently. Then he opened his palm, letting her pull away if she would.

Marguerite saw the question in his eyes. He would let her go, here and now, if that was her choice. She simply had to walk away.

In her mind, she thought of the night he'd kissed her and the shaken longing he'd provoked. She'd been unable to forget the way he'd made her feel or the tremulous emotions within herself.

Your father has already decided upon your marriage. Callum MacKinloch has no place in your life, the voice of logic demanded.

She knew that, just as she knew the rest of her life would be commanded by others. Though she longed to speak up, to tell her father she wanted to make her own decisions, he never listened to her opinions. He simply reminded her that he wanted what was best for her life. It was hard to argue when he'd given her so much.

'I have to go back,' she murmured at last. 'They'll be searching for me.' The words were leaden and she suspected that Callum would be gone in the morning. Loneliness stretched out within her at the thought.

He lowered his hand, his face devoid of any emotion. She wanted to say something, to make him understand how little power she held. But instead, she locked away the words, afraid of hurting him with the truth.

Callum escorted her back and with every step, he felt her slipping further away. Though she'd been glad to see him, both of them knew he didn't belong here. Still, he'd hoped for a chance.

Inside him, he closed off the numbness, accepting her decision. Just having these moments with her had been more than he'd hoped for. Of course her father would have chosen someone else for her to marry, someone with noble blood.

Not a prisoner, locked away from the rest of the world. Not a man with hardly a penny to call his own.

The dark tension warred with his instincts, but pride forced him to release her hand. No matter how many miles he'd travelled, if she'd made her decision, there was nothing more he could do.

She curled her palm around the pendant, her blue eyes holding back tears. He turned away, the ache burning a hole inside of him. Perhaps it was best to let her go.

'Wait.' Her voice held a quaver that he didn't understand. Before he could take another step, Marguerite closed the space between them.

His pulse faltered at her plea, but he shielded his thoughts and waited for her to speak.

'I don't want you to go,' she whispered.

Hope roared through him, that she might give him this chance. He touched her face and Marguerite stood on her tiptoes, winding her arms around him.

He held her so tight, their bodies merged into one. There was so much he needed to say to her and he struggled again to speak. But the words would not come.

For a breathless moment, he drew back to study her. His mouth hovered above hers, waiting for her consent. She lifted her mouth to his and the physical hunger consumed him. Her kiss evoked every moment that they'd spent apart, the empty loneliness that had made each day interminable.

He put his desires and feelings into the kiss, not caring about anything else but this moment. The woman he'd dreamed of was standing before him, and he intended to savour the forbidden moment.

'Will I see you again?' she murmured.

He nodded and pointed toward the fire, where he'd set up camp. She could come to him at any moment, though he knew better than to seek her within her father's castle.

'My father is leaving for England at dawn,' she told him. 'I'll try to come after he's gone.'

As she spoke the promise, Callum saw the hint of worry in her eyes, as if she were afraid of someone discovering their secret. He didn't care at all, for she'd given him a shred of hope.

And for that, he'd risk everything.

Chapter Five

'Good morn to you, Marguerite.' Her mother's sister, Lady Beatrice, opened the shutters, revealing the morning sunlight. The matron was plump with blonde hair the same colour as her own. A silver cross nestled between her large breasts, likely to draw attention to them. 'You'd best hurry to say farewell to your father. He'll be leaving for England within the hour.'

Marguerite sat up, murmuring a polite response, while her mind wandered back to the nightmare from last night. Beneath the coverlet, her hands were clenched, her heartbeat unsteady. Although it was only a dream, there was enough reality in it to frighten her. In her vision, she'd been with Callum, kissing him deeply. He'd laid her back upon the grass and she'd welcomed him into her arms.

Only to have him seized by her father's men and killed for touching her.

Fear took command of her, for she knew it could easily happen if she were not careful. It was dangerous to meet with him or to let her defences weaken. Callum was a man her father would never approve of. Wild and fierce, he was a fighter who had survived a torturous life. Yet she could not deny the desire he'd awakened inside her. She wanted desperately to see him again, but now she questioned whether or not to go.

'I've brought the silk and samite for you, along with the earl's measurements,' her aunt continued. 'You can begin sewing this afternoon.'

'Sewing?' She'd missed the first part of the conversation and frowned at the sight of the blue material.

'For his wedding tunic,' Lady Beatrice reminded her. 'Your father wishes your husband to see your accomplishments. What better way than to make the earl new garments, embroidered by your hand?'

The matron sent her a bright smile. 'He'll be proud to wear something made by his bride.' She began setting out lengths of silk upon the small table near the window. 'If you work each day, you'll finish by the time he arrives from England. The Duc did not wish you to be bored in his absence.'

Normally, spending several hours sewing would have been a pleasant way to spend the day. Today, however, it made her want to cry out with frustration. She suspected her father had done this in an attempt to keep her locked away in her room.

But she had other plans for this morn.

Marguerite allowed Lady Beatrice to help her get dressed, while she eyed the outside sun with longing. 'I will do as my father commands, of course,' she lied. 'But after he leaves, I was planning to ride.'

'That will not be permitted,' Beatrice said, shaking her head. 'We have our orders that you are to be kept safely inside the castle.'

'Like a prisoner?' Marguerite mused.

Her aunt's face clouded with confusion. 'It's for your safety, Marguerite. We wouldn't want you to be lost or, worse, to be abducted by a Scot.' She shivered, gripping her arms. 'I can only imagine what you must have endured with them.'

Marguerite said nothing, recognising that Beatrice would never understand. She moved to touch the fabric, examining the tight weave. The price of the silk might have fed the MacKinloch clan for a year, which was sobering.

She'd never stopped to think of how her father's wealth surrounded every part of her life, whereas Callum's family struggled for their food and shelter. During the battle a few months ago, their fortress at Glen Arrin had burned. Had they managed to rebuild their homes? How many had died?

Though she had dwelled with them for only a short time before Cairnross and Harkirk had attacked, she'd been accepted as one of them. Nairna and Laren had worked alongside her, almost like sisters. And the freedom was like nothing she had ever experienced. Here, she could hardly walk below stairs without a man guarding her. It was stifling, living this way.

Her aunt began chattering once again, but Marguerite didn't hear the words. Her mind was consumed with how to find a way out of the castle for a few hours, in order to meet with Callum. Her best opportunity would come, as soon as the Duc departed.

'Come, Marguerite,' her aunt insisted. 'Your father will be waiting below stairs. He'll want you to wish him safe journey.'

She took Beatrice's hand and followed her, casting another look at the blue silk and samite. Somehow, she had to make her escape.

She came on foot. Through the trees, Marguerite's saffron gown bloomed like a golden flower caught within the forest. Callum stood waiting for her, near his tethered horse, Goliath. Upon his shoulder, he carried his bow and quiver of arrows to protect them from any harm.

The sight of her made his pulse quicken. He was torn between wanting to steal her away and discovering how to win her heart. She'd kept her promise to return, but he hardly knew what she thought of him.

Ever since the first moment he'd seen her, an invisible pull had bound him to her. There was nothing he wouldn't do for Marguerite if it kept her safe and made her happy.

Though her fine gown marked her as a duke's daughter, when he looked upon her face, he saw the woman who had saved him from death. She was a quiet beauty that he couldn't relinquish.

When she reached his side, he repressed the urge to pull her into an embrace. His hand clenched around the bow and he nodded in greeting.

Marguerite offered a hesitant smile. 'Good morn to you.'

Callum gestured towards his fire, motioning the question of whether she had broken her fast. She saw the remains of the boar meat he'd taken and shook her head. 'I've eaten already.'

She twisted her hands together, reaching for the silver chain around her throat. When she pulled it free, he saw the pendant hidden beneath the silk gown. She'd kept it.

Her eyes held nervousness, but he made an effort not to frighten her. After so many months, they were strangers again. It would take time before she learned to trust him.

He beckoned to her to come closer and introduced her to his black stallion. Marguerite reached to touch Goliath and the horse nuzzled her hand. 'He's a handsome creature.' Her eyes met his and a flush of shyness came over her cheeks. Murmuring to the animal, she stroked his head and distracted herself with getting acquainted.

She looked flustered, as if she didn't know what to say or do. Moving between them, he took her hand in his. She was scared and it wasn't surprising. He'd removed her from the castle, bringing her out here alone. He had to do something to make her relax, to understand that nothing had changed between them.

Taking her hand, he lifted it to his own hair and drew it downwards in a petting motion. A smile flickered at her mouth. 'You're not a horse, Callum.' But the tension evaporated and she let out a half-laugh when he nuzzled her hand. With his hands upon her waist, he lifted her on to the horse, swinging up behind her.

'Where are we going?' she asked.

He pointed beyond the trees, north of the castle. Far away where none of her father's men could find them.

Marguerite started to protest, but he ignored her, urging the animal through the trees to the meadow beyond. He held her securely against him as he quickened the pace, letting the animal take them away.

In the open clearing, he urged the horse faster, holding her tight as he let Goliath run. The stallion loved nothing better than to go fast, the landscape blurring around them. He guided them over the hills, until they reached a small, silvery loch. His horse was glad to stop for a drink and Callum lifted Marguerite down while Goliath took his fill.

'For a moment, I was afraid you were trying to steal me away to Glen Arrin,' she breathed, a furtive smile upon her lips.

Would you want me to? he wondered.

Unlike most men, he could not speak words of flattery or tell her his thoughts. He had to rely on his actions to show her what he wanted.

With his hands resting upon her waist, he tried to let her see the thoughts within him.

If I could, I'd bring you back with me.

His hands moved up her arms, like a lover's. Her skin prickled with goose flesh, but she remained utterly motionless, her blue eyes caught up in his. 'I don't know what to say to you,' she whispered.

His answer was to touch a finger to her lips. *Say nothing at all.* He took her hands and brought them to his chest. Furtively, she rested her fingers upon his heartbeat.

'I think your heart is beating as fast as mine is,' she admitted, raising her hands to his shoulders. Her touch explored him, moving down his arms, and then up again. He didn't move at all, thankful that she'd read his thoughts. Only he wanted her hands upon his bare skin.

'I shouldn't be here right now,' she murmured, 'but I don't care.'

Neither did he. Her father was gone and they had a

few hours before the others would come to search for her. By then, he would bring her safely home again.

Marguerite's hands moved up his neck, then her hands threaded into his hair. The sensation of her touch brought him closer to temptation. He wanted to kiss her again, to taste the sweetness of her mouth and give in to his own desires. The blinding pleasure of her hands was pushing him closer to the edge. But then, with a mischievous smile, she petted him, as she had done earlier to his horse.

His answer was to seize her wrists and capture the kiss he wanted. He took command of her mouth, stealing her breath, and giving her no chance to escape him. She didn't understand the power she held over him. His hands moved into her hair, tearing the veil aside until he could slide his fingers into the silken length.

Don't play games with me.

Her lips were swollen, her breathing tremulous. But she understood now that he wasn't one of her father's men who would defer to flirtation or small touches.

Her face was pale, but there was no fear—only an answering desire. He hadn't brought her here for teasing, but neither would he harm her.

Taking her hand in his, he led Marguerite to sit upon a boulder overlooking the loch. The late morning sun had risen higher, casting its warmth. 'It's beautiful here,' she offered. Drawing her knees beneath her gown, she stared out at the silvery water. 'There was a lake near my father's castle in Avignois,' she admitted. 'When I was a little girl, I used to watch my sisters swim. I was too frightened to join them.'

He sent her a questioning look, and she added, 'I never learned how.'

But he saw the interest in her eyes. Bending down, she removed her shoes and dangled her bare feet into the water. 'It's not as cold as I thought it would be.'

Callum watched her, wondering if she would trust him. They were alone, with no one to intrude. Stripping off his tunic, he waded into the water, never minding that his trews would get wet. He came before her, the water reaching just above his knees, and held out his hand.

'I can't go into the water,' she said. 'My gown would be soaked.'

He didn't pressure her, but tilted his head in an invitation to join him. Wariness lined her face, as if she didn't trust him.

'I'm not certain it would be a good idea. I really am a terrible coward.' She tried to smile, but beneath it he saw a hint of fear. Possibly fear of the water, but it might be a fear of getting closer to him. Especially after the kiss he'd stolen.

He sent her a slow, sinful smile. *Come to me, Marguerite. If you dare.*

She gathered her skirts and stood up, eyeing him with wariness. Callum dipped his hand in the water and flicked a splash of water at her. Marguerite let out a light shriek, laughing as the cold droplets rolled down her throat beneath her gown. 'Don't. Really, I shouldn't.'

He reached into the water and cupped both hands full. Eyeing her with wickedness, he led the threat hover between them.

'You wouldn't dare.'

In answer, he sloshed the water toward her, angling it so that it just missed her gown.

She leaped back with her skirts still clutched in

her hands. 'Enough. I surrender.' But her eyes were laughing.

He emerged from the loch, dripping wet, and came to stand before her. Her gaze moved over his bare skin and there was interest in her eyes. She'd seen him unclothed before and sensual memories invaded his mind, recalling how she had bathed him.

He brought his wet hands to the jewelled girdle at her waist. She stared at him, covering his hands with her own while he unfastened it.

Trust me.

Her face paled, but he dropped the girdle upon the grass, waiting for her to make the choice.

'If I were still a little girl, it wouldn't matter, would it? I could try to swim if I wanted to.'

Callum nodded in reply, moving his hands to loosen the surcoat she wore.

'M-my father never allowed me to try swimming. He told me I wasn't strong enough, that I might drown.' In her eyes, he saw the war of feelings, as if she were torn with indecision. He drew his hands up her nape and she shivered before him. With his thumb, he brushed gently against her mouth, as if to tempt her.

'He will be gone for the next fortnight,' she continued, turning her back to him. 'To bring back the man who will be my husband.'

Her confession fired up Callum's jealousy, darkening his mood. He'd come here to fight for her, to show her another fate if she wanted it. He wasn't about to stand aside and let her wed someone else. Not if he could convince her otherwise.

She drew her hair over one shoulder, baring her throat to him. 'Will you help me take this gown off?'

His answer was to rest his hands upon her skin, letting her feel the warmth of him. Slowly he unlaced the saffron surcoat and helped her lift it away. The gown beneath it was tightly fitted to her arms. He rested his hands upon her shoulders, awaiting permission. Goose flesh rose upon her nape and she murmured, 'May I borrow your blade?'

Confused, he stepped back and handed it to her. Marguerite took the knife and used it to tear out the stitches that held her sleeves in place. 'I didn't bring scissors, as I sometimes do. But now we can remove it.'

When he hesitated, she raised her arms. 'Go on,' she whispered. 'But leave my chemise.'

He knelt at her feet, gathering the hem of the gown. As he raised it high, his hands grazed her waist and over the curve of her breasts. The linen chemise was soft, barely covering her flesh, and he gritted his teeth against the urges rising within him. When she was free of the garment, he couldn't stop the urge to touch her. While his hands encircled her waist, resting below her breasts, he brought his mouth to the silver chain resting upon her nape. His lips edged the chain, and he drew it out with his fingers, moving the pendant beneath the chemise to nestle against her bare breasts.

A sigh escaped Marguerite and it was all he could do not to drag her to him, stripping away the last barrier between them. His mind tormented him with visions of claiming her, using his mouth and tongue to awaken her passion.

She turned to face him, her body shielded by the linen. With her palms upon his chest, his heartbeat quickened. 'Teach me to swim, Callum.'

* * *

She was playing a dangerous game. Marguerite saw the emotions race across Callum's face and worried that she'd gone too far. Perhaps he'd brought her here to enjoy time together in a beautiful place and she had dared to reveal more of herself by shedding the outer gowns. Her bare arms attracted his notice, although her chemise covered her body.

He took her hand and led her into the water. It was cold, but not unbearably so. With every step, the water grew deeper. Past her calves, to her thighs, and finally her waist. Her chemise moved within the water and though Callum continued to walk at her side, she could feel the strain in his demeanour.

He looked like a man who was fighting against himself but the darkness in his eyes tempted her instead of making her fear him. Already he'd given her a glimpse of the physical heat that was hers for the taking. His kiss had been savage, unrelenting. And he tempted her in a way that no man ever had.

Her hands grew wet, but he didn't let go. And once the water covered her breasts, she gasped at the sudden drop in temperature.

'This is far enough.' She crossed her arms over her chest, for her breasts puckered within her chemise. Against the thin linen, she worried he might see too much.

You could have refused to swim, she reminded herself. *This was your doing.*

Callum drew her to face him and she saw the water lapping his muscled chest. The fierce desire to touch this man, to be consumed by him, was rising within her. No longer did it seem that they were worlds apart.

There was only this moment between them and the un-named feelings.

He reached down and picked her up, cradling her in his arms. His hands rested against the back of her knees and a violent shiver came over her. When he laid her back in the water, she was barely aware of him straightening her limbs. His dark eyes held her captive as his hands rested beneath her spine.

She was floating on the water, not understanding how. Her chemise was soaked and clung to her body. No doubt he could see the darker nipples beneath the linen and he made no effort to hide his gaze. His eyes passed over her, like a man who couldn't stop himself. He adjusted his grip to hold her with one arm, while the other traced the curve of her cheek, moving down her throat. The contrast between the heat of his hands and the freezing water held her locked in place.

Every part of her wanted him to go further, to move his hands over her aching breasts, to touch her where no man ever had.

The ripples of water held her suspended and she fought the urge to hold on to Callum's arms. Slowly, he moved to stand behind her, until he dropped his hands away. She was floating with nothing to hold her above the water. Panic filled her and she tried to sit up, flailing in the water until he caught her, guiding her torso back to the surface. Once again, he straightened her body, adjusting her position until her hands were outstretched, her legs straight.

He held the back of her head, standing behind her once more. His arms rested beneath her shoulders and she was intensely aware of his moulded strength. He was an archer, a man who could command the bow and send an arrow flying with one pull on the taut string. Those same strong arms held her gently but with the quiet reassurance of a powerful stature.

Marguerite lifted her eyes to his. From her position, he appeared upside down. His steady gaze reminded her that he wasn't going to let anything happen to her. *I'll keep you safe*, his eyes seemed to say.

She watched him, wanting more than his hands upon the back of her head. 'Kiss me,' she whispered.

Instead of bringing her back up to stand before him, Callum bent down to her lips. From the upside-down position, her mouth tantalised him, her cool lips surrendering. Whether she knew it or not, her plea fired the desires he'd tried to hold back. At the sight of her slender body, revealed to him through the thin white linen, it was a good thing he was standing in cold water. The curve and dusky tint of her breasts aroused him like hot oil upon fire.

He kissed her gently, then slid his tongue across the opening of her mouth.

Marguerite couldn't stop her intake of breath, and when her mouth parted, he invaded her with his tongue. The sensation turned her soft in his arms, her hands reaching for him. He held her in the water, and the kiss became the prelude of every way he wanted to know her.

Her tongue slid against his in a caress, and he took her deeper, letting the kiss turn hotter. He burned for her, body and soul. The water lapped against her skin the way he wanted to touch every inch of her. She reached up to his neck, holding on for balance while her eyes closed.

I want to be on top of you, your skin beneath mine.

His hands came under her knees, catching her before she could slide under. Against her breasts, the wet fabric of her chemise clung to her nipples, making them tight and hard. He imagined moving his mouth down to taste her, swirling his tongue on her until she moaned with need.

She held on to him, turning in the water with her arms around his neck. The water was too deep for her to stand, so she moved her body against his, her cool skin pressing upon him. Instinct made him want to lift her hips, wrapping her slender legs around his waist until he could penetrate her in one stroke.

She was watching him with sudden awareness, her mouth softening as she studied him. 'Callum?' she whispered. It was both a question and a plea.

He couldn't. Not now, not when she didn't know what she asked of him.

Instead, he strode back into shallow water, bringing her back until she stood waist-high in the depths. He broke from the kiss and dove away from her, his body slicing through the water in smooth strokes.

The physical exertion was what he needed right now, the driving need to punish himself. She was innocent and didn't understand what he wanted from her.

His arms broke through the water, swimming hard as if to run away from the man he was.

You're unworthy, the voice taunted. *She's far too good for you.*

He swam endless laps, the water so cold it numbed him from inside. When at last he returned to her, Marguerite stood upon the shore, shivering. On her face, he saw worry.

'Did I do something wrong?' she called out.

He strode through the water, heedless of the droplets rolling down him. No, this was his fault. His feet sank into the sand as he walked closer.

She didn't understand the effect she had upon him, but he wanted to reassure her that he'd regained his grip on sanity. When he stood before her, he reached out to a wet lock of her hair and smoothed it over one ear. He let his eyes speak for him, while his palm rested against her cheek.

It's not your fault. Never yours.

She watched him, her blue eyes worried, but her hand reached up to cover his. 'I know it's cold,' she murmured, 'but will you take me back into the water? Just for a little while?'

Callum eyed her and acquiesced, though he was freezing. He strode into the loch and led her with him. When Marguerite reached the deeper water, he moved her to her stomach. His arms balanced beneath her breasts and legs, lifting her to the top of the water.

'Don't let me fall,' she warned.

He shook his head and she tilted her head to look at him. The feeling of her slender body in his arms was a gift and he tightened his hold to reassure her.

Never.

Callum adjusted the position of her body, holding her with one arm while he showed her how to move her arms. Marguerite tried to swim as he had, but didn't know how to kick her legs.

He reached out to her thighs, opening them slightly as he guided one leg up and down in a fluttering motion. Her skin was cool and firm in his hands. But when he reached to guide her other leg, her face went down into the water. Instantly, he lifted her up and she coughed, holding him tight as she stood up.

'I—I'm sorry,' she apologised. 'I should have been moving my arms, but when my face went under, I was too frightened.'

He smoothed back the hair that had escaped from her braid, his hands upon her cheeks. *Don't be afraid.*

Her answer was to cling to him, resting her cheek against his chest. He embraced her and the ache inside him spread deeper.

'I don't know what's happening between us,' she whispered. 'And I know I shouldn't come to you when I'm betrothed to someone else. But I had to.'

In her voice, he heard the traces of guilt, as if she knew she was betraying her family. He rested his forehead against hers, while both of them shivered.

Nothing mattered any more. Not his clan, far away to the Northeast. Not the stranger she was supposed to marry. Only this moment.

'Could you build a fire?' she asked. He nodded and led her out of the water to sit upon the large boulder. He gathered wood to make a fire, steeling himself against the bitter wind. Marguerite was shivering hard, but he built up the tinder and struck flint until he had a small blaze going. Once he beckoned to her, she huddled as close to it as she dared.

'Swimming was harder than I thought it would be,' she admitted, resting her chin upon her knees. 'But thank you for trying to teach me.'

For a time, she simply sat with him and it didn't matter that neither of them spoke. The quiet time together felt right. When she sent him a glance, she flushed, as if remembering the kiss they'd shared. She took her hair over one shoulder, wringing out the water, finger-combing it to dry.

The motion caught his attention and the longing to keep her with him, to see her in intimate moments like these, was all-encompassing.

His hands dug into the damp sand when she knelt, peeling the wet chemise away from her skin while trying to dry it.

He picked up a fallen stick, intending to toss it into the fire, but he traced it through the dirt, still watching over her. Marguerite frowned, then she studied him with interest.

'Do you know how to write?'

The idea hadn't occurred to him. He shook his head, but then, a sudden flash of inspiration gripped him. Though he couldn't read or write, *she* could.

And if she could teach him, it would give him a way to talk to her. The idea exploded within his mind with the fierce desire to make his thoughts known, to break free of his silent prison.

Callum held out the stick to her, waiting in the hopes that he was right.

His hand closed over hers and he guided the stick back down to the dirt. Marguerite knelt and he pointed to her, then to the ground.

Teach me what you know.

She began to write curved markings, eyeing him with uncertainty. 'It's my name,' she said. 'Marguerite.'

Callum caught her hand and took the stick from her. Then he pressed her hand upon his and struggled to trace over the letters she'd printed. He couldn't quite duplicate the lines, but it was close.

'You want me to teach you how?' she murmured.

Yes. She couldn't know how hungry he was for words, for a way to express the thoughts inside him. If she could teach him anything at all, it would be a gift beyond price.

'Few men can read,' she warned him. 'And it takes many years to learn to write. It's not just the letters.'

He shook his head and forced her hand atop his. *I need to learn.* He struggled to write her name again, though one of the curving letters that dropped lower eluded him.

'In which language?'

An unexpected laugh broke forth from him. Though he supposed she was serious, he hardly cared at all. Any language was better than the endless silence. Callum pointed to her and then to himself.

'Both?'

He nodded and took the stick back. She adjusted his fingers to help him with the grip. 'I can try. But it takes time. More time than we have.'

He didn't care how long it took. He would practise until his fingers bled, if he had to.

But there was a shadow in her mood. 'They watch me, Callum. I may not always be allowed to come and see you.'

He drew her up to stand before him, cupping her face in his hands. She covered his fingers with her own, but didn't pull back. Instead, she closed her eyes and he rested his forehead upon hers.

'I'll do what I can to help you,' she promised.

'Where were you?' Lady Beatrice demanded, when Marguerite returned to the castle. There was no answer she could give. Her hair was still wet, and she knew her gown was bedraggled and damp. Instead, she offered no explanation, walking through the Hall and up the winding stairs to her chamber.

Inside her room, she found pieces of silk cut out and laid upon her bed. Seeing the physical reminder of her impending wedding made her stomach twist. She didn't want to be given to a man like an offering. She didn't want to lie meekly upon her wedding bed, letting a stranger take her virginity.

'You left the castle,' Beatrice accused, closing the door behind her. 'Against your father's orders.'

Marguerite took a comb and struggled to free the tangles from her hair, allowing her aunt grumble as much as she liked.

'You seem to believe that you can do as you please,' the matron remarked, lowering the bar across the door. 'But you are greatly mistaken. While your father is away, he left *me* in command of this castle.' Her eyes glittered with fury. 'You have no right to defy me, Marguerite.' A tight smile edged her aunt's face. 'And there will be a punishment for your behaviour.'

The comb caught in a snarl of her hair, and Marguerite said quietly, 'You cannot have me beaten. My father would never permit it.'

'No,' Beatrice acknowledged, 'but there are other ways to gain your submission. The Duc has been entirely too yielding when it comes to discipline. You left the safety of Cairnross to go and live with the Scots.' Disgust filled the woman's face, as if Marguerite had dwelled amongst rats. 'He should have punished you for that. But his heart was always too soft. You will not find the same leniency with me.'

Marguerite rested her hands in her lap, meeting her

aunt's fury with a passive look. She'd never witnessed such a temper from her mother's sister, and half-wondered if there was another reason for it.

'Your door will be guarded,' Beatrice informed her. 'You will spend the rest of this day and all day tomorrow sewing. If you try to leave, your guards will receive fifty lashes.'

'Why would you threaten innocent men for my actions?' She couldn't possibly understand why Beatrice would do such a thing.

'Nothing at all will happen, so long as you remain in your chamber.'

Marguerite stared at the matron and a chill faltered within her skin. She didn't care about her own punishment, but she couldn't let another man suffer on her behalf. It was clear that her aunt had guessed as much.

'Furthermore, you will not eat for the next day. Your hunger will serve to remind you of your duty.'

It was too much. Marguerite stood up and confronted the woman. 'What gives you the right to deny me food? My father will hear of this, if you dare.'

'He may not agree with my methods but by then, it will be too late, won't it?' With a dark smile, her aunt departed.

Marguerite ran to the door and opened it, only to find two men armed with spears. They barred her path and she saw that one of the soldiers was an older man. He wouldn't survive fifty lashes.

With great reluctance, she closed the door again. And wondered how she would ever get out.

Chapter Six

A day had passed and there was no sign of Marguerite. Callum had explored every inch of the forest, wondering if she'd remained absent by choice or by necessity. He watched over the castle gates, but as the morning went on, there no sign of her.

When the second day had passed and she didn't come, his suspicions went on alert. If she hadn't come, then there was a reason.

Idly, he reached down and picked up a twig from the ground, trying to hold it in his hand like a quill. He'd spent most of the night practising, trying to memorise the patterns of lines and curves that formed her name.

He needed her to show him more. He had not been able to speak for almost two years, and he was impatient to find a way of communicating. Although none of his brothers could read, they could learn.

This was a way of breaking through the cursed silence. If he could tell Marguerite what he wanted…if he could somehow convey it in written words, it might bridge the distance between them.

It also gave him a reason to seek her out. A reason

to be with her each day. She held the power to break through his silence. The power to give him back his voice.

In his mind, he conjured up the soft lines of her face and her vivid blue eyes. He couldn't explain what drew him to her side, binding him in invisible chains. There was nothing he wouldn't do for her if she asked it of him.

He watched the castle for the next few hours, as afternoon evolved into twilight. The urge to see her, to know that she was all right, could not be denied. In her father's absence, there was no way to know what prevented her from leaving.

They watch me, she'd warned. Was that why she hadn't come?

In his mind, he considered a hundred different ways to get inside the castle, but most involved the risk of discovery. He didn't know how large the Duc's retinue was or whether they would notice him. On the first night when he'd slipped inside the grounds, there had been a large crowd to hide among. Tonight, he would be exposed.

But then his luck changed.

He spied a man driving a cart filled with casks of wine. Callum moved swiftly from the trees and caught the edge of the cart, swinging his feet underneath. He used his strength to pull himself out of view beneath the cart, as the wheels rolled forward. The merchant greeted the soldiers at the gate and received permission to enter the castle.

Callum gripped the underside of the platform as the cart drove towards the kitchens. It was a strain to hold himself beneath it, but at last the merchant stopped the cart. When he began unloading the wine, Callum seized his chance, dropping to the ground. As men took casks and brought them within the kitchen, he waited for the right moment and joined them, hoisting a small barrel over one shoulder to keep his face hidden.

The men were stacking the casks in the cellar and when they left, he secured a hiding place behind them. Time was his ally now.

Gradually the hours passed until Callum guessed the others were sleeping.

He ascended the stairs and made his way towards the Hall. Inside, the trestle tables were pushed against the wall and men were sleeping upon the floor. Callum found a bit of leftover bread and meat on one of the tables and hid it within his tunic for later.

Inch by inch, he kept his back to the wall as he neared the staircase on the far side. He moved soundlessly past the others and trod quietly on the steps, listening for anything that would help him find Marguerite. She would be sleeping within her own chamber, away from the others.

In the darkness, he kept his back to the stone wall, searching for any threat. In his hand, he gripped a dirk.

Ahead, he spied two men guarding one of the chambers. He studied them, wondering if Marguerite was inside. The problem was how to get past the guards. Even if he did manage to distract them, there was no way to know if she was there.

But he had to try.

Her door flew open and Marguerite sat up from her bed, stifling the urge to scream. Standing before her was Callum, while her guards lay unconscious upon the ground. They weren't dead, thank God, for one of them moaned, clutching his head.

She threw back the coverlet and ran across the room into his arms. 'I'm so sorry I couldn't come to you. I have been locked in my room the past two days.' She held him tightly, breathing in his scent. Oddly enough, he smelled of bread. Her stomach roared with hunger, for Aunt Beatrice had given her nothing this day, except a bowl of pottage and sour wine. She'd continued her punishment beyond the first day and the lack of food had made Marguerite dizzy.

Callum's face hardened with anger, and his embrace tightened. When he eyed her attire, Marguerite realised she was still wearing only her chemise. She opened her trunk and chose a crimson cote, but Callum shook his head, pointing to a darker blue gown. He helped her to pull it on, then took her by the hand, leading her out of her room.

Marguerite hesitated. Though she wanted to be free of her imprisonment, she was afraid of what would happen to the guards. Would Beatrice have them flogged, as she'd threatened? But then it was clear that the guards had not willingly let her go. It might be an idle threat, nothing more. Either way, she wasn't about to remain her aunt's prisoner any longer.

Callum led her down the steps, into the darkened Hall. One of the dogs lifted his head and whimpered. Marguerite moved forward, touching the animal's head so he would know her scent. The dog licked her wrist and started to follow, but she pressed him back, whispering for him to stay.

Her heart beat faster, her veins thrumming with fear as she followed Callum outside.

'We'll be seen,' she murmured against his ear. 'I don't think there's any way for us to get out.'

He didn't seem concerned at all. Taking her hand, he walked past the first wall, then motioned toward the soldiers. She didn't understand what he meant, but all she could do was let him take the lead. He waited a moment while a few guards strode past the entrance. Marguerite held her breath, running with him toward the open gate.

He was simply planning to walk out, wasn't he? When she eyed the guards at the top of the gatehouse, she suddenly realised why. All of their attention rested upon the forest ahead, seeking potential invaders. They weren't at all aware of what was happening behind them.

Callum wrapped one arm around her shoulders. He guided her to the side of the outer wall and Marguerite pressed her shoulders against the stone, keeping tightly to the shadows. Callum inched his way all along the wall until they reached the far corner. Then he got down upon his stomach, crawling through the darkness toward the ditch.

This is madness, Marguerite thought, as she followed him. Her long gown made it difficult to crawl and she heard the sounds of insects buzzing around her face as she crept along the ground, following him. When Callum reached the ditch, he waded into the water, up to his thighs. Strong arms reached for her, lifting her on to the opposite side.

Marguerite continued on her knees until she reached the edge of the forest. Once they were inside, Callum led her deeper, making her walk within a stream, presumably so that dogs could not track her scent.

It was miserable, being wet, cold, and hungry, but she forced herself to follow. She walked until the exhaustion heightened her dizziness. Voices of doubt reminded her that this was a grave mistake. Aunt Beatrice would search for her and when they found her, Callum would suffer.

You should go back, while you can, her conscience ordered. But she was so weak from hunger and the despair of the past two days, she couldn't bring herself to do it.

When at last they reached Callum's sleeping space, he built a fire for her. She huddled close, trying to hide the tears of exhaustion and fear. He came up beside her, first removing one shoe, then the other. He dried her feet with his own tunic and placed them across his lap, letting her warm them near the flames.

A thickness rose up in her throat and she swallowed back the tears. Why had she left? It was foolish, dangerous, and such a mistake. So many people would be harmed by her desire to leave. What right did she have to disobey her family? Defiance would bring nothing except suffering.

The fire crackled in the evening stillness, the only sound to break the silence. Callum touched her bare feet and massaged the soreness, as if in silent apology for the nightmare of trying to escape the castle. The sensation of his hands on her was heart wrenching, for she was torn between the desire to touch him and the worry of being caught.

When he offered her bread and meat from a fold of his cloak, she nearly attacked him like a savage. She savoured the soft bread and firm crust, so hungry was she. Callum eyed her strangely and she admitted, 'My aunt punished me for leaving the castle by taking away my food. I've had little to eat these past two days.'

His expression turned so fierce, she didn't know what thoughts were raging inside him. He stood, searching through his bundle of supplies before bringing out a cloth-wrapped hunk of meat. Marguerite wanted to weep at the sight of it, but forced herself to eat slowly. He fed her until she could eat no more, and then she closed her eyes, drawing up her knees.

Callum arranged a sleeping place for her and gestured for her to come and lie down upon the blanket he'd set out. She stretched out and he came up behind her, pulling her body against his. His body was warm and she felt safe against him, as though he would do anything to take care of her. He drew his cloak around her, covering them both.

For now, she let herself fall into sleep, pushing back her fears of what would happen in the morning when her disappearance was discovered.

Having Marguerite in his arms was the sweetest torment Callum had ever endured and a gift he'd never expected. Her slender body rested against his, her tangled hair tucked under his chin.

There would be an uproar in the castle when they discovered her gone. Even now, they were likely searching for her. But when he'd learned that they'd locked her away, he'd lost sight of reason, needing to get her out. Had he known at the time that they were denying her food, he might have committed a more unthinkable crime.

How anyone could mistreat this woman was impossible to believe. In her sleep, she burrowed beneath his cloak and her backside nestled against the arousal he'd tried to hold back. He wanted her with a fierce, instinctive need, but he couldn't dishonour her by surrendering to the desires rising within.

Only in his mind could he lower her gown, baring her skin…cupping her breasts in his palm while he kissed her. His pulse quickened as he remembered the sight of the puckered nipples when he'd taken her swimming a few days ago. The white linen chemise had clung to her curves, revealing her naked beauty to him.

He imagined kissing those breasts, touching her everywhere. The way a husband would.

The knife of reality slashed through his dreams. Another man would share her bed, filling her with children. Giving Marguerite the life he couldn't.

Unless he convinced her to leave everything behind. He had no idea if she would ever consider it.

Callum sat up, adjusting his cloak so she could continue to sleep with it. He covered her and reached for his bow and quiver. The need to hunt came over him, to pour his frustration into physical exertion.

He moved quietly through the forest, searching for game. As he crept among the trees, he thought of what to do now. No one knew he was here, save Marguerite. He could take her back to Glen Arrin if she wanted to go.

But then, why would she? He could give her nothing. A life with him made her little better than an outlaw. She didn't deserve to live that way, hiding from her family. The sobering reality made him question what to do.

The wilder side of him wanted to ignore the consequences and steal her. She'd come with him this far, hadn't she?

But if he spent his nights with her, he wouldn't last long. The scent of her skin, the softness of her body pressed against him, had ignited his lust until he'd had to walk away. If she stayed, he would claim her as a lover would, learning her body, filling her with himself.

He clenched his bow, trying to calm the rising storm of lust. When he heard footsteps behind him, he spun, an arrow fitted to the bowstring.

'Don't shoot,' Marguerite murmured and he lowered the bow. A lock of her hair hung over one shoulder, tendrils of gold framing her face. Her blue eyes captivated him, but he held his ground. 'Are you all right?'

He gave a single nod. She looked as if she wanted to say so many things to him and didn't know how to begin. But worst of all, he saw the defeat in her eyes.

Without allowing her to speak, he shouldered his bow and closed the distance. He took her face between his hands and kissed her, reminding her of the night they'd shared together. Her lips were soft, yielding to him as he tried to convince her without words to spend the rest of her nights with him.

But she lowered her head at last, confessing, 'I didn't sleep well. I kept worrying about what will happen when we're caught together.'

Not if. *When*, she'd said. As if she were already giving up.

'I have to go back, or too many people will be hurt.'

He'd suspected she would say this, but neither did he want her to return to a place where she was held prisoner. Words of argument were locked away inside of him and though he tried to move his mouth, nothing came forth.

Marguerite reached up to touch his cheek. 'I suppose I shouldn't have come with you last night.'

His answer was to kiss her again, pulling her close as if he could absorb her into his own skin. Her mouth was open with shock, but he wouldn't release her, demanding that she respond.

There were no words to tell her what he felt, but damned if he'd let her walk away. He kissed her roughly, demanding her response.

No man will ever touch you like this. No one will ever make you feel the way I do.

Her mouth met his with her own desperation, kissing him back while she held him for balance. Callum backed her against a tree, moving his knee between her legs until she was seated upon him. 'What are you—oh,' she breathed, as he shifted his weight against her. Her head leaned back and he kissed her again, his tongue moving inside as he rocked her core.

A shudder broke over her and when he pulled back, he saw the dawning pleasure in her eyes. He'd meant only to balance her, but the secret response of her body reacting to the pressure of his thigh fascinated him. He trailed his hands down her back to rest upon her hips. Marguerite opened her eyes and the vivid blue entranced him.

Her breathing quickened and she began to press herself against his thigh, colour rising in her cheeks as he bent to kiss her throat. The flush of her arousal only heightened his own need and he drew her higher, pulling her leg around his waist. Instinct commanded his mind, though he knew he was taking things too far.

He didn't care. Since he had no words to wield as weapons, he had no qualms about using his touch instead. He wanted to seduce her, to bring her such pleasure she would never think of leaving him.

But then she began to move against him, of her own accord. 'I've never felt this way before,' she breathed, pulling him into another kiss. 'I want you in a way I don't understand.'

Her body trembled against him, her thighs tightening. He reached to lift her higher, wrapping her legs around his waist. Fiery and passionate, Marguerite continued the stroking rhythm, lifting her hips against his erection. He pressed her back against one of the trees as her breathing quickened.

Control fled him and he supported her weight with one arm, moving the other beneath her skirts. He needed to touch her, craved it beyond all else. His hand cupped her bare bottom beneath her skirts, and she shifted her hold around his waist.

'Callum,' she murmured, but her voice wasn't a protest. It was a demand.

Maddening lust gave him the courage to bring his hand between her thighs and when he touched her damp curls, she gave a throaty moan.

'Dieu,' she whispered. With her plea, he touched the wetness, exploring her intimate skin as if to mark her as his. She trembled, her lips swollen from his kiss, but he saw the pleasure breaking forth as her breath grew hitched.

He stroked her slowly, not wanting to hurt her, but she behaved as if he were torturing her. Not knowing whether he should pull his hand away, he held still. 'Please,' she begged. 'More.'

He dipped his fingers within her wetness and her legs squirmed. She was exquisite, her body so tight against his hand. Using a soft rhythm, he thrust his fingers within her and she ground her mouth against him.

He now understood why men killed one another out of jealousy. The visceral need to mark her, to ensure that she wanted only him, was filling his veins in a primal way. He burned for her, wishing he could remove the barriers between them and be the man to claim her innocence.

Abruptly, she convulsed against him, her body racked with violence. For a moment, he feared he'd hurt her, only to see a look of languid passion on her face.

Slowly, he lowered her down. Marguerite pressed her face against his chest, her arms around his waist. His body was so rigid, the physical frustration hurt. But he merely stroked her hair, holding her.

'I don't know what to say to you,' she murmured. 'I should be ashamed of what I did, but I'm not.' Her blue eyes held the fire of longing and she held his gaze. 'I wanted more.'

Marguerite was shaken by the experience, though she tried to pull her thoughts together. Her body was liquid, her legs hardly able to walk. It was dangerous being around Callum, for he made her inhibitions vanish.

She wanted him as her lover. She wanted to lie with him, to feel the intimacy of his body inside hers.

But if she dared to reach for another future, her father wouldn't hesitate to use his power against the MacKinloch Clan. She was his pawn, not permitted to have any say in her marriage. And with every moment she spent with Callum, the suffocating resentment rose higher.

The Duc wasn't the one who had to wed a stranger and welcome him into bed. He didn't seem to care what Marguerite's desires were. It was about strengthening his political ties, increasing the family wealth. Not about her wishes.

The question was, did she dare to fight for what she wanted, knowing that it would likely fail? It was too late to stop her father from bringing back another potential husband. But perhaps there was a way to appeal to him, to somehow make him see that there could be advantages to allying with a Scottish clan.

Callum took her hand and led her back to the fire. He dropped down to one knee and picked up a twig. He drew in the dirt for a moment and when he stood, Marguerite saw her name written in the earth. Had he spent the past few days practising? She'd only written her name once for him. The letters weren't perfect, but they were legible.

'You learn quickly,' she said, startled that he could have made such progress. She welcomed the distraction of teaching him more letters, for it kept her mind off the staggering pleasure he'd given her. Or their unknown future.

Callum took her by the hand and led her to a log. There was unrest carved into his face, the tension of a man who had been denied his own release. The sting of shame made her wish she could do something for him.

And when she saw his attempts at her name written within the dirt, she understood that he'd brought her here for another distraction.

Marguerite sat down and studied the words. He must have written her name nearly fifty times. It touched her that he'd practised for so long.

As he swept the dirt aside with a pine branch, he handed her the twig once more. She held it for a moment and said once more, 'It's not enough. Even if I teach you the letters, I don't think you can—'

Impatiently, he cut off her words, touching a finger to her lips. Then he guided her hand down to the dirt in front of them. There was determination in his eyes and a will to learn that she'd not seen before.

This might be his only way to communicate. The only way to unlock the voice inside of him. She understood that, even if he didn't know how difficult it would be.

'I can try to teach you,' she said, 'but I don't know if there is time enough for you to learn.' It had taken her years to master writing and she doubted if her efforts would do anything at all for him.

He pressed the twig into her hand, nodding for her to begin.

Callum drank in the knowledge faster than anyone she'd ever known. Marguerite had never seen anything like it. She'd written the alphabet and Callum had practised each shape, struggling with the curved letters. He'd worked as hard as he could, shaking out the stiffness in his fingers.

She'd demonstrated each letter and sound, showing him how to write simple words. Throughout the lesson, his eyes were intent upon the ground. He struggled to string the words together, and although his spelling was disastrous, at least he was starting to understand how to put the sounds there.

Mor, he wrote.

She added an 'e' to correct him, and wrote as many

words as she could think of, until her fingers were getting scratched from the branch she'd used.

'You're doing well,' she complimented him. He'd written and rewritten the words at least a dozen times, practising them over and over, as if his life depended on it.

And it might, if he stayed here too long.

Her fingers were aching and she massaged them, sitting back against the log. 'I think that's enough for now,' she said, rising to her feet. 'I have to return. They'll be looking for me.' The evening sun now rimmed the horizon in red and gold, and she couldn't stay much longer.

He bent down and laboured over the letters, until he stood back to let her see the word. *No*, he'd written.

'I can't stay and you know this,' she said quietly. 'They would accuse you of abducting me, no matter what I say to defend you.'

He set down the stick, his dark eyes filled with frustration. But he had to understand the truth of her words. Already she had spent far too much time alone with him. If they were caught together, she didn't doubt that they would take him prisoner. She couldn't let that happen.

'If I can come back to see you, I will,' she said. 'It may not be for some time, but…I'll try.' She sent him a half-hearted smile. 'You have many letters to practise until then.'

The likelihood was that her aunt would keep her locked away, unable to leave until the Duc returned. Marguerite would suffer punishment for what she'd done. But she held no regrets at all.

Callum extended his hand, but instead of leading her back, he drew her palm to his waist. For a long moment, he cupped the back of her neck, keeping his forehead pressed to hers.

'I don't know what will happen to us,' she whispered. 'I wish—' Her words broke away, for wishes were worth nothing at all. Instead, she closed her eyes, holding on to him. For now, she could only hold fast to the moments slipping away like water through her fingers.

At her side, Callum took her hand and pressed it to his chest. The firm reassurance and strength only dug deeper into her heart.

She suspected he would wait for the rest of his life, if she asked it of him. And it simply wasn't fair.

Chapter Seven

The sound of dogs barking drew closer to their position within the forest. Callum fitted an arrow to his bow and stood before her.

'They're going to find us if I stay here any longer,' Marguerite said. And though he knew she was right, it didn't mean he was going to step aside and let them lock her away again. He'd been imprisoned and tortured before and he'd endure it in a moment if it meant protecting her.

But she turned to him, forcing him to lower the bow. 'I need to face them myself.' Her voice came out with a tremble and he shook his head.

'If they see you, you would bear the punishment for my rebellion.' She gave him a broken smile, adding, 'The only way I'll ever be free is if I speak to my father.' Her hand moved to touch his cheek. 'Stay back, Callum. Let me try to fight for what I want.'

Though he understood her desire, he had no intention of letting her face them alone. How could he hide away like a coward, letting her bear the brunt of their anger?

'They won't hurt me,' she told him. 'And if they deny me food again, I'll speak to the servants. Surely they would help me, if it meant gaining a reward from my father.'

She moved in, winding her arms around his neck. Though her hair was tangled, her face still held the satisfied flush of fulfilment he'd given her. He wasn't about to let her go alone.

He might be able to watch over her without her knowledge. He could infiltrate the castle, guarding her as best he could, until she gained her father's permission to come back with him.

It will never happen, his mind taunted. *The Duc will never accept a broken man such as you.*

He dulled the voice of reason and gripped Marguerite in a fierce embrace. When he pulled back, he saw the tears glimmering in her eyes, though she tried to send him a reassuring smile.

'I'll be all right.'

He didn't believe it, even as he gestured for her to walk towards them.

But first she stood on her tiptoes to give him a last kiss. It was the softest touch, like a farewell. And when she turned away from him, a sense of foreboding intruded, as if their shared dreams would never happen, no matter how hard they fought.

Callum climbed a large oak nearby and hid himself within the branches, watching as she walked towards the sound of the dogs. She moved with her head held high, offering no excuses for her actions. And when the riders caught up to her at last, they seized her, lifting her atop one of the horses before they stole her away from him.

* * *

'I should have you beaten for your disobedience,' Lady Beatrice said coolly. 'Never have I seen such behaviour from you. I can promise you, your father will hear of this.'

Marguerite held her shoulders back, keeping her silence. She had decided not to answer any of their questions, nor make excuses for what she'd done. Like Callum, she intended to lock away her words.

'You've caused everyone a great deal of trouble,' her aunt continued. She took Marguerite by the wrist, squeezing so tightly that a bruise would form. 'I can't understand why you would go off into the forest. And I do not believe you were taken against your will.' She pulled Marguerite towards the stairs, forcing her to return to her chamber.

When they reached the door, Beatrice stopped. 'The guards outside your room confessed that they saw a man who took you. A Scot, they believe.' Her aunt's gaze grew cunning. 'Or am I wrong?'

'And where would I have found such a man?' Marguerite countered, unable to hold her silence any longer. 'I know none of the nearby clans.' She stared up at her aunt. 'Perhaps I was the one to free myself. The men would be too ashamed to admit they were bested by a woman.'

'You expect me to believe that?'

No, but she refused to endanger Callum by letting anyone believe he was involved in her escape. So far as she knew, only the guards had encountered him and the lie might work. It was all she had.

'I don't expect you to believe anything I say.' She

walked into her room and sat down before the fire, warming her hands.

Her aunt closed the door behind her. Beatrice's mood seemed to discolour the air with rage. She took deep breaths, as if to control her temper. 'You spent a night away from the castle. You, who can hardly dress yourself, much less take care of a household. Your father entrusted Duncraig Castle to me and he gave strict instructions about keeping you here.'

'Imprisoning me, you mean.' Marguerite stood up and faced her aunt. 'I'm not as helpless as you think I am.'

'You've never done anything except wield a needle and smile prettily at your father. He indulged you in anything you wanted, after your mother died.'

'I was grieving—'

'And so was I,' Beatrice snapped. 'She was my only sister.' Her face twisted with frustration. 'When my husband died, the Duc might have brought me into his household, but I will not stay in a barbaric country such as this. Soon enough, I'll coax him back to France where I belong.' Her aunt sent her a calculating smile. 'I have your father's favour, you know.'

From the insinuation in Beatrice's voice, Marguerite suspected precisely what sort of favours the matron had granted the Duc. It sickened her to think of the pair of them together.

'He can't wed you,' Marguerite argued. 'It would be against the laws of the Church.'

'There are many ways he can provide for me.' Beatrice crossed her arms beneath her voluptuous bosom. 'And believe me when I say that he will do *anything* I ask of him. You had best remain in your room for the next sennight if you want me to hide your secrets from him.'

'I have no secrets.'

'Liar.' Beatrice reached out and cupped her chin. 'Even if it wasn't in the past two days, you've been touched by a man. You might have taken a lover, even. What do you think your bridegroom will say if he finds out you are no longer a virgin?'

In spite of her efforts, Marguerite couldn't stop the flush on her cheeks. She had allowed Callum to touch her in ways he shouldn't have. She had given in to temptation and the guilt weighed upon her.

'I am a virgin still,' she said quietly. But had she remained with Callum, she doubted if she could have kept her virtue. She wanted him more than any other man. And she didn't know how to get out of her betrothal agreement to the Earl of Penrith.

'Get out of my chamber,' she ordered her aunt. 'And cease treating me like a prisoner.'

'You will be guarded at all times,' Beatrice said. 'Until your father returns.' She crossed the room and stood at the door. 'And as for your former guards? They each received fifty lashes on your behalf, Marguerite.' Venom laced her tone and she finished by saying, 'Remember who holds the power here.'

After her aunt had gone, Marguerite closed her eyes. Somehow, she had to find her own power.

Callum stood in the shadow of the trees, far below Duncraig Castle. Though Marguerite hadn't wanted him to follow her, he intended to watch over her and somehow gain a means of protecting her within the castle.

You're unworthy of her, the voice inside him mocked. *There's no place for you here.*

He knew it, but he wasn't going to dwell among the trees like an animal. He wasn't going to abandon Marguerite, despite the danger to himself.

The afternoon light skimmed over the hills, casting shadows over the castle walls. He cleared his mind of the doubts, steadying his resolve. From the size of the castle and the men he'd seen during his first encounter, it was a large household with many servants. Surely they would need another. And although he couldn't speak, he could show the others that he was strong enough for any task. Sometimes actions held more weight than words.

His pace slowed as he neared the drawbridge. Inside the gates, he saw the soldiers guarding their post. They locked their spears, barring his way.

At first they spoke French and he shook his head, not understanding their words.

'What do you want?' one demanded, in heavily-accented English. They were eyeing his horse, for that made it apparent he wasn't a beggar. Callum met their gaze evenly and held out empty hands. Then he touched his mouth, in an effort to make them understand.

They eyed him with no idea of what he meant. Frustrated, Callum dismounted from his horse. With effort, he tried to speak, but it felt as if his throat were blocked, the words trapped inside. Nothing came forth, not even a single sound.

'If you've nothing to say, then be gone,' the first soldier ordered.

Callum stared at the man. They believed he was witless, didn't they? Good for nothing at all. His anger gained a foothold, rising higher. The idea of simply shoving the men aside sounded better than trying to make them guess what he wanted.

He gripped his horse's bridle and forced himself to calm down. There had to be another way. Callum lifted his eyes just beyond the guards and spied a man approaching. From the stranger's appearance, he appeared to be a fellow Scot.

The man's gaze narrowed as he drew nearer, just behind the guards. When he was within view, the stranger looked at Callum and turned back his sleeves. Upon his wrists were reddened scars like his own.

The man interrupted the guards and offered, 'He means no harm, lads. It's only my cousin, come from the north.'

Callum kept his face blank, not knowing why the man was helping him. His suspicions went on edge, but he made no effort to deny the man's words.

'Your cousin, is he?' the guard remarked. 'Why is he here?'

'After all the raids, I suppose he's looking for a new place to live. Am I right?' He stared at Callum, who gave a single nod.

Reluctantly, the guards let him through and the man brought him towards the stables. 'You can put your horse with the others, for now.' With a sidelong glance he murmured under his breath, 'You're a MacKinloch, aren't you?'

Callum inclined his head and the man smiled. 'I thought so. I knew your brother Bram. You were just a boy when I saw you last. Colin, is it?'

There was no way to correct the man, so he shrugged. It was close enough.

'I am Iagar Campbell.' The name was unfamiliar to

him, but the scars upon the man's wrist gave the clearest indication that he wasn't lying. Iagar seemed to notice his stare, and he added quietly, 'I was at Cairnross.'

When they reached the stables, the stable master began speaking in French, so rapidly that Callum couldn't follow any of it. Iagar answered on his behalf, and after a time the stable master grumbled and brought his horse Goliath to a stall.

'If you're looking for a place, this is the best you'll get. The others think we're good for nothing except shovelling dung.' Iagar winked at him. 'But there are ways to get what you want if you know how to ask.' He passed Callum a shovel and led him into one of the stalls. In Gaelic, he added, 'Go on and start. We'll talk later when there aren't any ears to overhear our conversation.' With a light slap to his back, Iagar left the stable.

Callum eyed the horse in front of him and guessed her to be Marguerite's horse. She was a light grey mare with delicate features. When he touched her nose, letting her learn his scent, she gave a whuff and then lowered her head to drink from a trench of water.

Over the next few hours, he worked until nightfall. The stable master Jean never took his eyes off him, but when he realised that Callum had done well enough cleaning the stalls, there was a noticeable difference in his demeanour.

'You don't speak, do you?' Jean asked, using English at last. Callum shook his head, touching a finger to his lips. The stable master studied him. 'You've earned a meal after the work you did. You're hungry, I suppose?' At his nod, Jean led him outside.

Torches lined the walls, the orange flames flickering in the twilight. Callum kept his face lowered, so as not to attract attention. He didn't doubt that the guards he'd attacked on the night he freed Marguerite would recognise him if he showed himself.

He followed Jean to the kitchen, where he saw a few other men and women gathering outside. 'You can get some table scraps here,' the stable master offered. 'And you can sleep in the Hall, as your *cousin* does.' From the emphasis he placed on the word, Jean had guessed they weren't related.

After he left, Callum found a barrel of rainwater and splashed his face, thoroughly scrubbing his hands until he was clean. He didn't suppose anyone would want to give him food, smelling the way he did.

He waited for over an hour among the others, his stomach raging for something to eat. Though he was accustomed to hunting for his own meat, he didn't have the choice of returning to the forest. The idea of begging for leftover food didn't sit well with him.

The cook was still busy preparing a light meal of sliced meat, baked salmon, cheese and assorted breads for the Duc's family. Seeing so many exotic foods made his mouth water. He noticed the cook struggling with a heavy iron pot of water. Without asking, Callum took it from the older woman and hung it over the fire.

She stared at him, her round face narrowed. *'Merci.'* Then she took a crust of bread and placed bit of the salmon on it, ladling a thick sauce over it. Callum's stomach roared with hunger at the sight and he accepted the food, nodding his thanks. When he bit into the warm fish, the succulent flavour was like nothing he'd ever tasted. He caught the cook's gaze and sent her a smile.

She spoke in French again, but he shook his head to indicate he didn't understand. Then she asked in English, 'Do you like it?'

Callum devoured the food and stood, coming close to her. The older woman's hair was grey and wrinkles rimmed the edges of her eyes. He took her hand and kissed it in thanks.

'Scottish devil,' she chided, snatching her hand back. 'If you think you'll get more food out of me by flirting…'

She turned her back to him and began rummaging through another part of the kitchen. Callum waited and she handed him a tart the size of his palm, dripping with cherries.

'You'd be right.' The cook's face cracked into a smile and Callum bit into the tart, the cherries oozing into his mouth. Never in his life had he tasted food like this. When he'd finished licking his fingers, he kissed the cook on the cheek.

'Make yourself useful by taking one of these trays to the Hall,' she ordered. 'Follow the others and if you value your life, don't spill a crumb. Or if you eat it before it gets there, I'll have you flogged.' She pointed to the heavy tray of herbed salmon and he followed the other kitchen servants to the Hall, being careful not to spill the sauce.

Inside, the large Hall was immaculate, with fresh rushes upon the floor. Callum held the heavy tray, absorbing the sights around him, searching for Marguerite. If she'd been locked away in her room again, he would do what was necessary to set her free.

But then he spied her at the far end of the room. She sat alongside an older matron, a shuttered expression on her face. She wore a ruby-coloured surcoat and a cream cote that hung to the floor with tightly fitted, draping sleeves. A veil and gold circlet rested upon her head. Around her throat, he spied the silver chain and the blue glass pendant rested upon the crimson gown. Although her expression remained serene, he sensed the unrest simmering beneath. Callum carried the tray and stopped before her, waiting for her to notice him.

When she did, her hand stilled upon the goblet of wine, panic etched on her face. She appeared frozen, not at all pleased to see him. It was as if he'd invaded her safe world, the uninvited guest whom she could never present to her family. Though she accepted a piece of salmon from his tray, not once did she look at him.

He gave no reaction to her dismay, slipping into the role of a nameless servant. Frustrated anger simmered beneath his skin, for he no longer knew if she wanted him here or not.

But when he followed the others back, he caught her stricken gaze and sent her his own challenge. He'd infiltrated the castle walls just to see her—let her come if she dared.

Marguerite waited hours before slipping away from her guards during the evening entertainment. Distracted by the storytelling, they hadn't noticed her disappearance. But they would. She had only moments to warn Callum.

She found him standing outside the stables. He'd stripped himself of the tunic and had poured water over himself. Though the night air was warm, his skin puckered from the cool droplets. She saw the reddened scars upon his back and the strong muscles that corded along his upper arms and torso.

She remembered what it was to touch his skin, to taste the firm mouth that stole away her wits, leaving her breathless.

'You can't be here, Callum,' she whispered. 'Please. You have to go.' Couldn't he understand that if they were caught together, his life was in danger? Beatrice hated the Scots and she wouldn't hesitate to punish him or, worse, have him killed.

'If they find me with you—'

Her words broke away when he led her into the shadows. There was no light and she couldn't see anything, not even his face.

'Don't do this,' she whispered. 'I'm trying to keep you safe. If anything happened to you…'

He drew closer, his dark eyes shadowed with persistence. It had been such a mistake to let him touch her as he had in the forest, for now he'd glimpsed the secret desires within her heart.

He took her hands, lifting them to his shoulders in a blatant invitation. Marguerite's fingers moved to his throat where she felt the rapid pulse. Her own heartbeat echoed his, for she was caught without knowing what to do. Like the apple of sin, he offered her a temptation she didn't want to refuse.

Callum pressed her back against the wall, supporting her as his warm breath silenced her protests. *She cared.*

He sensed how distraught she was, but he wasn't going to abandon her. Not after they'd hurt her before.

'It's too dangerous for me to see you any more, Callum,' she murmured. 'My father will return soon. And my new…betrothed husband will come with him.'

His hands stilled on either side of her as the coldness slid through his veins, freezing into anger. Was she giving up?

'I am grateful to you for protecting me,' she whispered. 'And I am glad that you are healed. But it has to end between us.'

No. He wasn't going to stand back and let her fear dictate the future. He gripped her hand and drew it back to his throat. Reminding her that he couldn't speak, but it hadn't stopped him from coming here.

She was his and he intended to fight for her.

His hands moved up to cradle her head, his thumbs edging her temples. He wanted her to feel his touch, to know the thoughts inside of him. When his fingers passed down her cheeks, there was wetness from her tears.

'I don't want you here any more.'

In the heated darkness between him, he knew it was a lie. She was trying to drive him away, in order to protect him. Didn't she know that he would do anything for her?

A sliver of frustration irritated his pride, for he didn't intend to hide. If she wanted to be with him, he could take her away right now. But she was faltering. He could see it in her divided loyalty, her uncertainty of whether she could turn her back on her family, seeking a life with him. Leaving her made it too easy for her to forget what there was between them.

Callum ignored her soft struggle to move away and held her captive. Against his hands, he felt the harsh beating of her pulse. He moved his mouth to kiss the trembling vein and her hands came up to hold his head.

Aye, she was lying to him. He sensed it in the way her hands dug into him, pulling him closer. He nipped at her throat, moving up to her chin, then capturing her mouth.

There was desperation in her answering kiss, but she didn't try to free herself. She kissed him back, her mouth meeting his as he took possession. Never would he stand aside and let another man take what belonged to him. He wouldn't cower before a duke or hide in the shadows out of fear.

Like a brand, he kissed her hard, provoking the heat that had always been between them. He slid his hands between them, just to the underside of her breasts. And when he grazed the hardened tips, reminding her of the way he'd pleasured her, she gasped against his mouth.

Don't ever deny what's between us.

Abruptly, he released her and walked away. He wasn't leaving, not after all they'd endured.

A heaviness clenched Marguerite's heart when he left. The vast emptiness inside was all-consuming, for he'd thrown down a gauntlet of his own, challenging her to fight. She made herself to walk back to the Hall, forcing back the tears.

Even though she wanted him desperately, she understood the challenge that lay ahead. Until she'd convinced her father to end the betrothal with Lord Penrith, there was no hope of being with Callum.

Guy de Montpierre would be furious if she refused the marriage. He'd given her a life of privilege and she recognised his God-given right to choose her husband.

To deny it and rebel against him made her ungrateful and selfish.

The good-girl daughter cringed at the thought of asking him, while the woman who had spent the night in Callum's arms wanted nothing more than to spend all of her days with him. No matter what happened.

She might fail…but she had to gather her courage and try.

Chapter Eight

'MacKinloch?' came a whisper from the back of the Hall. 'Come with me.'

Callum spied Iagar Campbell beckoning to him. He rose, following the man outside. It was late at night and most of the castle inhabitants were asleep. The darkness made it difficult to follow Campbell to the stables, for the torches were sparser in this area. Though he didn't know if anyone else was there, he supposed it was safe enough to hear what the man had to say.

They stopped, just inside the doorway. Iagar loosened his tunic, revealing reddened marks around his throat. Then he lifted his wrists, revealing the scars that could only have been formed by manacles. 'I was freed a few years ago,' he admitted. 'But I remember what they did to you at Cairnross.'

Callum studied the reddened marks. Though it was possible that Campbell had been chained alongside him, he didn't recognise the man. Whether or not it was true, he waited for the man to continue.

'I remember you as a boy,' Iagar said, leaning against one of the stalls. 'Your brother took punishments for you.' His expression turned angry and his fingers dug against the wood of the stall. 'It shouldn't have happened. Not to any of us.' Anger and bitterness laced Iagar's voice and Callum suspected that the man had lost someone close to him.

'But now we're fighting back against the English.' Iagar's eyes gleamed with ambition. 'We're forming our own group of men to reclaim the lands stolen from us. To put an end to the suffering of our kinsmen.'

Callum folded his arms across his chest, understanding that they wanted him to be a part of their rebellion. Although he recognised their purpose, he had no desire to be involved.

'Aren't you going to say anything, MacKinloch?'

Callum unsheathed the dagger at his waist and touched his mouth with it, implying that his tongue had been cut out.

Iagar paled, his face tightening. 'Then you, of all men, have a reason to want vengeance.'

Callum kept a veiled expression on his face. He was here for Marguerite, not to start another fight with the English.

Iagar offered, 'Come and join us. We have a small hut outside the castle grounds and we could use another Scot. Another man we can trust.'

He started to shake his head, but Iagar urged, 'Take some time to make your decision.' He eyed the scars upon Callum's wrists. 'There are other prisoners left, not far from here. I think you remember what it was like, living in English captivity. We're going to free the rest of them. No matter what the cost.'

Over the next few days, Marguerite sensed Callum's presence everywhere she turned. At meals, he served her food. In the morning, she saw him standing outside her window, leading horses out for the hunters. And today, when she walked through the garden, she had seen her name written in the earth beside the herbs she tended. It was as if he'd countered her declaration with a defiance of his own.

I'm not leaving.

She knelt down and touched the dirt where he'd printed her name. Seeing his awkward handwriting reminded her of when she'd taught him the letters. Guilt pressed against her conscience, for she'd not been able to give him any more words to communicate. It felt as if someone were tearing her in half. Her heart was with Callum and her mind here. And she didn't know how to respond to the way he was fighting for her. Until her father returned, she could do nothing.

Sweeping the dirt clean, she began writing his name in the space. He might not recognise it, but he would understand that she'd answered his silent message.

'What are you doing, Marguerite?' came her aunt's voice from behind her.

She dropped to her knees, hiding the words beneath her skirts. Reaching out to pull a weed from the herb garden, she answered, 'I believe it's obvious enough.'

'You should be sewing your bridegroom's wedding tunic,' Beatrice chided. 'He will come in a few days, and you've barely finished any of it.'

Because I don't want to marry him. Because I have to find a way to reason with my father.

She held her silence and a moment later, her aunt gripped her by the arm, jerking her up. 'Answer me when I speak to you, or I'll have you locked in your room again.'

Marguerite's anger blazed. She pried her arm free from her aunt's grasp and felt the rush of indignation filling her up inside. 'Try it again and see what the others think of you. Already they despise you for what you did to those soldiers.' Though she hadn't seen either of the men, it dismayed her to think of how they'd suffered after her escape.

'It was *your* fault,' Beatrice corrected. 'Had you stayed in your room and obeyed me, it never would have happened.'

Marguerite was so stunned by her aunt's self-righteous attitude, she could make no reply. There was no sign of remorse upon Beatrice's face.

'It would not be wise to make an enemy of me, Marguerite,' she said quietly. 'I'll expect to see you in your chamber within the hour.'

She stared at the woman, her shoulders squared. Beatrice turned and left her there, and Marguerite wondered exactly how much damage the woman had done in the Duc's absence. She'd been so concerned with Callum, not once had she paid heed to the castle inhabitants.

Behind her, two guards shadowed her, as if she were about to run away again.

'Come.' She beckoned to them. They were different from the first two men who had guarded her, but she suspected they would have the answers she needed. 'I would like to know what happened to the two men who guarded me in my room.'

The taller guard was bearded, his brown hair cropped short. 'They were whipped, my lady.'

'Did they survive?'

The second man nodded. 'Barely. Thomas has been

abed since it happened. He was too old to receive fifty lashes. John took twenty more of them, on his behalf.'

Marguerite shuddered at the thought. She took a breath and asked, 'Do they blame me for it?'

The bearded guard shook his head. 'They know it was the fault of that *peau de vache*.'

Marguerite knew she ought to chastise him for comparing Beatrice to a cow, but she let the insult go. 'I would like to see the guards who were injured, if I may.'

'She will not allow it,' the first man protested.

'Do you not believe those men deserve compensation for what they have suffered?' She fingered the pearls upon her bodice, as if to remind them of her wealth.

They exchanged a wary glance and she pressed further. 'My father would never allow food to be denied me, nor innocent men be punished. Beatrice has stepped beyond her authority and I intend to see it stopped.' She held out her palm. 'Give me your knife.'

The bearded guard obeyed and Marguerite cut off four pearls from her bodice. Giving two to each of them, she added, 'Your loyalty belongs to me. Not to her.'

The two men were listening now and she continued, 'In front of my aunt, you may accompany me at all times. But when she is gone...' she cut off two more pearls and handed one to each '...allow me my freedom to go or stay as it pleases me.'

The guarded bowed his head in obedience. '*Oui*, my lady. And if you so desire, we can take you to the two wounded guards so that you may speak to them.'

She nodded her agreement and began walking back towards the tower, with the guards following behind. When she crossed by the stables, she saw Callum against the far wall, holding the reins of her father's destrier. She sensed him watching her, though he kept his head averted. His silent rebellion unnerved her, for she remembered the strength of his arms and the conquering touch of his mouth upon hers.

As she moved past him, her body grew sensitive, remembering how he'd awakened her with his touch.

And something within her snapped. What good was it to push away the man she wanted, behaving like a coward? She had precious time before the others arrived. Was it not better to steal whatever moments she could?

As she followed the guards to go and tend to the wounded soldiers, her mind raced with ideas on how to seize what she wanted.

At dawn, Callum heard Marguerite enter the stables. She ordered the stable master, 'Prepare my horse. I am going riding this morn.'

'But, Lady Marguerite, what will your aunt say?' Jean protested. 'I thought your orders were not to leave the castle grounds while your father was away.'

Marguerite smiled. 'The guards are outside my bedroom door. According to them, I am still inside sewing.' She nodded towards Callum. 'I will take one of your men with me, as an escort. That one will do.'

That one? Callum sent her a sidelong glance, wondering what she was up to. She was behaving as if she'd never seen him before and his suspicions deepened.

Marguerite didn't spare him a glance, but when the stable master began to argue again, she pressed something into his hand. 'I've been held prisoner for days now. If I am gone for a few hours, no one will know. And you will be rewarded for your silence.'

The stable master inclined his head. 'As you say, my lady.'

Callum finished saddling Marguerite's horse and his own mount, leading both outside the stables. He assisted Marguerite on to the animal and she rode forth from the gates with him behind her. He let her take the lead, but instead of going through the forest, she rode west, towards the sea. He hadn't realised they were so close, within only a few miles.

Marguerite stopped to let the horses drink, before continuing towards the coast. Not once did she speak to him and he couldn't guess at her reasons for bringing him here. She clearly did not want anyone to eavesdrop on their conversation.

When she drew her horse to a stop, he saw the grey waters of the sea and dark clouds hovering above. Seagulls circled the rocks, while the hill descended into a large stretch of sand. Marguerite dismounted and let the horse graze while she walked downhill. He followed, but as she continued her slow strides across the beach he caught her hand.

Why? he asked in silence.

She reached within her bodice and withdrew the silver chain and glass pendant. 'You never left. Even when I asked you to.'

In answer, he touched her chin, cupping her soft cheek. Golden hair rested upon her throat and she reached up to remove her veil, tossing it on the sand. 'I don't know what will happen when my father returns. It frightens me, what he will do if he finds out about us.'

Her hands reached to cover his and she continued, 'But I have a few days left with you. I don't want to lose them before I have to.'

The words fired up a hope he hadn't dared to feel. He captured her palm with his and led her down towards the sea. Marguerite leaned her head against his shoulder as they walked and he drew her closer.

Beneath her calm demeanour, he sensed the unrest simmering. Tension lined her face, mingled with defiance. She'd brought him here for a reason, but for what, he couldn't guess.

She let go of his hand when they reached the shoreline. Driftwood and shells lined the sand, along with a fallen log. He followed Marguerite there and she leaned down to pick up a stick.

'I promised to teach you more words,' she said, offering him the stick.

But he didn't take it. Instead, he reached out to touch her chin, wishing he could read her thoughts. Something was making her anxious, but she wouldn't reveal it to him.

'If you want, I'll try to teach you more writing,' she blurted out, her words rushed. 'Or perhaps you could give me another lesson in swimming?'

There was an edge to her voice, a nervousness about her demeanour. Though she might believe swimming was a way to spend time together, it wasn't a good idea. The moment he saw her slender body, wet from the waves, he'd want to touch her again. And God help him, if he did, he didn't think he could stop.

The summer air was cool and he motioned for her to wait a moment. He built a fire for them and when it was burning bright, he picked up the stick again and sat beside her.

'Show me the letters you remember,' she said.

He wrote out the alphabet that he'd spent countless

hours memorising. Some of the shapes still eluded him, but his hand was growing steadier with the practise.

She bent to help him with the letter S, her hand upon his. When she leaned so close, her delicate scent ensnared him. He wanted to lay her back in the sand naked, touching her body until he learned what made her sob with pleasure.

The stick nearly snapped in his hand and he forced himself to concentrate.

'You've learned so fast,' she remarked, kneeling beside him. 'It took me years to do as much as you have.'

He took the stick and wrote her name, then his own.

'You saw it,' she murmured. 'I wrote it for you in the garden, hoping you would find it.'

At her timid smile, he set down the stick and faced her. Her hands moved up to touch his shoulders and she rested her cheek against his in a light embrace. 'I'm sorry for what I said a few days ago. I was afraid that if you stayed, you would be in danger.'

He'd known that, but hearing her say it made him hold her closer. Words stumbled in his throat, yet he couldn't get them out.

But now he had another way. Pulling back from her, he picked up the stick and thought for a moment. He struggled to remember the shapes of the letters and the spelling.

Finally, he wrote in the sand: _Mine._

Her expression softened with emotion. 'Yes. I am yours. For as long as I can be.'

It wasn't the promise he wanted. He wanted her for always.

The words revealed the truth he'd suspected. Despite what there was between them, she was still her father's daughter. Her loyalty to her family was stronger than any feelings she held towards him.

It was sobering to know that he was asking her to choose between them.

But then she leaned in and kissed him. Her lips were soft and in the touch of her mouth upon his there was a decision. She'd found a way to come to him, and no matter how long it lasted, he intended to make the most of it.

A breathless sigh escaped her when he bent to kiss her jaw and the delicate skin of her throat.

'I want this day with you,' she demanded. 'A few hours with no one to stop us. No one to tell me what sort of man I should wed.' She stared hard at him and a dark blush covered her cheeks. 'I want to feel the way you made me feel a few days ago when you touched me.'

She was playing with the fire of his lust and God only knew where it would end. Callum stared at her, letting her see how badly he wanted her. Taking his hands, she brought them to the back of her gown.

'Help me take this off,' she murmured. After he loosened the laces, she raised her arms. As he removed each layer, he saw the gooseflesh cover her skin.

When she was in her chemise, he paused, not knowing how far she wanted to go. 'Leave it for now,' she answered. 'Teach me to swim, and then…' Her words trailed off, her shyness overcoming her.

He wasn't about to let his mind ponder what she meant by those words. Instead, he removed his tunic and took her into the water. The waves moved against her, and she clung to him for balance.

'It's c-c-colder than the lake, isn't it?'

When they reached a depth that was just above her waist, he lifted her up, stretching her on her stomach. She struggled against the waves, but tried again to swim. With her hair dipping below the water, she fought, churning her arms and kicking her legs. He released her without warning and, as she continued to move, she suspended herself in the water. It wasn't smooth or particularly strong, but she did manage to swim.

'Look!' she cried out to him. 'I'm not sinking.'

He gave a slight smile, moving into a different position that forced her to swim to him. When at last he stopped, she moved her arms and kicked until she caught his waist and stood up. 'It wasn't so bad this time. At least I remembered to move my arms and legs.' Her teeth chattered, but he warmed her in his embrace. A breathless smile lit up her face, as her arms came around him.

She was shivering and when he pointed to the water, asking if she wanted to swim again, she shook her head.

'I want you to help me get warm,' she whispered.

Her body pressed against him and he wondered if she knew what she was asking. The waves sloshed them, but he guided her out of the water. Sand caked their legs and she shivered, holding on to him.

Callum led her back to the fire to get warm, adding more driftwood to increase the heat. He took her discarded cloak and spread it out before the fire, gesturing for her to sit upon it. Marguerite ignored him, standing before the flames with her hands outstretched. Her expression had gone distant, as if she were lost in thought.

She turned to look at him, a question in her eyes. In that moment, he saw the uncertainty in her face, mingled with fear. He met her gaze with unyielding strength. No matter what happened, he would remain at her side. She was the woman who had risked everything to save his life, the woman who had brought him back from the brink of madness. The woman he would die for.

And then she stared straight at him, her hands lifting her chemise away until she stood naked before him, wearing nothing except the glass pendant.

Chapter Nine

Marguerite could feel the hunger in his eyes, the desire for her. A thousand voices were crying out within her head, warning her not to do this. She was promised to another man and she had no right to betray her intended husband.

But the idea of letting a stranger claim her virginity felt so wrong. Callum was the man who held her heart and she wanted to be with him. If her new husband learned she was not a virgin, he might cast her out. Or refuse to marry her, if she revealed it.

It was a way out of the betrothal.

The idea of surrendering to Callum, letting him become her lover, was a dangerous move, one that could destroy both of them. But if her efforts failed and she could not avoid the marriage to the earl, at least she could give this part of herself to Callum. He would never hurt her and it was something they could share together.

'You should remove the rest of your clothes,' she murmured. 'Let them dry by the fire.'

He moved before her, and she saw his eyes lingering

upon her bare skin, drinking in the sight. Though she felt awkward revealing everything to him, she made no move to cover herself. She watched as Callum removed his own clothing. When he stood naked before her, she was struck by the power of his body, the fierce lines of heavy muscle and skin. As an archer, his arms were lean and strong. She ached to touch him, to discover how to bring him the same pleasure he'd given her.

Callum hadn't made any attempt to come near her and she realised he was waiting for her to grant permission. She took his palms and laid them upon her breasts. His hands filled up with her, cupping the smooth weight of them. The warmth of his touch sent another shiver through her. His thumbs moved across her nipples and they hardened beneath the caress.

She hardly felt the cool air of the wind, transfixed by him. His dark hair fell over his shoulders, down his back. There was nothing tame about him; he was like a wild creature who wanted to possess her.

Marguerite rested her hands upon his chest muscles, exploring the hard flesh, watching the way his face transformed. He did the same to her, fingering her erect nipples and stroking her breasts. Then he lowered her to the cloak, resting upon his side as he made her comfortable.

His eyes turned dark, wicked, as he took her hands and lifted them above her head. He locked them in place, while he bent his mouth to taste the bud of her nipple. A surge of need echoed between her legs, causing moisture at her intimate place. She felt the hard length of him against her thigh and wondered what it would be like to take him inside her.

He released her wet nipples and took the glass pendant, rubbing the smooth shape upon her erect tips. The sensation was foreign and he used it, along with his tongue, to torment her further.

His mouth and tongue suckled hard, drawing a deep response inside her. Marguerite reached for his shaft, curling her fingers around his length. His breathing quickened and he lifted his mouth from her breast, watching her as she explored his manhood. He covered her hand, showing her how to move against him in a rhythm.

If it was possible, he grew larger in her hand, and she saw the fierce pleasure transforming his face. Abruptly, he pulled away from her and she felt the cool breeze of the wind upon her skin. His mouth moved down to her thighs, above the sand, tasting and teasing her. With his fingers, he touched the intimate slit between her legs. She trembled when he slid a finger inside her, lazily stroking the wetness.

His mouth was moving everywhere, over her thighs, making her feel so vulnerable. She was arching, trembling as the need for him overtook her. He sat up, guiding her to straddle him. With his mouth, he kissed her hard, rubbing her against his heavy, thick shaft.

Marguerite reached down to the blunt head of him and moved it against her slick opening. She wanted to feel him deep inside, to be taken and conquered by this man.

His face was taut with need, his hands gripping her hips as she lowered herself. It was too tight to take him and she let him rest only a fraction inside of her. But when he lifted her up, lowering her again, he moved deeper.

She understood, then, what she had to do. Slowly,

she raised her hips and sheathed him a little further. She found a slow rhythm and her body seemed to adjust to his size, stretching and growing wetter with each penetration.

But then his hands curled beneath her bottom, forcing her to increase her pace. Though he didn't pull her down, she found herself growing more excited, her body straining for more. Her breathing came in rapid gasps as she moved upon him, the thrusting length of him filling her up.

And though she felt tight as he invaded, he dulled it when he sat up and took her breast into his mouth. With his tongue, he tasted her nipple, holding still as she grew accustomed to him buried within her. Gently, she raised up again, experimenting with the sensation as his tongue gloried against her breasts.

He gripped her lower back, his hand moving between their joining. She felt his fingers caressing the sensitive flesh above her entrance and a ripple of shock flooded through her. A moan escaped her and he pulled his hand away.

'No, don't stop,' she whispered. He returned his fingers to her hooded flesh, and she showed him where to touch, until she was shaking from the way he rubbed her. He was thick and hard inside of her, but he remained motionless.

The double pressure of his manhood and the movement of his fingers made her raise her hips back, seeking the rush she wanted.

'It feels good,' she admitted, and Callum never relented, keeping up the rhythmic pressure of his hand until she bucked against him, thrusting in counterpoint to his tantalising strokes.

The heat built up inside her, a shimmering crest of pleasure, until she shattered against his hand, clenching him deep inside. He grabbed her hips and thrust hard, forcing her to ride him, the intensity of her climax convulsing her again and again.

He laid her back on to the cloak, still moving in slow penetrations, and she lifted her knees to take him deeper. He was merciless, demanding that she give every part of herself to him. And when he plunged against her, taking his own release, he groaned and continued to drive deeply inside her while she clung to him, lost in her own storm.

When he rested against her, upon her skin, she heard a single whispered word, 'Marguerite.'

'You spoke,' she breathed. 'Callum…you said my name.'

He wasn't aware of anything, only the immense satisfaction of his body joined with hers. Had he said anything at all? He tried to make his mouth move, to let out her name again…but nothing happened. Again, he struggled to bring out the words, but the invisible wall prevented him.

'You spoke. I know you did.' Her bare arms came around his neck, holding him in a tight embrace. A smile came over her and she drew her hands up to clasp his hair. 'I want to hear it again.'

He struggled to form the word, but the longer she watched him, the more awkward he felt. If what she said was true, he'd spoken without thinking. Without trying.

He withdrew from her body, angry at himself for being unable to fulfil such a simple request. Picking up her chemise, he started to bring it to her, when he spied the sail of a ship approaching on the horizon. From the speed of the wind, it would be here within half an hour, and the occupants might see him and Marguerite before then.

Callum tossed the chemise to Marguerite and heaped sand upon the fire, extinguishing it. He donned his own clothing, but she looked worried at the sudden change of his mood. 'I don't understand. What's wrong?'

He pointed out at the approaching ship and her expression paled. 'That could be my father.' Fumbling with the linen chemise, she hurried to dress herself. Callum helped her with the cote and surcoat, handing her the veil to cover her wet hair. Marguerite had barely put her shoes on before he pulled her into a run to the waiting horses. He gathered the reins of her mare, helping her to mount.

She started to wait on him, but he slapped the horse's flanks, urging the animal to go on. There was no time to delay. He could shadow her from a distance, but she had to return to the castle quickly.

If it was the Duc arriving, she needed to be safely back in her chamber before anyone discovered her gone. He didn't know if she'd succeed, for there was so little time.

Callum urged his horse into a gallop, keeping several paces behind her. As he rode, he thought of the husband the Duc was planning to bring back for Marguerite. A cold rage drowned out reason, replacing it with jealousy. If he'd had an estate and a title, he could gain Marguerite's hand in marriage. He could be the one to claim her as his wife, the way he'd taken her body just now.

Making love to her had been the most priceless gift she could have given him. The idea of her sharing that experience with someone else, of letting another man take her, was akin to driving a spear through his chest.

He couldn't let her go. All he could do was pray she would make the decision to walk away from this life and leave with him.

Marguerite gave her horse over to Jean when she reached the stables. Her guards eyed her mussed hair and dishevelled clothing, but said nothing. Embarrassment flooded her cheeks and she felt as if everyone knew what she had been doing.

When Callum rode in behind her, he disappeared into the stables, presumably to care for the horses. She didn't know what he'd thought of her actions but inside, her body was still trembling from the fierce reaction he'd evoked.

Lady Beatrice glared at her, but Marguerite passed by the woman and spoke not a word. She went straight to her chamber and ordered a bath. Though she'd believed that her father would travel on land, the ship she'd seen was large enough to carry his entourage and horses. It was entirely possible that they had returned early, especially travelling by sea instead of on horseback.

As her maids helped her to bathe and dress during the next hour, she thought of how Callum had spoken his first word in so many years. Of all the words he could have said, he'd chosen her name.

Her heart softened at the memory, for there was no other man she could imagine sharing her life with. Yet, she was deeply afraid of defying her father. Never in a thousand years would the Duc understand why she would want to cast off the wealth she was surrounded by, in order to wed a Scottish warrior.

Callum was the man who made her blood race, who'd given her a forbidden taste of passion. The man she loved.

Marguerite touched the glass pendant and held it as she finished bathing. Her maids said nothing as they helped her don a clean blue gown and surcoat. Around her hips, she wore a slender golden girdle set with sapphires. They braided her wet hair and hid it beneath a veil.

Outside, she heard the commotion and the sound of horses approaching.

'The Duc!' one of the soldiers shouted, and a cheer resounded among the men as they gathered to greet him.

So. He'd returned early. Marguerite forced herself to go below stairs, her heart pounding. She feared that he would recognise the guilt in her face, or worse, that someone might tell him where she'd gone.

With each step, her skin grew colder, until she stood at the entrance to greet him. Callum emerged from the stables and when the men arrived, he took their horses. Not once did he look at her, his face devoid of any expression. It was to protect both of them, she knew, but it bothered her more than it should.

Her stomach plummeted when her father approached, though she forced a smile upon her face. The Duc rode alongside another man, whose height equalled his own. The man, whom she suspected was the Earl of Penrith, had fair hair like her own and he offered her a slight smile of welcome. He was impeccably dressed in a midnight-blue silk doublet, with dun-colored chausses and a dark cape. A jewelled sword hung at his side and Marguerite idly wondered if he knew how to use it.

Her father had chosen a man whom most women

would consider handsome and strong. She ought to be well pleased, but all she wanted to do right now was weep.

Do not betray yourself, she warned. *Behave like a duke's daughter.*

Guy de Montpierre strode forward, the man at his side. 'Marguerite, I would like to introduce you to Peter Warrington, the Earl of Penrith.'

She curtsied to Lord Penrith and he sent her a kind smile. Taking her hand, he brushed a kiss upon the back of her palm. 'I am well pleased with this betrothal, my lady.'

He released her hand, and her insides felt as if they'd been turned into stone. Even standing before this man felt like a betrayal to Callum. She couldn't find the words to speak a simple greeting, so she nodded and stepped back.

'We will draw up the necessary documents this evening and have them signed and witnessed on the morrow,' her father claimed. To her, he directed, 'Arrange for a meal and good wine for us.'

Marguerite murmured her agreement, wanting to leave them both. Her mind was caught up in turmoil, and as she departed, she saw Beatrice moving closer to the Duc. Though her father gave no greeting, Marguerite noticed the subtle interest in his eyes. It was quite possible that Beatrice could influence him and she had no doubt that her aunt would fill his ears with stories of her misbehaviour.

But he could not punish her in front of the earl, thankfully.

While Marguerite gave the orders for their meal, she noticed Lord Penrith standing at the entrance, watching her. After she spoke to the servants, Marguerite cast him a look, wondering if the earl was the sort of man who would understand her wishes.

She felt nervous beneath his gaze, not knowing what to say to him. He crossed the Hall and when he reached her side, he asked, 'We have a little time before the meal is prepared. Perhaps you might wish to show me the grounds until the food is ready?'

Though she nodded her agreement, leading him from the Hall, she didn't want to spend any time with this man, nor lead him to believe that they could have a successful marriage.

The earl started walking within the inner bailey and offered her his arm. Marguerite took it and he said, 'You appear frightened of me. There's no need.'

'We've only just met,' she admitted. 'I don't know you at all.'

He stopped walking and regarded her. 'Your father told me many stories of your beauty and your virtue. I thought he was exaggerating, as all fathers do. But it seems, in this instance, he was right.'

Not about my virtue, Marguerite thought. As if in response to her thoughts, she saw Callum leading another horse into the stables. The look on his face was emotionless, as if he didn't care whether she was there or not. It dug into her feelings, making her wonder if he knew that she had no choice. The invisible web of captivity was closing in on her and she didn't know how to unravel it.

'It has been a difficult year,' Marguerite confessed to the earl. 'The last man I was betrothed to turned out to be a liar and a murderer.'

'Cairnross was a powerful man,' Lord Penrith said. 'But anyone could see that he was cruel.'

'And you are not?' she prodded.

He sent her a chagrined smile. 'I am a man of many complexities. But I am not cruel. And I have every intention of treating my wife with the greatest respect.' Though his tone was light, she sensed something else behind his claim.

Raising her eyes to his, she saw friendliness there, but nothing more. He did not look upon her with a lustful eye, nor as a man bent upon possessing her. She let out a slow breath. Even so, she would withhold judgement until she knew this man better.

As they continued walking throughout the grounds, she was intensely aware of Callum. Though he ought to understand that she had to be courteous to her father's guest, she could feel the silent accusation. And she sensed his jealousy, burning into her with a darkness that chafed her heart.

It was wrong, letting the earl believe that she could possibly be his wife. Dishonourable to stand at his side and let the lies of omission make her into a woman she wasn't. When they reached the garden, she stopped walking.

'Lord Penrith,' she murmured. 'I wish to be honest with you.' She reached for the edges of her courage, hoping he would understand.

'Have I done something to offend you?' he asked, his eyes narrowing.

'No.' She searched for the right words, to make him understand. 'But you have journeyed a great distance on my behalf and I do not believe I would make a good wife for you.'

He stopped walking. 'And why is that? I have been here only a few minutes.' His gaze narrowed upon her and, before she could speak, he predicted, 'Or do you have feelings for someone else?'

Slowly, she nodded her head. 'You deserve a wife who could love you.'

A half-smile twisted his face. 'I have little interest in love, Lady Marguerite. It matters not to me whether or not we have feelings towards one another. Many a strong marriage was built upon friendship.'

She didn't know how to respond to that and now was not the time to admit that she'd given herself to another. The earl's statement confused her, for she'd believed he would be angry or bothered by the fact that she cared for someone else. Instead, he didn't appear to mind at all.

They finished their walk, but as Marguerite passed the stables, she couldn't stop herself from looking back. Callum was no longer there.

When she reached the entrance to the keep, she saw the knowing eyes of her aunt Beatrice.

'She's a fine lass, isn't she?' Iagar remarked, later that night. Callum stood near the back of the Hall with the other men, eating a large piece of bread the cook had given him. He didn't have to ask who Iagar was talking about, but ignored the statement.

'You were gone with her for a while,' Campbell continued, a leer upon his face. 'Did the Lady Marguerite take a liking to you?'

He stood and gripped Iagar's throat, shoving the man against the wall. Rage filled every part of him, that the man would suggest anything against her. Even if it was true.

Callum held Iagar just long enough to warn him, before dropping him to the ground. The man coughed, gripping his throat. There was a flash of anger on his face, but he quelled it.

'You should put your strength to another use, MacKinloch. We're leaving tomorrow night to raid a garrison south of here,' Iagar told him. He kept his voice low, adding, 'You could help us free the prisoners.'

Tension knotted inside Callum at the mention of captives. He didn't want to be involved with the other men, to stir up trouble with the English. Yet, he remembered the restlessness he'd endured while in chains. The feeling that no one would come for him. That he would die, locked away from the world.

Upon the dais, he spied Marguerite sitting with her betrothed husband, the Earl of Penrith. Jealousy sank its claws into his mind. He didn't like the man watching over her, fascinated by his bride.

The thought of the earl touching Marguerite sent off a blaze of fury inside him. Without realising it, he was gripping his knife. A primitive side of him wanted to abduct her from her father's castle, to take her north where no one would ever find them.

She belonged with him. Only she had been able to unlock the years of silence, letting him speak again. And after the morning he'd spent in her arms, he wasn't going to let her go.

His companion sensed his distraction and pressed further. 'Join us at Sileas's home, when the castle is abed. We'll talk further.'

Iagar started to walk away, but he turned back. 'You remember what it was like, MacKinloch. Hoping someone would free us. And season after season, we were in chains.'

The man's words brought back the nightmare of those years. Callum sobered, remembering well enough what it was like to pray for help when none came. Each day of suffering was like a scar upon his mind.

But he refused to agree to Iagar's request, for he was here for Marguerite. He stood against the back wall for hours, watching over her. And only when she retired for the night, climbing the stairs, did he finally retreat to the stables.

Chapter Ten

Tangled dreams warred within Callum's mind. He was standing atop a stone tower, watching as his brother Alex fought to save his daughter's life. Lord Harkirk had taken the young girl hostage, baiting them in an attempt to slaughter both Alex and Bram.

The bow felt awkward in his hands, though he'd never ceased practising. From this distance, he couldn't strike Harkirk without the danger of harming the child.

His brothers fought below, while he held his arrow steady, waiting for an opportunity. In the eyes of Harkirk, he saw a man who revelled in torture and death.

Then he saw Lady Harkirk and the pain upon her face. She had been trapped in her marriage, just as he'd been chained and at her husband's mercy. But she had been the one to save him, convincing Harkirk to accept the bribe and release him.

The brave courage in her face reminded him of Marguerite. Without hesitation, Callum released the arrow, watching it strike down the man who had been responsible for so much suffering. At last, Harkirk was dead.

The memory shifted again and they rolled over Harkirk's body. But instead of the baron's face, he saw the frozen expression of Lord Penrith.

Callum awakened from the dream, shaken by what he'd seen. He'd killed Harkirk, months ago, just as he'd sworn to do. But instead of setting him free from all the nightmares, the death had plagued him for an unknown reason.

And then, to imagine killing Penrith… It made him wonder what sort of man he was becoming. It had enraged him to see Marguerite walking with the man, resting her hand upon his arm. The pair of them made a striking couple, both of them wealthy and attractive. The earl had looked upon her with the eyes of a man who appreciated what he saw.

Callum was forced to watch them together. He didn't know if he could remain here, not knowing whether or not Marguerite would find a way to escape the marriage. Violence and unrest simmered within him, and he might provoke a fight if he saw them together.

He had to find a way to release the anger building inside him, before he did something he regretted.

Marguerite found Callum waiting for her outside the stable, when she went out riding with her father the next morning.

His face was shielded, but in his expression, she saw a rigid exhaustion, as if he'd barely slept at all. Upon his back his bow and quiver rested, as if he were prepared for any threat. He held the reins of both horses, leading them forward until he stood a short distance away.

The Duc noticed the weapons and strode over to

take his horse. His eyes narrowed. 'You're not one of my men.'

'Forgive me, Monsieur le Duc.' The stable master approached and said, 'He is Iagar's cousin and needed a place to work. He's helped in the stables this past sennight and has done well here.'

Callum met the Duc's eyes with a steady look of his own. Marguerite wondered if she should intervene and vouch for Callum. Instinct warned her to say nothing, though she saw him watching her surreptitiously.

'I know your face,' Guy said. 'I've seen it somewhere before.'

When Callum gave no reply, the Duc demanded, 'Well? Have you nothing to say?'

'He cannot speak, Monsieur le Duc,' the stable master intervened. 'His tongue has been cut out, so we believe.'

'Has it?' Her father studied Callum and his eyes hardened as he turned to Marguerite. 'Do you know this man?'

She didn't know what to say, afraid of betraying them both. Never had she lied to her father, but she had also seen his ruthless nature. If Guy de Montpierre knew what had happened between them, Callum would pay the price with his life.

'No,' she said quietly. 'I do not know him.'

Callum handed over the reins and helped her on to her horse. The touch of his hands upon her waist evoked the memory of how he'd gripped her bare hips the previous morning. She'd lost herself in abandonment, the forbidden touch arousing her as she took him within her body.

Marguerite couldn't look at him, for her cheeks were

burning from the vision. Was she making the right decision by lying to her father? She didn't know.

But she saw the coldness on Callum's face, at her denial, and there was nothing she could say to him. He never once met her gaze, behaving like a mere servant.

It broke away the pieces of her heart, for this wasn't where he belonged. Callum was a fighter, like his brothers. He was a servant to no man and she couldn't bear to treat him as such.

He didn't like this situation any more than she did. Would he leave, as she'd wanted him to, days ago? Or would he stay, forcing her to see him, reminding her of what she stood to lose?

Guy mounted his horse and led her away from the castle, towards the coast. Marguerite knew it was only an excuse to speak to her alone. Her nerves grew brittle, half-afraid of what he would say.

When they were half a mile from the gates, her father slowed the pace of his horse, riding alongside her.

'What do you think of the Earl of Penrith?' His expression remained neutral, as if waiting to gauge her response. 'We finished drawing up the betrothal agreement last night and it will be signed and witnessed this day, if you agree to it.'

Marguerite didn't know how to answer. If she admitted that she had no intention of wedding the earl, he would demand to know why. Her courage faltered and she hedged her answer. 'Lord Penrith is still a stranger to me. I can only hope he will be better than Lord Cairnross.'

'Cairnross never once mistreated you, did he?' Guy's tone was defensive, irritated at her accusation.

Marguerite stopped her horse and regarded her father. 'He killed my maid. I left the fortress because it wasn't safe to remain there.'

'He wouldn't have dared to hurt you,' her father argued, dismissing the idea.

But his rationalisation only heightened her anger. 'I couldn't know that. And you were already gone to Edinburgh, so I had to make the decision on my own.'

A cold expression slid over her father's face. 'What you did was reckless and dangerous. Going off with strangers and a clan chief you didn't know. They could have violated you, or—'

'They did not harm me,' she interrupted.

'The fact remains that you lived with a group of savages, like a common peasant.'

She stared at him in disbelief. 'Is that what you thought of the MacKinlochs? They gave me sanctuary, putting their own lives at risk. For *me*, a woman they hardly knew.' It outraged her that he would call them savage.

'I spoke on their behalf to the king. Whatever debt was owed to their clan, I have satisfied. Now we must lay the past to rest.' His voice softened, but the iron within it was unmistakable. 'Beatrice told me that you disobeyed my orders and spent a night alone in the forest.'

Marguerite didn't deny it and the fear began closing in. 'She locked me in my room. I was angry.'

'She was protecting you, according to my orders.'

'I was given no food for over a day. I needed to get out of the castle.' Colour flooded her face and she struggled to think of a way to explain her actions.

The Duc eyed her with suspicion. 'There is a rumour

that a man helped you escape the castle.' His back stiffened and his gaze became piercing. 'Whether or not it is true, I think you understand me perfectly, Marguerite. You will marry as soon as possible. It is why I chose a man who doesn't care whether or not his wife is a virgin.'

Her cheeks flamed with humiliation, for he was right. She'd willingly surrendered her body to Callum, with no regrets. Never had she experienced anything like his lovemaking and, to her shame, she wanted him again. To wake up in his arms, to share his life and bear him children would mean everything.

Before she could speak, her father added, 'You should know that there are noblemen who refused to have you, after your association with the MacKinloch Clan.'

'Then they weren't honourable men,' she responded. 'I owe a great deal to the MacKinlochs.' Her heart caught as she thought of Callum once more. 'I have no regrets over the choices I made.'

With a sigh, he drew his horse to a stop. 'You always did have a soft heart, Marguerite. Like your mother.' A faint smile creased his mouth and her frustration dissolved.

Guy was still the father who had sat her upon his knee, telling her stories. He'd been the only parent she'd known, for her mother had died when she was barely two. Though she'd been fostered with another family in Navarre, their relationship had always been close. He'd visited her often, bringing gifts.

'Don't be afraid of this marriage,' he reassured her. 'I believe Penrith can provide everything you would ever want.'

She tried to smile, but he'd spoken the same words when he'd arranged her betrothal to Cairnross. 'Can you…delay the betrothal a little longer?' she asked. 'I want to be certain he is a good man.' Once the formal agreement was made, it was nigh impossible to break it.

Her father reached out and cupped her chin. 'As I said before, there can be no delay.' He turned back towards the castle and Marguerite followed him, keeping a slight distance behind.

Once he entered the gates, she saw other men arriving, friends come to witness the betrothal. She held back, feeling uncertain about all that had happened.

A faint cracking noise sounded behind her. When she turned, she saw Callum upon his own horse, watching them from the trees. What was he doing here?

He beckoned and Marguerite cast a nervous look back at her father. The Duc might come after her if he discovered her missing, but then she could spare a moment or two.

Curiosity won out, so she rode forward to him. Callum took her reins and urged both of the horses deeper into the forest, until they were well out of view of the castle gates.

When he drew the horses to a stop, he dismounted and lifted her down.

'What is it?' she breathed. 'What has happened?'

His eyes turned fierce and he framed her face with his hands. Against her cheeks, she felt the warmth of his breath.

'Mine,' he said harshly. His mouth came upon hers, branding her with a kiss that took apart her senses. She kissed him back, glorying in the rush of desire that pooled through her. He touched her upon her spine, his hands moving down to her bottom. She held him close, feeling the sensation of his body against hers.

When she pulled back, her lips felt sensitive and swollen. 'Yes, I am yours,' she whispered.

Hearing his voice was a gift she'd never expected. There were a thousand questions she wanted to ask, but she was afraid she would only frustrate him if he couldn't find the words. Callum looked as if he wanted to say more, but the only words he could manage were, 'Come. Now.'

He wanted her to leave with him for Glen Arrin at this very moment. Upon his horse, she saw supplies to last for several days. And though it tempted her, she could not abandon her father and home without any word of explanation. The Duc would only send an army of soldiers after them and there was not enough time for them to reach safety.

'I can't,' she told him. 'I need time to persuade my father.' When he looked unconvinced, she added, 'If I go with you now, they'll find us.' She rested her palm upon his cheek. 'They would hurt you and your family. I can't let that happen.'

Callum struggled to speak again and she waited, hoping he could let out the words. In the end, he closed off his thoughts and lifted her back on to her horse.

She rode back to the castle, but he remained behind, watching.

Seeing her with the earl was like a slow poison, blistering him with jealousy. Callum spent the remainder of the day working on countless tasks to distract him from thinking of them together. He'd eavesdropped on the man's servants, for if there was any hint of cruelty, he would hear it from them.

But most had a jovial mood, behaving as if they were well treated. They were here to serve Penrith and to bring back his bride to England. Callum wasn't about to let that happen. He'd kidnap her first.

The endless waiting was trying his patience. He didn't believe she could extricate herself from her father's command, any more than she could escape the marriage. The only reason he hadn't ignored her wishes and carried her off was because it would hurt her. She cared about her father and was loyal to him, just as he was close to his brothers.

But with every moment she spent here, it was too easy for her to fall into their trappings. He was powerless to stop it and frustration seethed inside him like an unholy creature clawing its way out. His hands itched for a bow and arrows and as the afternoon waned, he retrieved them. An hour spent practising might ease the frustration rising inside him.

Callum left the castle gates, starting towards the forest, when he heard voices ahead. It was Iagar Campbell, along with a handful of others. All were armed.

Iagar had mentioned trying to free some prisoners and although he didn't know the details, it didn't matter. He yearned for a fight, to use his weapons and release the restlessness plaguing him. Though he was wary of joining them, there was no greater cause than to grant another Scot his freedom.

Deliberately, he stepped upon a dry stick and the cracking noise alerted the others.

'MacKinloch,' Iagar greeted him. The others stared

at him with distrust and their discussion ceased at once. 'Did you decide to join us, then?'

Callum gave a single nod and raised his bow in answer.

One of the older men, Sileas, stared at him with a suspicious eye. 'Why would you want that one? He's no good to us. A half-wit, isn't he?'

The cold anger clenched beneath his skin, rising for a fight. Were it a younger man who'd spoken, he might have unleashed his temper, proving who the real half-wit was. Instead, he took slow steps towards the man, in a silent threat.

Iagar intervened, placing himself between them. 'I know the MacKinlochs,' he said. 'They're loyal to our cause.'

Doubt and distrust marred the mood, causing dissent among the men. Iagar reminded them, 'We could use an archer.' He sent a questioning look towards Callum. 'If you're willing.'

There was risk involved in this fight, for he didn't know the men or where they were going. Yet neither could he remain in the castle, watching Marguerite with her intended husband. If he didn't occupy himself somehow, the jealousy and madness would consume him.

He inclined his head in agreement.

Before Iagar could speak again, another man intervened, 'We don't even know him.' Staring hard, he added, 'He might tell the Duc about the raid.'

'He can't speak,' Iagar responded. 'There is nothing to fear.'

Sileas's eyes gleamed, a thin smile spreading over his face. 'Then he couldn't betray us if he wanted to.'

Callum made no effort to prove him wrong. Though

he'd spoken a few words to Marguerite, each one had been a struggle. He didn't know what was preventing him from speaking, but the morning he'd spent as her lover had somehow slashed through the barrier of his voice. He was fighting for every word, hoping that somehow he would regain enough of his voice to convince her to leave with him. Being around her was changing him inside, healing the scars of his imprisonment.

As the men continued discussing their plans to raid a garrison a few miles to the south, he thought of all the nights he'd spent, wishing someone would save him. He'd been a captive since the age of twelve and the years of imprisonment had changed him. He didn't know how to live like a normal man, or how to carve a life for himself.

The thought dug into his conscience like a dull blade, scraping the heart of his frustration. He needed a purpose, a way to provide for the woman he wanted. And the only thing he knew how to do was wield a bow and fight alongside his brothers. It might not be enough.

'He's got a horse, hasn't he?'

The unexpected words broke through Callum's musing, snapping him back to attention. Before the others could voice their opinions, he shook his head in refusal. No one was going to take his horse from him.

'We'll get there faster with horses, MacKinloch,' Iagar protested. 'We need yours.'

But the stallion was his only way to return to Glen Arrin, his homeland. He wasn't about to let them use his horse and possibly lose it in a raid. Callum unsheathed his dirk in a dark warning. He shook his head in refusal.

Iagar raised his hands in false surrender. 'It was only

a suggestion. We'll leave it here, if that's your wish.' But the words held a note of anger, echoed by the men who looked irritated at his refusal.

Callum lowered the dirk and returned it to his belt, ignoring their grumbling. The horse was safer left behind in the stables than with these men.

He hung back while the others disappeared into the darkness. Iagar moved to walk alongside him. 'I'm glad you've joined us, MacKinloch. We've a greater chance of succeeding with more men.'

His fist clenched around the bow he'd slung over one shoulder. The lines in Iagar's face relaxed, and when they had gone far enough away from view of the castle, they stopped to build a fire and light torches.

This raid was a reckless effort, but if they freed even a few prisoners, it was worth it to join them. Callum cast a look back at the castle, hoping he wasn't making a mistake.

Chapter Eleven

It took them over an hour to reach the garrison. Callum wondered how any of them knew where they were going, but the older man Sileas guided them there until they reached the river, where they extinguished their torches. The wooden fortress was small, with perhaps a dozen guards. Barely more than an outpost, it was no threat to anyone.

Uneasiness crawled through Callum's stomach, making him wonder why these men had chosen such a small target. And whether there were any prisoners there at all.

He'd stopped Iagar, pointing to his scarred wrists and then to the fortress.

'If there are any prisoners there, we'll free them. I promise you.' Iagar gripped his shoulder and added, 'Stay here. We'll need you to guard our backs.'

Callum slowed his pace, taking his position behind them.

'Let none of the English soldiers escape,' the older man warned. 'Otherwise, they'll bring reinforcements.'

Callum gave a nod, but inwardly, he didn't like this. He doubted if there could be more than one or two prisoners, not in an outpost this small. But he had a greater range by staying outside the fortress with his weapon. He fitted an arrow to the bowstring while Iagar, Sileas and two other men crawled on their stomachs toward the gates.

The shadows shielded his presence as he waited. After several minutes passed, he heard the battle cries of the men as they charged forward with dirks and spears. One of the guards shouted, only to be cut off in the middle of a word.

It was part of any raid, he knew. Even so, it didn't diminish the sense of unrest building within him. He'd expected a fortress the size of Cairnross, where they would infiltrate the walls and break the prisoners free, as best they could.

Instead, this felt wrong.

He held an arrow fitted to the bowstring, watching for any sign of prisoners being freed. When none came, he wondered what had gone awry and decided he should go in to help.

Callum kept his arrow taut, ready to defend himself. His eyes blurred against the brightness of the torches when he first entered the fortress.

After his eyes adjusted, he stared in disbelief at the bodies littering the ground. There were no prisoners here at all. Only English soldiers who had been murdered.

Callum saw Iagar raise a dirk and fury rose up inside of him. He opened his mouth, a roar rising in his throat for them to stop and lay down their weapons. But it came out as nothing but a breath of air. His mind was raging, the words trapped. He couldn't voice a single command.

The slaughter sickened him. Aye, he'd been taken prisoner as a child by men like these, growing up in chains. But not all of the soldiers deserved to die. The fury within him transformed into revulsion.

Iagar and the others began looting the bodies and Callum retreated into the darkness. These men were nothing but murderers and thieves.

His hand gripped the bow in a fight to control his anger. If he could have found his way back to the castle alone, he'd have gone immediately.

'MacKinloch,' he heard Sileas call out, 'aren't you going to join us?' The man stood with his back against a wooden wall, while he held a sword from one of the fallen men.

His answer was to release one of the black-feathered arrows, embedding it in the wood behind Sileas's head.

Sileas raised the sword, his temper blazing. 'What was that for, ye son of a cur?'

But Callum fitted another arrow to his bow, aiming directly at the old man's heart.

Because you deserve to die for what you've done.

Iagar stepped beside him. 'Put down the bow, MacKinloch.'

Callum spun and aimed the weapon at the man he'd believed was an ally. He'd been wrong. They'd come here to loot and to kill, not to save men's lives.

Backing away slowly, he let them know that he wanted nothing to do with them. Especially because, as Sileas had predicted, he could tell no one what had happened here.

The following day, Marguerite found Callum swimming in the loch, north of the forest. The sky held streaks of rose and lavender and she sat upon a large stone, watching him. His body tore through the water in long strokes, at a punishing pace. His shoulders flexed and she waited for him to finish, hoping to share the gift she'd brought. Around her neck, she wore the pendant he'd given her. She touched the cool glass, feeling suddenly nervous around him.

The last time she'd been with Callum, he'd asked her to leave everything behind to be together. She wanted to, but despite her attempts to speak with the Earl of Penrith in private again, her father wouldn't allow it. Perhaps he'd sensed what she was trying to do. Before she could voice a protest, the betrothal agreement had been finalised, signed and witnessed.

You're weak-willed and cowardly, she berated herself. *You don't deserve your freedom, if you aren't able to speak for yourself.*

Worry rooted inside her that she couldn't break free at all. Yes, she could have refused to sign the document. But the Duc would demand to know why and somehow the truth would come out. He would seek retribution against the MacKinlochs if she admitted she'd become Callum's lover. It was a dangerous game she'd begun, one she feared was impossible to win.

When at last Callum ceased his swimming, he stood up in the water. His dark eyes caught hers and she saw the trouble brewing within him. He looked angry, like a man returning from battle.

Emerging from the water, he didn't seem to care as he walked to her unclothed, the water rolling down his skin in droplets. His black hair hung past his shoulders, wet and pushed back from his face.

Like a sleek predator, he watched her. Silently reminding her of the way he'd run his hands over her skin, awakening feelings she didn't understand. Seeing him in the morning light, she wanted to touch where the sun gleamed over his muscles, illuminating flesh.

'I—I brought you something,' she murmured, averting her gaze from his body. But as she bent to retrieve the pouch, his powerful legs were so close she could reach out and touch him.

Her lungs constricted with nervousness. When she stood up, his manhood had grown thick and heavy, aroused by the sight of her. Marguerite shivered, remembering the heat of his body moving over hers.

Keeping her eyes averted, she held out the pouch. 'It's a quill and a bit of parchment. I thought you might like to try writing upon it.'

'Marguerite,' he said. In his voice, she heard the unspoken questions. He took the pouch and tossed it back on the hillside, dragging her close. His arms closed around her, gripping her in a tight embrace. Against her hips, she felt the hard length of his arousal and the answering rush of desire within herself.

His mouth moved to her lips, taking her in a kiss that insisted she belonged in his arms. He was ruthless, demanding a response that pushed away all of her fears, reminding her of why she needed him. Why she had to sever the betrothal and face her father's wrath.

When his hands moved to the laces upon her gown, he stared at her in an unspoken question.

'I can't,' she whispered. Not now. She didn't deserve affection or pleasure, when she'd failed to fight the betrothal. The lies she'd told her father and the earl were encircling her, strangling her hold upon honour.

Callum took her face between his hands, staring

into her eyes. She saw the dark possession and a hidden frustration within them. He touched his forehead to hers. In his eyes, she saw the future she wanted, the man she desired.

'I will find a way to free myself,' she vowed. 'And when I have, I will come back with you. I swear it.'

Her hands moved to thread through his dark hair, stroking the back of his head. She touched him, crossing her arms around his neck, letting her hands slide down his naked back.

His lips pressed a light kiss against her jawbone. It sent a shiver through her, reminding her of the time when he'd kissed her in other secret places.

As he got dressed, Marguerite couldn't escape the thought that something else was bothering him, but he had no words to tell her. There was tension in the way he held himself and a sense of trouble.

She retrieved the pouch and offered it to him. 'Do you want me to teach you more words?' Inside the pouch, she showed him her gift of parchment and a quill, as well as a container of ink.

He eyed them, but did not accept the pouch. Darkness shadowed his mood and she couldn't guess whether or not she was the cause of it.

'Would you rather I hadn't come?' she asked. 'If you've no wish to learn more writing, I won't force it upon you.' She set them down on the ground, wondering if she'd misunderstood him.

He was fighting against himself, struggling for the words. His mouth moved, but no other sounds came out. The frustration built up higher until he seized a stone and threw it hard into the water, where it splashed and sank.

'Callum, tell me what it is.'

It was the wrong choice of words. He spun on her, his rage filling him up. She realised that he'd been trying to speak. In his stance, she felt him tremble with anger and frustration.

It hurt to see him like this and she tried to console him in an embrace. 'It's all right.' As soon as she touched him, she realised that pity was a mistake. He didn't want her sympathy. She raised up on her tiptoes and brought her mouth to his, hoping the kiss would ease him.

Callum kissed her back, the dark heat of his mouth seeking absolution. When his tongue threaded with hers, she clung hard, tasting his anger, meeting it with her own guilt. There was a wildness to him, like a man trying to consume her. She shuddered beneath the onslaught and heat, offering herself in solace.

His hands moved to the ties of her gown and she knew if she remained silent, he would take her again. He would lay her back upon the grass, filling her up and giving her unspeakable pleasure.

Callum bared the nape of her neck and shoulder, causing shivers with the warmth of his mouth. His hands came up to touch her breasts and her nipples hardened against the silk. She struggled to maintain her composure, but the sweet torment made her hesitate. More than anything, she wanted to be with him again.

You don't deserve it. Not until you've broken free of the earl.

Though it hurt to push him away, Marguerite reached back and caught his hands, drawing them down to his side. 'Last night, I signed the betrothal agreement.'

The look of betrayal on Callum's face made her feel

like she'd turned away from him. 'I'm going to talk with both of them today,' she said. 'I promise you.'

But within his brown eyes, she saw the doubt. He didn't believe her.

There were no words Callum could say. He'd believed that she would refuse the betrothal and free herself. But it didn't seem that she had the will within her to stand up to them.

He saw her step back, watching him. Though he tried to keep his face expressionless, she saw through the surface to the frustration beneath.

'I blame myself for being too afraid.' Her voice was anguished and she turned away from him. 'But if I make a false move and reveal my feelings, my father will hunt you down and kill you. I can't risk that.'

Though he wanted to move forward and touch her shoulders, he forced himself to remain in place. Each day here was another moment in purgatory. Heaven lay just within his reach…but until she broke the ties, he could do nothing.

'You're angry with me, I know.' Still she didn't turn around to face him, keeping her gaze downcast.

'Not…' *with you.*

He stared at her hollowed shoulders, the broken posture.

'I wish I could have done something to stop the betrothal from happening,' she admitted. 'But I was powerless.'

Aye, he understood that feeling. Her words conjured up the harsh memories of last night and the dead soldiers. Innocent men had been slain and he'd done nothing to stop it from happening. He'd ignored the premonitions he should have heeded. Instead he had believed Iagar's false words.

It had resulted in murder. The bleakness crept over him once again, strangling him with the wish that he could go back and change it.

'You must know that I don't truly want this marriage to Penrith,' Marguerite said, risking a glance back at him. 'But no one hears what I'm trying to say.'

He knew exactly what that felt like. From deep inside, he summoned the words, tearing them free.

'Fight, Marguerite.'

Fight for us. If you can't tell the Duc what you want, then there's no hope.

But the rest was too difficult, too far beyond him. He took a breath and tried again.

'You…'

She waited to hear him speak, her blue eyes filled with regret. In his mind, a thousand words sprang forth, words he wanted to say. Words she needed to hear.

You are the only woman I've ever wanted. You kept me alive when I wanted to die. Without you, I was less than a man. But neither of us can continue this way.

He could see that she felt as trapped as he did.

'I what?' she asked, hoping for more.

But his mouth moved without sound, his throat refusing to relinquish the words. He tried again and the inability to communicate made him fight even harder.

In the end, he stared hard at her, unable to voice more than a single word. 'Choose.'

'Monsieur le Duc, the messenger you sent to the English garrison returned a moment ago. He claims there was an attack last night. No survivors are left.'

'They're going to blame us for the massacre,' the Duc said, pacing across the floor. He sent a dark look toward Xavier, the captain of his guards. 'We're the closest to the outpost.'

'My men were all accounted for last night,' Xavier answered. 'Whoever did this was not one of ours.'

Guy's face turned grim and he ordered, 'Assemble a group of soldiers, and find out who it was. It falls to us to mete out justice. Or else the English King Edward will see to it.'

The Duc sat, reaching for a cup of wine. His hand curled around the silver, while inwardly he tensed. Though he held estates in Scotland, passed down from his Norman ancestors, his position here was untenable. He'd hoped to secure a strong marriage for Marguerite with the Earl of Cairnross. But his daughter had run off to live with a Scottish clan, for reasons he couldn't fathom.

Oui, Cairnross had proved to have a cruel streak. But most powerful men did what was necessary to maintain order.

From across the room, he saw Marguerite standing at the doorway, her face pale. She'd overheard his words, no doubt.

'What will you do?' she asked, moving closer. Xavier, the Captain of the Guard, exchanged a look with him, as if to ask permission. Guy inclined his head.

'We will find the murderers and execute them for their crimes,' Xavier admitted.

Her lips tightened into a line and she pointed at his hand. 'What is that you're holding?'

The Duc hadn't noticed the arrow until now. He sent

his captain a questioning look and Xavier held up the shaft. 'We found this embedded in the wall.'

'Black feathers,' the Duc noted. 'Interesting.' Few men used arrows with distinctive feathered tips. He tried to think of whether any of his archers used arrows like those, but he couldn't quite imagine it.

Marguerite's face whitened. She murmured excuses to leave, and her behaviour struck him as unusual.

His eyes narrowed upon the doorway and he turned to Xavier. 'She knows something. Follow her.'

'What have you done?' Marguerite demanded. It was nightfall before she'd been able to slip away from the castle. Over and over, she'd worried about the arrow, terrified of what it meant. Her throat ached with unshed tears, and her hands clenched as she tried to keep her hysteria under control.

Callum studied her, his eyes questioning. She went on, 'Nearly a dozen men were murdered last night at the English garrison. They found one of your arrows there.'

His expression didn't move a single muscle. Like a wall of granite, he revealed nothing at all.

Shaken by it, she whispered, 'Were you there that night?'

He inclined his head in a nod and her heart plummeted. She stared at him in disbelief. 'And did you kill those men?'

He shook his head. Though she wanted to believe him, her pulse clamoured within her chest. 'Why would you go with them? There was no reason for it.' Knowing he couldn't answer, she unleashed her anger. 'Don't you know that they'll find out? My father plans to execute any man who was there last night.'

Her tears broke free, in spite of her resolve not to cry. 'Do you think I want to see you hanged, your head cut off like a traitor?'

Callum caught her hands and his mouth tightened with his own anger. She tore her hands free, the tears running freely down her face. The fury and fear gripped so hard within her, she was shaking.

'What happened that night?' she murmured.

Callum crouched on one knee, brushing the pine needles away to reveal the dirt beneath. After thinking for a moment, he wrote: *Prisuners*.

Marguerite shook her head, not understanding. 'But there weren't any prisoners there. It was just a small outpost.' Taking the twig from him, she adjusted the word he'd misspelled.

He shrugged and wrote again: *Not my kil*.

'Then why did they find one of your arrows there?' *I was angry*.

'Who was responsible for it? Were my father's men involved?' She stared at the dirt, waiting for his answers.

Scots.

A hundred more questions crowded inside her, but she stopped asking. There was no point to it.

She wanted to rest her cheek against his chest, holding fast to the man who held her heart. But if she dared to defy her father now, the Duc might accuse Callum of leading the attack upon the garrison. And he would die for it.

He came to stand before her. Although she couldn't look him in the eye, she felt the quiet intensity of his presence. She continued to let out the tears, wishing he could somehow talk to her.

But there were no words at all. Only the quiet stare of a man whose silence would be viewed as guilt.

'You can't defend yourself,' she whispered, finally meeting his gaze. 'They'll take you prisoner and I can't do anything to stop them. Not if you can't speak.'

And though he *had* spoken on a few occasions, it seemed he had little control over the words. Whatever had caused him to lose his voice was still holding him captive.

'You should leave now,' she ordered, feeling broken at the thought. 'Go back to Glen Arrin, before they find you.'

He shook his head, folding his arms across his chest. She couldn't understand why he wouldn't try to save himself. Didn't he realise what he would face?

A faint noise caught her attention and she froze, as if someone were watching them. Whether or not it was an animal, she needed to return.

Marguerite reached for his hands, her pulse racing. 'I know you don't want to leave, but you must.' She stared into his deep brown eyes. 'You saved my life in the battle. Now let me save yours.'

He threaded his hands into her hair, but his expression was inscrutable. 'No.'

'Why? Would you rather die?' She gripped his head, the anger blazing through her. 'Do you think I'll stand aside and let that happen?'

'If…leave, you…wed him.' His brown eyes were nearly black with his own shielded frustration and she pressed herself closer, trying to use any means possible to convince him.

'I would wed Satan himself if it kept you alive.'

She raised her mouth to his, needing to show him,

without words, what he meant to her. Their lips mingled and in the strength of his arms, she felt whole. She wanted Callum to stay, to help him break through the wall of his silence. He was starving for words and he needed her help. But there was no choice. He had to leave or face his death.

Callum kissed her hard, his arms holding her close as if he could capture her spirit. As he slid his tongue against her mouth, she opened to him, her hips moulded against his.

Every last thought in her mind disappeared when his tongue slid against hers, reminding her of the way he'd made love to her. His body went rigid, his hands moving over her bottom, bringing her closer.

Marguerite surrendered to the instincts roaring inside, her swollen lips kissing him hard as his erection strained against her softness. She was trembling in his arms, wanting so much more than she could have. Her breath quickened in her lungs and desire clouded the thoughts spinning in her mind.

'Marguerite,' he said, pulling back to look at her. In his dark eyes, she saw the man who held no fear at all for their future. He didn't seem to care that she was betrothed to another.

He wanted no other woman but her. And though she wanted to fight to be with him, never would she let him die. Not when she could save him.

'Do you want your father to know?'

Marguerite turned around from the door to her chamber. In the hall stood the captain of her father's guards, Xavier.

'What do you mean?' She turned to face the man. His thin face was smug and she didn't trust him at all.

'I followed you tonight. And I saw you with the Scot. The mute one who works in the stables.'

His knowing look made Marguerite's heart catch. If he told the Duc that she'd kissed Callum, there was no knowing the depths of her father's fury. She stared at the captain, not wanting to reveal anything to him.

'What will you pay for my silence?' he prompted.

The threat reached down past her fear and squeezed the throat of her anger. Drawing upon it, she took a step towards him. 'What would you pay to keep yourself alive?'

Ice hung from her voice as she withdrew her eating knife and pointed it towards him. 'All I have to do is tell my father that you tried to hurt me. That you tried to force your attentions on me and you'll feel the lash upon your back. Perhaps worse.'

'It would be a lie.'

She forced a thin smile. 'But he would believe me, not you. So if you dare to spread stories to my father, remember what I can do to you.'

He stared at her, his expression as hard as iron. She'd made an enemy this night, for no doubt he'd hoped she would line his pockets with silver. But she was not about to let him threaten her.

After he left, she couldn't calm the beating of her heart. Though she tried to appear serene, inwardly she was drowning in fear for Callum. They would find him if he didn't go.

Marguerite went inside her chamber and sat down while her maid tended her gown and hair. Her lips were still swollen from Callum's kiss, her body on edge. Outside, it had begun to rain and she worried about him dwelling among the trees.

She stared at her chamber and the small bed with soft sheets and warm coverings. All her life, she'd lived in the finest castles and houses, wearing expensive gowns and dining upon exotic foods. This was her life and her father would never allow anything less.

But it was no longer what she wanted.

Marguerite dismissed her maid and went to stand at the small slit of a window, watching the darkness outside. If she were wed to Callum, she would never again live in a castle or wear gowns like this. There would be no maids or servants.

She'd enjoyed the time she'd spent with the MacKinlochs, but it had been so different. They fought to survive, instead of worrying about which husband would bring the greatest status. When she looked around at her life, it felt selfish and shallow.

She closed her eyes, resting up against the wall of her chamber. Her only hope was to speak with the earl, to somehow convince him to let her go.

This time, her father never protested at all when she asked to ride alone with the earl. Though Lord Penrith seemed amenable enough, she dreaded telling him the truth. She took the lead, bringing him away from the castle, to the hill overlooking the sea.

At the sight of the blue waves smoothing the edges of sand, she thought of how Callum had taught her to swim and the morning she'd spent in his arms. Guilt flushed her cheeks, but she had to speak with the earl and make him understand why she couldn't wed him.

Once they stopped the horses, the earl held the reins

and regarded her. 'You implied before that you didn't want this betrothal.'

She shook her head. 'But not because of you.'

His blue eyes turned thoughtful and he held out his hand to her, inviting her to walk. 'Are you so certain it would not be a good marriage?'

'It would be wrong. And though my father will be furious with me, you deserve my honesty.' Her cheeks burned, but she forced herself to continue with the confession. 'You deserve a virgin bride for your wedding bed.'

He said nothing for a long time, turning away from her while he thought. She expected anger or a biting response. Instead, he stared out at the sea.

'I have made many mistakes in my life,' Marguerite continued. 'But it would be a greater mistake to let you believe that I would be a good wife. I cannot wed you.'

The earl's expression turned musing. 'You know nothing about me, Lady Marguerite.'

She waited for him to continue, and he added, 'I, too, know what it is to care for someone else. Someone unsuitable for marriage.'

When he looked back at her, she saw the echoing shadow in his eyes, but he masked it with a sardonic smile. 'I see no reason why we cannot find another solution that would benefit us both.'

'What do you mean?'

'Keep your lover,' he suggested. 'Have him join us in England, if that is your will. So long as you are discreet, I won't stop you.'

Shock rendered her speechless. She had no idea how to respond to such an offer. 'And what if I bore a child from him?'

The earl shrugged. 'Then I will not have to share your bed.' The look in his eyes spoke of a man who didn't want to perform his marital duty. 'I made this betrothal because I need an heir for my lands. If you provide it for me, I care not who the father is.'

'I don't understand.'

His face held a trace of bitterness. 'A lady such as yourself wouldn't. But I think we would do well together. I like your sense of honour. And you.'

Her gaze lowered to the ground. 'Let me go, Lord Penrith. Please.'

'No,' was his answer. Though he spoke the word lightly, she sensed the steel beneath his tone. He was a man who possessed his own authority, one with a resolve to equal her own.

He softened his refusal by giving her hand a gentle squeeze. 'Consider my offer, Lady Marguerite. A respectable marriage, a strong alliance…and a blind eye toward your lover. It should be enough for you.'

Perhaps it should, but it wasn't. She didn't understand his nonchalant attitude toward infidelity. Most men would be furious to learn that their brides were no longer innocent. But the earl was unlike the other suitors she'd met.

Lord Penrith returned to the horses and waited to boost her back on to her saddle. He glanced back at her and in his eyes she saw a man resolved to keeping this betrothal. Though she didn't understand his reasons for making the marriage, something bothered her about his behaviour. 'I am sorry,' she told the earl, 'but I must speak with my father. I cannot marry you.'

His face was like a block of smooth marble, unyieldng. 'Ask, if that is your will, Lady Marguerite. But I have no intention of breaking our agreement.'

Callum spent most of the morning considering what to do. Marguerite's insistence that he return to Glen Arrin weighed upon him. Though he understood that she didn't want him implicated in the murder, if he left now, she would be lost to him.

She'd signed the betrothal agreement, and her father would coerce her into wedding the Earl of Penrith. He was convinced of it.

Aye, walking away now might save his life, but his life was nothing more than an empty shell without her. He wasn't willing to let her fears dictate his actions. Why should he hide like an outlaw because her father held power? If he fled, it was as good as admitting guilt.

Callum slung his bow over his shoulders and took the long walk to the castle, intending to return to the stables. At his waist, he carried the pouch of parchment, quill and ink that Marguerite had given him. Though it might not be needed, at least he could write a few words to defend himself.

Before he reached the castle, he saw a gathering of men, just outside the gates. Among them, he spied Iagar.

'MacKinloch,' came the man's voice. 'We're leaving Duncraig. You'll come with us.'

Callum sent Iagar a stare and shook his head. Did the man think he was going to blindly obey strangers? Keeping a neutral expression on his face, he continued his walk when Iagar blocked his path.

'They've taken Sileas for questioning. He's going to break if they torture him. And who do you think he'll blame for all of it?' Iagar's tone turned menacing. 'I'm trying to save your ungrateful arse, MacKinloch. Come with us and save yourself.'

Callum kept walking, not even bothering to look at the man.

'You were with Lady Marguerite when you escorted her on her ride the other day.'

At those words, Callum stopped. Was the bastard threatening her? His hand clenched around his bow and he fought to keep his expression shielded.

'She's a bonny one, the lass is. What do you think her father will do to her when he learns she's been with a Scot?' Iagar dropped his voice to a whisper. 'Was she good? Should I have a taste of her, after you're dead?'

Callum spun, his hands reaching for Iagar's throat but found, instead, the point of a dirk at his throat. 'You don't have a choice in this, MacKinloch. If you stay, you die.'

Not if he could help it. Callum seized the man's wrist and squeezed until Iagar released the weapon. The man's face reddened as he struggled to free himself from his grasp. He stared hard, letting the man know he could crack the bone if he wanted to.

'Die, then, if that's what you want.' He bent to pick up the dirk and Callum never took his eyes off the man as Iagar retreated.

'But if you betray us, it's your death. And hers.'

Chapter Twelve

When she returned from her ride with the earl, Marguerite was startled to see her aunt speaking to Xavier, the Captain of her father's Guard. The two soldiers who had been her escorts were bound with rope.

After she gave her horse over to the stable master, Marguerite hurried forward. Her aunt had a gloating expression upon her face, one she didn't understand.

'Why are these men being detained?' she asked Beatrice. 'They are my guards, are they not?'

'They stole from you, Lady Marguerite,' Xavier answered. 'They took pearls from you and tried to use them for their own compensation.'

'Thievery is not tolerated here,' her aunt added. 'They will each lose a hand for what they've done.'

'It was not thievery,' Marguerite said, stepping between them. 'The pearls were a gift to them and to the men you punished. As compensation for what they've had to endure.' She drew herself up to face her aunt, adding, 'Surely you cannot punish these men for what was freely given.'

'Take them below,' her aunt ordered Xavier. 'My niece and I will discuss this.'

The false look of benevolence on Beatrice's face re-pulsed Marguerite. She darted forward and seized the blade from Xavier's waist. With a few slices through the rope, she freed the men and ordered them to go. Turning to Beatrice, she commanded, 'You will not take them prisoner.'

'You overstep yourself.'

'No.' With the knife still in her palm, she advanced upon her aunt, feeling the sudden rush of danger in her veins. 'I have had my fill of you attempting to take my mother's place. This is my home and you are nothing more than my father's *putain*.'

Beatrice's eyes gleamed with rage. 'I will not tolerate such insults from you, Marguerite.' With a hand, she dismissed Xavier. Only when she was certain the men were safe did Marguerite lower her knife.

'I told you not to make an enemy of me, Marguerite,' her aunt said calmly. 'You lied to the Duc about our…conflict.'

'I spoke the truth. You tried to starve me in my own home. And you punished innocent men.' The anger rose up, nearly blinding her with its intensity. 'And now you think to punish more of them?'

A thin smile spread over Beatrice's face. 'I am not without mercy. If you say that you gave jewels to these men, so be it. But your father will not be pleased to learn that you granted favours to his men.'

She didn't miss the implication in the matron's words. 'I granted no favours. Only compensation for their trouble.'

'You mean bribes, so they would let you meet your lover in the forest,' Beatrice corrected. 'Xavier told me about him. One of the MacKinlochs, isn't he?' She took a step forward, grasping her skirts as she climbed the stairs leading into the Hall. 'I saw him near the stables just now.'

The rush of fear swept through her, leaving Marguerite speechless. *Dear God, no. Let it be a lie.*

She masked her emotions, keeping her tone firm. 'You will not threaten him.'

'I don't have to,' Beatrice said. 'Xavier is taking him to your father now, for questioning. I would suggest that you be careful about what you say. He was carrying a quiver filled with black-tipped arrows, just like the one they found at the outpost.'

As her aunt slipped inside the Hall, Marguerite turned back and saw Callum surrounded by soldiers. He made no move to fight them off, but went into their custody without argument.

God above, she didn't know how to save him without implicating them both.

Guy de Montpierre stared at the Scot standing before him. It was the mute who had taken shelter in the stables. One of the soldiers had taken a quiver from him and held up a black-feathered arrow.

'Is that yours?' the Duc asked.

The Scot gave a single nod, his face shielded without emotion or fear. Eyeing his guards, Guy motioned for them to draw in closer, to prevent the archer from making an escape. He suspected this man had something to do with the attack on the garrison, but why would he have returned to the stables? Already he'd heard of several other Scots who had disappeared and he'd sent men after them. But this man's behaviour spoke of a man who possessed great courage, or else he was the greatest fool. Curious, he gestured for the man to sit. 'Can you speak at all?'

The man gave no answer, but opened a pouch at his waist and held out a piece of parchment. Intrigued, the Duc allowed him to sit. Few men could write and he wondered if a priest had taught him.

The Scot struggled to grip the pen, but he wrote only two words. The first was MacKinloch. The second was Marguerite.

At the sight of his daughter's name, a cold fury took command of his temper. If this man was a MacKinloch, then he had lived with Marguerite during the time she'd taken sanctuary with them. His suspicions darkened and he was beginning to see a pattern in his daughter's behaviour. The thought of her having anything to do with this Scot enraged him. If he'd harmed her in any way, Guy wouldn't hesitate to give him a traitor's death.

Beatrice's suggestion, that she had been meeting a man in secret, suddenly held a grain of truth. *Mon Dieu*, the Scot must be the reason for Marguerite's reluctance to wed.

'What does my daughter have to do with this?' Guy demanded. It was an effort to keep from killing the man right now.

MacKinloch set down the quill, giving no answer at all.

'Send for Marguerite,' the Duc ordered. In the minutes before her arrival, he glared at the Scot. *If you've hurt her in any way, you answer to me.*

But there was only the quiet stare of defiance in the man's eyes.

* * *

When at last Marguerite appeared in the Hall, she touched her hand to her heart in fear. So. She did know the MacKinloch clansman.

'You lied to me,' the Duc said coolly. 'You said you didn't know this man. But he claims he's a MacKinloch.'

Marguerite's face blanched, but she nodded. Embarrassment flooded her face, but she admitted, 'Callum MacKinloch is his name. His brother Alex is the clan chief.'

'Why did he come here?' the Duc demanded. *And why did you lie?* It wasn't at all in Marguerite's nature to tell an untruth, and, from the way she avoided looking at the man, his suspicions magnified.

'I don't know why.'

'Marguerite,' he warned, crossing the room to stand before her. 'Tell me what you know of this man.'

Fear made her cheeks whiten, but she said, 'I saved his life, when he was Cairnross's prisoner. He protected all of us in the battle, before you came with your men. That's all.'

'Is it?' He didn't believe her. Likely she was trying to protect the man. 'Did you teach him to write?'

Tears welled up in her eyes, but she confessed the truth. 'Yes.'

To do so meant that she'd spent time with MacKinloch. The thought made him want to flay the Scot alive. Guy's hands curled into fists at his side, and at that moment the Earl of Penrith moved into the Hall. His eyes moved to Marguerite and she sent him a silent plea.

MacKinloch's gaze moved upon both of them and Guy didn't miss his possessive stare. This Scot somehow believed he could force his way into Marguerite's life.

Guy didn't care what lies had been spoken, nor what had happened in the past. He wouldn't allow any man to threaten his daughter's future. Especially not a common Scot who couldn't even speak.

Lord Penrith came forward, interrupting. 'This morn, Lady Marguerite and I came to an understanding about our betrothal.'

There was reassurance in the man's gaze. When he turned to his daughter, Guy saw the wrenching pain in her blue eyes. To her credit, she did not deny the earl's claim. Penrith came to stand beside her, taking her hand in his. Whatever had transpired in the past would not be held against Marguerite. The alliance was not in danger and when Guy eyed his daughter, she gave a silent nod.

The Duc turned back to the Scot, wanting to know more about the murdered Englishmen. 'You were there on the night the garrison was attacked, weren't you?'

Callum gave a nod.

'He witnessed the raid,' Marguerite interrupted. 'The arrow you found was his, when he tried to stop the men.'

Before he could say anything else, Marguerite continued, 'I warned him not to stay here, that you might blame him for it.'

And so he would, if the man were guilty. In his daughter's voice, he heard the shaking fear and he intended to use it to his advantage. To MacKinloch, he asked, 'Why were you there that night?'

The man wrote a few words on the parchment and held it up.

'He thought there were prisoners being held at the

outpost,' Marguerite said, deciphering the handwriting. 'He wanted to free them.'

'And why should I believe that you were innocent of wrongdoing?'

MacKinloch said nothing, setting the quill down. His hard stare challenged the Duc, almost daring him to take him prisoner.

'He came to you, instead of fleeing like the others,' Marguerite interrupted again. 'And when he gives you the names, you should punish those responsible for the murders.'

'I have no reason to give my trust,' he countered. 'But I will question MacKinloch further.'

She came forward and took his arm. 'I know what that means.' In her blue eyes, he saw the terror and it only confirmed his belief that Marguerite held feelings for the Scot. 'No torture,' she pleaded. 'I beg of you, let him go.'

Guy gave no response, his gaze fixed upon MacKinloch. There was no trace of fear on the man's face, only acceptance.

'I will use whatever means are necessary to find the truth,' he replied, removing Marguerite's hand from his arm.

'Please,' she whispered.

The Duc let her draw her own conclusions. Often, the very threat of torture was enough to break a man. Especially one who had endured it before.

He signalled for his men to take Callum MacKinloch into custody. 'Escort him below. I will have words with him later.'

His daughter looked stricken, but she gave no argument. Only after MacKinloch was gone did she turn to him. 'I have given you nothing but obedience my entire life. I've agreed to marry a man of your choosing and asked nothing for myself in return.'

In her voice, he heard the fear and unshed tears. 'Father, I ask only that you let him return to Glen Arrin.'

'Did he touch you?'

She lowered her head and shook it in denial. But he saw the guilt and embarrassment on her face. Another lie.

By God, he was going to tear the Scot apart.

'Monsieur le Duc—' The earl moved between them and took Marguerite's hand. 'Whatever happened in the past will remain there. I am well aware of your daughter's feelings and I believe we will have a stronger start to our marriage if it begins with forgiveness.'

Guy studied Lord Penrith, wondering if he spoke the truth. There was no trace of anger upon the man's face and it did seem that he didn't hold Marguerite at fault.

A fraction of the tension eased from his shoulders. 'What say you, Marguerite?'

Her face held misery, her mouth downcast. But she nodded her agreement. 'I will go through with the marriage.' She stared back at him, her face pale. 'But if I find out you have harmed Callum, I will not marry the earl or any other man.'

Her obstinacy took Guy off guard. 'You've no right to issue warnings to me, Daughter. You should be grateful for the earl's benevolence.'

'It is a vow that will be broken, if you dare to threaten him.'

She meant it. Though her voice remained quiet and calm, he heard the sincerity in her tone. It seemed his daughter had grown a spine after all.

A dull regret spread through him, that it had come to this. He couldn't understand what Marguerite could possibly see in the Scot. The man was so poor, he had nothing at all to give her. No doubt he was using her heart, trying to better himself by attracting her attention.

His daughter was far too gentle and soft-hearted for her own good. And he'd move the moon from the sky to keep her safe.

'I vow that I will not harm him,' he said. But then, there were ways of assuring that MacKinloch would never see Marguerite again. Ways that ordinary men wouldn't survive and Guy didn't have to lay a hand upon him.

The broken relief in her face bothered him and she insisted, 'As long as he is safe and alive, I will keep my word.'

But she didn't look at the earl, nor was there any hope of affection between them. Guy gave a nod, vowing to put an end to whatever was between her and the Scot.

Her acquiescence was the only reason he kept MacKinloch alive.

Two days later

'You're pacing,' the earl remarked.

Marguerite stopped and realised he was right. They were inside the solarium and Lady Beatrice was sewing in the corner. She sent a look towards the matron, and Lord Penrith guessed what she wanted. He spoke quietly to the older woman and, soon enough, they were alone.

Marguerite felt the walls closing in on her. Callum was being held in the storage chamber below ground, guarded night and day. 'They won't let me see him,' she admitted. 'I fear my father may not have kept his word.' It felt strange confessing this to the man who wanted to wed her.

The earl crossed the room and took her hands. His palms were warm, his face concerned. 'Thus far, he has.'

Marguerite studied him and remarked, 'Would you release me from this marriage, if I asked it of you again?'

He went quiet for a time, his hands still holding hers. 'No, Lady Marguerite. I intend to wed you, just as we agreed.'

'Why?' She stared at the earl, unable to understand him.

'As I told you before, I need an heir and a wife. The Duc has offered a generous dowry for you, one that will help me rebuild my estates.'

'Any other woman could do that for you.'

'No.'

She let go of his hands, holding herself around the waist. 'I am sorry, but I cannot give Callum up. I belong with him.'

'We will marry in a few days, and I will bring you back to England,' Lord Penrith said. 'There you will be lady of my estates and govern them in my absence. The rest of my household will see a husband and wife who are good friends. But I will not share your bed.'

She paled. 'Why? If you seek an heir, then—'

His face took on a derisive smile. 'My tastes do not run toward women.'

Understanding dawned upon her. It explained why he had not once tried to kiss her or seek her affections. The earl wanted her friendship, but nothing else.

'You see, then, why I do not mind if you keep a lover, so long as you are discreet. No one need know of it.'

She closed her eyes, admitting, 'Callum would never agree to it. His family and home are in Scotland.' She took a breath and faced him. 'There must be another way.'

The earl took her hand again. 'Your father has made his wishes clear and so have I. If you wed me, you can have all that you want, Marguerite. Or if you refuse, your lover will face the accusation of murder.'

Bitterness slashed through her at the thought. She knew how angry Callum would be if she wed the earl, but she could see no other way of saving his life.

'What does my father intend to do?'

'After our marriage, he will send the Scot back to his clan. In the meantime, he will hold him for questioning.'

She closed her eyes, distrust washing over her. 'Will you send word to the MacKinlochs in Glen Arrin? His brothers might be able to help.'

'I can, yes.'

She heard the unspoken words, *If you go through with our marriage*. Though she didn't know if she could make that promise, she was grateful for the earl's assistance.

'I need to see Callum,' she pleaded. 'I need to know that he hasn't been harmed.'

The earl drew closer, his hand moving to her nape. 'I can arrange it.' The look in his eyes haunted her and she didn't understand it. 'You could be with him this very night, if you so desire.'

A shiver washed over her as his thumb edged her jaw. 'Remember, Marguerite. I need a child from you.'

* * *

Dark bloodstains marred the stones and chains rested upon the floor. Callum reached for one of the manacles and his lungs tightened. Though the soldiers had not chained him, he was still a prisoner. He paced across the small space, well aware of the man guarding him.

The Duc hadn't come. Nor had anyone questioned him. He'd let Callum remain in the darkness, knowing that the waiting would only bring him closer to the madness captivity could bring.

Every hour, every moment that passed in darkness, made him lose track of the days and nights. There were no other prisoners here and the isolation brought him back to the darker times he'd endured.

Callum retreated to the far wall, sitting down upon the dirt floor. How many times had he felt the lash upon his shoulders, the taunts of the soldiers? He'd been broken apart so often, it was a wonder he was still standing.

He closed his eyes, the past welling up inside him. The air within the space was cool and musty, like the night he'd nearly died. They'd separated him from Bram and brought him directly to Lord Cairnross.

Callum clenched the iron manacle, the weight heavy within his palms. That night, they'd stripped him of his tunic, using rope to bind him to a post. He'd stood with his back to Cairnross and the men laid the sharp blade of a sword against his throat.

'You are so young, boy,' Cairnross had said. *'Barely eight and ten, aren't you? You've grown up in chains. And your brother has caused us more trouble. Tonight it ends.'*

His teeth clamped together as he stared down at the dirt. Don't speak, *he warned himself. But when the* lash struck him, he bit hard until he tasted blood in his mouth.

'Your brother will pay for his mistakes with your life,' Cairnross said. 'The moment you cry out in pain, my men will slit your throat. Or you'll be beaten to death. The choice is yours.'

Horror filled him at Cairnross's declaration. Callum fought to free himself from the post, but the ropes abraded his wrists so tightly his skin burned. The lash struck, again and again, and he bit his lip so hard, the pain mirrored that of his back. The sword blade rested between his throat and the post, and fear consumed him.

He didn't want to die. He'd never had the chance to live, or to escape the chains that had bound him in darkness. His body trembled beneath the onslaught of the lash, his knees weakening.

'Cry out, damn you!' Cairnross shouted.

He refused to give the man the satisfaction. Deep within his mind, Callum found a place of silence. A place of strength where no one could touch him. Aye, he might die this night. Likely would. But he wouldn't give them the satisfaction of making him scream. He locked away the sounds, his knees folding. He expected the sword to bite into his throat, but it didn't. The soldier kept it pressed to his throat, but didn't break the skin.

As the minutes passed into an hour, the blows slowed down. From deep inside, he fought against the punishing lash, reaching for the place of peace within himself, a place where there was no pain.

And still he made no sound.

The soldier holding the blade began murmuring a

prayer in Latin. Callum didn't understand the words, but he recognised the offering of mercy.

Would this be the moment when the sword ended his life? No longer could he stand up. His body slumped against the ropes, his back raw and bleeding. Cairnross had already left, granting him a small victory, for Callum hadn't voiced a single sound.

'Leave him,' the soldier holding the sword ordered. 'He'll be dead, soon enough.'

Instead, Bram had found him. His brother had cradled his broken body, openly weeping as he'd tended Callum's wounds. He'd kept vigil and prayed over the next few nights when a fever had struck hard, leaving him to fight for his life.

But he'd survived it, at the cost of his voice.

The soft tread of footsteps drew him out of the vision. Marguerite came down the stairs, a determined look on her face.

He was hardly aware of her orders to the guards or why she was here now. The walls seemed to close in on him, heightening his discomfort. She'd been right—he shouldn't have returned. The intense need for freedom was rising higher until it couldn't be denied, but they wouldn't let him go.

'I tried to come sooner,' she whispered. 'I swear to you, I did.'

He didn't ask how, but when her arms came around him, he closed his eyes and breathed in her scent. When she touched his back, he shuddered at the phantom pain from his memory.

'Are you all right? Did anyone harm you?'

'No,' he managed. He drew her into his lap, his

back pressed against the wall. With her in his arms, she pushed away the shadows, bringing him back to the present.

'You're trembling,' she whispered. 'Let me warm you.' Her arms came around his neck, her body nestled as close as she could.

That she'd come this night, risking everything for him, was more than anyone had ever done.

You're going to '…marry him, aren't you?' The words were harsh in his throat, and he couldn't quite voice the full sentence.

'You're speaking,' she breathed, and he heard the surprise in her voice. 'I've never heard you say so many words before.' She leaned in and kissed his mouth softly.

Only because of her. Marguerite had somehow reached inside him, unlocking the words. He didn't question how or why, but he repeated the question. 'Are you…' *going to wed him?*

She seemed to sense what he was trying to say. 'I'll do whatever I must to save your life.'

Frustration boiled within him, that she would sacrifice herself. 'Don't,' he commanded against her mouth. He kissed her hard, taking her face within his hands. 'You're mine, Marguerite. Always were.'

'If I refuse, my father will hurt you,' she whispered. 'I couldn't live with myself if I caused that.' Her hands moved down to his back and Callum cast a look at the door.

'Do they…know…?' The last few words caught, and he forced himself to slow down. One word at a time.

'…know you're…here?' he repeated. He could imagine the Duc's reaction if he learned Marguerite was with him at this moment.

She shook her head. 'It's the middle of the night, and nearly everyone is asleep. Lord Penrith…' a blush coloured her cheeks at the mention of the earl '…he—he gave me the chance to say farewell to you.'

Farewell? As if she'd already made her decision to stay with him? His anger intensified toward the earl, and not for a moment did he trust that Penrith would want Marguerite left alone with a prisoner.

Callum tamped down the resentment and forced himself to respond. 'Did he?'

She reached out to his face and changed the course of their conversation. 'Who were the other men who killed the English soldiers that night?'

Though he named the others, he had little interest in what happened to them. It was the Duc's task to seek justice. Even so, Marguerite seemed to commit the names to memory. 'I will tell my father.'

It would do no good at all. He took a breath and spoke. '…won't believe you. My word…against theirs.'

Callum touched her cheek, watching as she leaned in to his palm. Regardless of whether or not the true guilty men were captured, he didn't doubt that the Duc would find some way of punishing him for the time he'd stolen with Marguerite.

He didn't care. His life had been worthless enough, but she had been a precious gift. One he'd never deserved.

Around her throat, Marguerite toyed with the glass pendant he'd given her. 'I'll try to get you out. I need to bribe more of the guards.'

It was a fruitless effort and he knew it. The only way he'd be allowed to leave was if the Duc agreed to it. For now, he wanted this moment with her.

'Stay,' he murmured against her throat. His mouth pressed against the pulse that thrummed beneath her skin. 'As long…as you can.'

She shifted upon his lap, straddling him. He hardened instantly, remembering how he'd taken her that day on the sand. In the dim torchlight, her eyes were luminous, her body arousing him.

'Do you…remember?' he murmured.

'I remember when you were inside me.' Her face transformed, revealing her own needs. 'It took my breath away.'

She moved against him and he drew his hands beneath her skirts, touching her bare legs. Her mouth opened in shock as his hands drifted up her calves, to the backs of her knees. A shiver broke over her and she drew her palms beneath his tunic.

'You're the only man I want,' she confessed, touching his chest. 'You're the man I want to wake up with in the morning. Not someone else.'

'Then don't,' he demanded. His hand moved higher, touching the curve of her hip, slipping between her thighs. *He'll never give you the same kind of pleasure I will.*

Her eyes closed, a gasp escaping her mouth as he drew his knuckles against her soft mound. She bit her lip, and he heard the clenched moan within her throat.

'Don't speak, Marguerite,' he whispered against her skin. 'Not…a sound.'

Against his hand, she was wet, wanting him so badly. He tormented her with the lightest touch, shifting his fingers intimately against her. Her breasts ached for his touch and she reached up, struggling to loosen the cote she wore. It was dangerous, being with him here, while the rest of the castle slept. At any moment, someone could intrude upon them.

There was no time for slow, gentle lovemaking. No, this was a desperate need, to take him into her body and savour the last time together. If the earl ever chose to share her bed, she would hold this memory in her heart.

Callum's hands moved out from beneath her gown to touch her shoulders. Marguerite sensed his hesitation and the fear that they would be caught together.

'Please,' she whispered, moving her hands down to his trews. Against her palm, she felt his heavy arousal and his breath inhaled sharply.

Silently, she touched him, exploring him through the rough wool. 'Be with me now,' she begged.

His answer was to lower the gown, drawing it down one shoulder. Her arms were trapped in the tight sleeves as he bared her breasts. Leaning down, he teased her nipple with his tongue. Tasting her, awakening the bloom of dark pleasure that he offered.

Against her hand, she felt his erection straining, growing harder. As he suckled her, she curled her fingers around him, rubbing against his shaft. He helped to free himself until she could feel the heat of his length against her wetness.

'No sound,' he whispered again, guiding her hips up. His thickness stretched at her entrance, but he entered her easily, as if he were made to be joined with her.

Her arms were pinned at her sides, and he lifted her a fraction higher, letting her slide upon him as his mouth kissed her bare skin.

Marguerite fought to keep from making noise as he started to thrust with a gentle rhythm, now using his mouth to encircle her breasts, in a nibbling warmth that he brought up to her throat and down her shoulder. His hands lifted her bottom and he was so hard that she ached as he sheathed himself within her. The torment of being unable to speak grew more intense, until he withdrew from her body, standing up.

She was about to protest, when suddenly he lifted her, balancing her back against the wall. Her skirts hung down, but he bunched them at her waist, holding her tight as he eased back inside. She was feverishly hot, drowning with need for him.

Though his voice was rough and broken, he told her of the night he'd lost his voice, and the horror of the sword against his throat. Her arms tightened around him as he thrust inside, telling her of how he'd almost died.

Tears welled up, but she let him release all the words, all the horrors.

'I survived,' he said, still inside her as he lowered her to stand. He guided her hip around his, and drew his fingers back between her legs. 'But you gave…a reason to fight. Reason to live.'

He kissed away her tears as his hands stroked and caressed her. With his body still sheathed within her, she felt as if she were being touched by both his hands and his manhood. The sensations were magnified and she guided his hands where she wanted them. His eyes burned into hers as he touched her until she was trembling. She moved against him, feeling him penetrate as his hands urged her closer to the edge.

'I love you,' she told him, locking her gaze with his.

The words transformed him and he stilled, their bodies joined together. His voice was hoarse, but every word was clear. 'Love you…Marguerite.'

Her heart warmed to know it and his hands moved in a caress while he entered her tenderly. He continued the deep penetration until the rhythmic caresses of his hands sent her past the brink. She bit back a scream; as she came apart, his mouth closed over her breast in a hot, wet suction.

'Love you,' he repeated. Then his movement changed from gentle into a man starving for her. He quickened his pace, thrusting against her so hard that she came again, half-crying at the intensity of pleasure.

No longer did she care where they were or that they might be caught. She wanted him to feel the same release that she'd found and she met him, her hips pushing in counterpoint to his. Gripping his hair, she wrapped her legs around his waist and he backed her against the wall again, his body moving in swift strokes. She saw the exertion on his face, welcomed the slick penetration of his manhood inside her, and he kept up the harsh pace.

'Don't…wed him, Marguerite,' he commanded. 'I'll…find a way for us. I swear.'

But as he let out a groan and spilled his essence within her, she could only hold him. Tears filled up her eyes, for there seemed no possible means of being with this man.

And it broke her heart.

Chapter Thirteen

She left him an hour later. The darkness enveloped him, leaving nothing but a memory. Her scent was upon him and Callum closed his eyes, leaning back against the wall.

Today. He was going to speak with the Duc and make his way out of the prison. He didn't doubt that Marguerite's father would leave him down here to rot, if he could.

The sound of the guards returning interrupted his plans. A man's voice broke through the silence and a chained figure fell upon the ground, only a few feet away. In the darkness, it was hard to tell who it was, but Callum spied the tell-tale marks of a whiplash.

'That you, MacKinloch?' Sileas demanded. The older man's hands were chained together, but he managed to come closer.

Callum said nothing, letting the man believe that he still lacked the ability to speak. The older man slumped against the wall beside him, his head resting between his knees. 'Hope ye said a prayer last night. For today's the day we die.'

He stared at Sileas, waiting for the man to continue. 'I gave them names. Told them you were with us.' A grimace twisted his mouth. 'We'll be hanged for it.'

He didn't doubt that the Duc would hold him accountable, regardless that he'd done nothing wrong. If for no other reason than that he'd dared to love Marguerite.

Through the next hour, he barely heard another word the old man said, for his mind was turning over ways to escape. At this moment, his hands were unbound and only the guards stood between him and freedom. He had to seize the one chance he had.

Within the stone walls, there were no weapons. No stones, no blades—nothing at all. Stealth and surprise were the only advantages.

The old man began mumbling prayers again and it was clear he'd already given up. Callum stood, moving towards the stairs and out of Sileas's earshot. At the top, the two guards blocked his way.

'I want…to speak with the Duc,' he demanded, frustrated with himself when his voice was still hoarse and the words stalled when he spoke.

The first guard seemed startled to realise that Callum could make any sounds at all. But he shrugged, answering, 'You will be taken before him at noon this day.'

'Why?'

The guard said nothing and Callum suspected that Sileas's claim, that they would be put to death, had truth in it. 'Who else?'

The guard named a few of the men who had gone on the raid, finishing with, 'The old man, yourself and Iagar Campbell.' His expression turned grim. 'You can't escape it, if that's what you're thinking.'

But Marguerite had sworn she would not go through with the marriage if he was harmed. Therefore, it was not likely she would be present to witness his death. Her father would invent an excuse.

'He wants you gone, MacKinloch. Because of the lady.'

Callum didn't doubt it. Guy de Montpierre wouldn't hesitate to punish him for touching Marguerite. Most men would be frightened to think of dying within a few hours. But he'd faced his own death so many times, it didn't distract him from his purpose. He would find a way out, at a moment when they least expected it.

He took a step backwards, as if he were returning, but stumbled forward, bumping against the guard.

He muttered an apology, falling back into the shadows. And as he retreated, he slipped the dagger he'd stolen beneath his tunic. The weapon would serve him well, when it was needed.

The afternoon sun rose high, spreading its light across fleecy clouds. Marguerite saw the prisoners gathered below, the same men whose names she had given to her father. Justice would be done for the murders.

A light knock sounded upon her door and when she called for the visitor to enter, she saw the Earl of Penrith standing. His expression appeared strained. 'You should come below, Marguerite.'

'I have no wish to watch men being hanged. Even if it was for murder.'

'What of your lover? Will you not let him look upon your face for the last time before he dies?'

His words startled her into numbness. 'Callum is here? But my father—'

'One of the guards whom I sent away that night told the Duc that you spent hours together.' The earl's gaze lowered to her waist. 'Could you have conceived a child?'

Her cheeks burned with shame. 'I don't know.' She still couldn't grasp the earl's willingness to accept a bastard as his own, if by some mercy she had conceived a new life.

'If you want him to live, his time grows short.' The earl waited and Marguerite gripped her skirts, hurrying outside her chamber.

She raced down the stairs and out of the Hall, down another flight of stone stairs before she reached the area where the men were being held. As Penrith had predicted, Callum was with the others. He stood behind them, his arms bound behind his back. A row of seven nooses hung from a scaffold, one for each man. Her father stood near the front, watching as the charges were read. Marguerite fled to the Duc's side.

'The captain of my guard, Xavier, warned me that you had met with the Scot. Is it true that you spent last night with him?' her father asked.

She couldn't answer. There were no words that would make him understand. Instead, she bolstered her courage and said, 'Execute him and I will not marry Penrith.'

'I am your father,' he whispered harshly. 'All your life, I've provided you with everything. And this is how you repay me? By giving yourself to a man who has nothing at all? Who will never give you the life I've intended for you?'

'It is my life,' she whispered. 'And he would wall

hrough hellfire if I asked it of him. Don't you know he
ould have left at any time? He stayed for *me*.'

'Then your face will be the last he sees when he dies.'

Her blood froze within her veins, her body numb
t the thought of Callum joining the other men. 'Don't
o this. He was innocent that night. He tried to stop
he others.'

'Marguerite.' Her father's voice held weariness. 'Do
ou truly believe this is about the murders at the gar-
ison?'

It was about her daring to love a man who was not
f the same wealth or class. About her surrendering her
irtue for love, instead of duty.

'If you kill him, I will never speak to you again,' she
varned. 'You will have no part in my life.'

She started to walk towards Callum, while they led a
risoner toward the gallows. Though Callum remained
till, she saw his eyes searching. He glanced at the row
f archers standing a short distance behind him, then
is gaze fell upon her.

Her heart sank and she drank in the details of his
trong face and long dark hair. She didn't care what she
ad to do, but she refused to stand and watch him die.

It will be all right, his eyes seemed to say. She
ouldn't understand how, for he was surrounded on all
ides. Even the Duc stood near the gallows to witness
he executions.

But then, without warning, one of the prisoners broke
ree of his ropes. Marguerite saw the man rushing to-
vards her father and horror filled her when she saw the
lash of his knife.

The blade glinted as he raised it high to stab the

Duc. Her father flinched, holding him back with all his strength.

A moment later, an arrow shot across the inner bailey, embedding into the prisoner's back. A second followed and he dropped where he stood.

The entire courtyard grew still and she saw the bow that Callum had seized from a nearby archer. Somehow, he'd broken free of his own bindings and saved her father's life.

The Duc stared at him, but there was no gratefulness in his eyes. Instead, he appeared furious that Callum had been the one to rescue him. He crossed the space between them, stepping past the body of his would-be assassin.

Their eyes locked and Marguerite hurried toward them. Something made her stop, however, when she saw the rage in her father's eyes.

'I don't know what role you played in that attack,' he began, 'but others say you should be hanged for it.'

'I killed…no one,' Callum said. 'Too late to stop them.'

The Duc eyed him with a hard stare before he turned his gaze back upon his daughter with an unspoken accusation. Marguerite felt the intensity of his frustration and hatred towards the man she loved.

'So you can speak,' he remarked. 'I wonder what else you've lied about.'

Callum gave no reply and Marguerite held her own silence. Both of them realised that one wrong word would mean his death.

Instead, she moved to her father and took his hand. Kneeling down, she lifted his hand to her forehead in a silent plea. *Let him live*, she prayed.

Guy's fingers rested upon her veiled hair and she could feel the trembling anger he held back. 'Take him north, into the mountains,' her father ordered, 'and leave him there.'

Shock flooded through her and she stood. The Duc moved away from her without casting her a single glance. His soldiers moved in to surround Callum, who made no attempt to escape their custody.

'I'll grant you your life, as compensation for mine,' the Duc acceded, 'but do not show your face to me again. Or to my daughter.'

The statement was like an arrow through her heart, piercing her hope. Marguerite never took her eyes from Callum, though they blurred with tears. The soldiers dragged him away, and he fixed his gaze upon her.

Remember, you are mine.

I won't forget you, she swore, in her own silence. *My heart is yours.*

And when he'd gone, she sank to her knees, feeling utterly lost.

They left him with nothing but the clothes on his back. No food, no water. No shelter. It was the Duc's way of offering a death sentence without laying a hand upon him.

He'd been blindfolded throughout the journey, giving him no means of knowing where he was. Callum could only estimate how far they'd brought him, praying that he would find some familiar landscape or a clan nearby.

The land was a bright green with mountains rising all around him. In this part of Scotland trees were less common, and with no horse, he had to walk mile after mile, with no way to guide him.

Worst of all, he suspected that Marguerite must have gone through with the marriage. Her father had spared his life, leaving her with little choice. Enough time had passed that she was likely the earl's wife now.

Like a slow torture, it dug into his skin, the thought of another man taking his place.

He stumbled to his knees beside a stream, drinking the cold water while he tried to exorcise the image from his mind. Aye, they'd let him live. And though he knew enough to survive off the land, every taste of food was bitter in his mouth. The damned helpless feeling was driving him into madness. He didn't know where he was or how to find her again.

And if he did reveal himself, the Duc would kill him where he stood.

You never deserved Marguerite, the voice inside him warned. *She was never yours to have.*

But for every day of the rest of his life, he would remember the pain in her eyes when they'd taken him away. She'd loved him, just as he loved her. She'd come to him in the darkness, bringing him into the light.

Callum climbed one of the hills, grasping at the silky grasses for balance. With every step, his lungs burned, his body fighting the weakness from hunger and lack of sleep. Doggedly, he continued on, until he reached the apex.

From all around, he could see the land, rising and falling in a sea of green. Tiny rivulets of water creased the hills, waterfalls that carved silver ridges into the surface.

The temptation pulled at him to simply lie here and let go. He would never have Marguerite, no matter how hard he fought for her. Even when he'd asked her to

eave everything behind, she hadn't come. And her fa-
her would never allow her that freedom.

Her life was too deeply woven into a world of nobil-
ty he'd never belong to. But in those brief, stolen moments, she'd given him a taste of heaven. He'd loved
ier with every breath, every part of his soul.

Upon the ridge, he watched the sun rise higher, spill-
ng over the land in rays of gold. The immensity of
iis isolation filled him with the vision of years spent
vithout her.

Sometimes he wondered if death would have been a
gift, to be with her until the last breath passed from his
ody. But he didn't want to give up on her, or let go of
hat dream. She'd wanted him as much as he wanted her.

No longer would he wait for her to make a decision
ir try to extricate herself from the tangled web of ob-
igations. She was meant to be his, whether or not any-
ne else believed it.

Callum stood up, his mind made up. This time, he
vouldn't ask. He would simply take her with him and
amn the consequences. She was worth dying for.

From his vantage point, he studied the landscape,
earching for anything that would help him gain his
earings. His eyes narrowed upon a small travelling
roup moving on horseback through the hills.

He began his descent, moving towards them at a
risk walk, and then a light run when he reached the
ottom of the hill. He would find his way back to her,
o matter how long it took.

The taste of the wine was bitter and Marguerite
hoked upon it. Her Aunt Beatrice stared at her, a nod
f satisfaction on her face.

A horrifying suspicion was confirmed when she tasted something that shouldn't have been in the wine

'What have you done?' she demanded, casting the goblet aside. Wine sloshed upon the ground and she couldn't know how much she'd drunk. Had her aunt poisoned her?

She saw the faint nod from her father and the look they exchanged between them.

'It will start within the hour,' Beatrice said, gesturing for a servant to remove the fallen cup.

'What will start?' Marguerite touched her mouth, the aftertaste of the herbal brew making her wonder what they were talking about.

'Come,' her father said, rising from his seat at the dais. The earl sat at her left, looking mystified at what was happening. To her betrothed husband, the Duc said simply, 'It is naught to concern you, Penrith.'

Marguerite felt the fear sliding deeper inside, as her father took her hand and led her above stairs. Behind her, Aunt Beatrice followed. He led her into her chamber and dismissed the maid who was inside, mending a gown.

Once the door closed behind the maid, her father spoke. 'Beatrice gave you a blend of herbs that will cast out any child you might have conceived with MacKinloch.'

Marguerite sank down upon her bed, her insides iced with terror. Though she didn't believe there was any child, their actions went beyond imagining. The idea that they would kill any unborn babe horrified her. Her hands went to her middle, and though she felt no effects from the herbs yet, she saw the look of grim determination on her father's face.

'Do you truly hate him that much?' she asked her father, while her aunt sat down in a chair.

'Oui,' he answered. 'He will gain no part of your dowry, nor will I let him take advantage of you. There is nothing at all he can give, Marguerite.'

Except love. She was shattering apart inside for her father would never understand the way she felt about Callum. When she looked into his face, she saw the blend of anger and worry. Once again, he was treating her like a little girl who had disobeyed him and had to be punished. In his eyes, she was incapable of making decisions for herself.

It bruised her heart to know that the father she'd loved all these years was more interested in his ambitions than his daughter's happiness. The brutal reality crashed upon her as the first cramps seized within her womb.

She huddled upon her bed, the pain swallowing her whole. How naïve she'd been to hope that, in time, he would come to accept her decision. He wouldn't. Never would he believe that Callum MacKinloch was good enough for her. Choosing a life with the man she loved meant breaking away from her family for ever.

Another pain struck and she doubled over, feeling as if a part of her were being ripped away. Over the next few hours, she lay upon her bed in misery, staring at the wall while her body responded to the herbal poison.

But she didn't cry. The hurt within her could not be released with tears. It went all the way into her heart, severing a little girl's adoration for her father. It cauterised any sense of obedience or loyalty she had once given him.

No longer was he the man who had pulled her upon

his knee, telling stories. No longer the man who tucked her head beneath his chin, holding her close while she played with the gold ring upon his finger. Nor the man who'd sworn to keep her safe at all costs.

He'd now become the man who had slashed apart her hopes, leaving her with nothing at all. And for that, she would never forgive him.

'Callum!' came the voice of his brother Bram.

Callum quickened his pace, startled to see his three brothers on horseback. An unexpected smile broke over his face at the sight of them. When they drew their horses to a stop, his brothers gripped him hard, all talking at once.

'We received word several days ago from Marguerite—'

'What are you doing here? And where's your horse?'

'—that you needed our help.'

Callum raised his hands and regarded them. 'Much has…happened. We'll talk over food.'

The sound of his voice seemed to stun them into silence. Alex was the first to recover and his smile was blinding. 'Your voice is back. Thank God.'

Bram let out a rush of breath. He raked a hand through his dark hair and managed, 'Aye. We've much to be thankful for.'

His youngest brother Dougal looked startled, but as he cared for the horses, he added, 'What about Marguerite?'

'I'm going back for her.' Callum explained what had happened and what his intentions were. Though sometimes his voice faltered, it was gaining strength. He gave them enough to make himself understood.

They made camp and his brothers offered food and mead to satisfy his hunger and thirst. In their presence, he felt their quiet support. They'd come to help him and it meant more than he could say.

Later that night, his brother Bram joined him while Alex and Dougal slept. They lay back on the grass, staring at the stars that dotted a darkened sky.

'It's dangerous, what you're about to do.'

Callum didn't deny it. 'You would do the same, were it Nairna.'

'I'd kill any man alive who tried to take her from me.'

'Then you know.' He reached into the pouch at his waist, fingering the frayed ribbon Marguerite had given back to him. 'Her father will never let her go. But I can't…let her marry the earl. Not now.'

'The Duc knows where we live. If you take her, he'll only bring an army after her.'

Callum leaned back, crossing his arms behind his head. 'He wanted me to die here. If I stay hidden, he might believe it.'

'Is she worth the risk?' Bram asked.

'She gave me back my voice.' He didn't mention that Marguerite had also given her innocence. The physical connection had gone deeper than he'd ever expected. When he'd joined with her, he'd found the other half of himself.

And he wasn't about to live without her again.

Chapter Fourteen

The ship awaited them, miles away on the coast, where it would take her south along the western coast of Scotland toward Wales. They would then continue the inland journey to the earl's estates in England.

Marguerite stared at her packed belongings, feeling lost and alone. Her father had agreed to the earl's proposition, that she wed him in England instead of here. After all the unrest and the bitter memories, it would be a better start for them. Not to mention it would take her far away from the MacKinlochs.

The bleakness went deeper than her skin, filling up her veins. She'd suffered over the past few days with pain and bleeding, until the herbs' effects had passed. Her body was weak while her mind felt blurred and uncertain. Marguerite forced herself to eat a small meal this morn, but barely noticed the food.

Had Callum survived? Though her father had ordered him bound and taken away, she didn't know if they'd abandoned him in the wilderness or murdered him. They'd given him no weapons, no food—nothing at all to survive in the harsh northern lands. And there was no way to know if his brothers would find him.

The thought of Callum's death had shifted her own desire to live. What reason was there to go on, enduring a marriage she didn't want, to a man who would never love her? It was as if her father were moulding her life out of clay, shaping and destroying her own efforts.

She was like an empty vessel, fired from her father's ambitions, with no power of her own. The cool anger was transforming her, making her wonder what reckless act would finally achieve her freedom.

Her maids dressed her in a rose surcoat and cream-colored coat, before braiding her hair and gathering it within a golden net. A white barbette covered her head, winding around her throat. Marguerite studied her reflection in a polished silver mirror. Although the woman before her appeared calm and serene, inwardly, the worry consumed her mind.

Before she departed her chamber, she went to one of the trunks and withdrew a bow and a quiver filled with black-feathered arrows. She'd taken them back from the guards after Callum's release.

'My lady?' one of her maids questioned, but Marguerite gave no answer. She kept the weapons at her side, walking slowly down the winding stone stairs.

Outside, her horse awaited her and she tied the bow and quiver to her saddle. Beyond the first wall, Lord Penrith was supervising the dowry goods being loaded into wagons. Marguerite kept her distance, watching over him. Of all the men her father could have chosen, there was nothing wrong with the earl. Were it not for her love of Callum, she would find no hardship at all in marrying the handsome, kindly man.

But her love belonged to the silent warrior who had captured her heart with a single look. He'd given her passion, making her feel alive. She might have given her promise to go through with this marriage, yet it would never change her feelings for Callum.

Right now, she felt as though she were being suffocated, her life pulled in directions it wasn't meant to go. She wanted an hour to herself, a time to grieve for her loss.

After the stable master assisted her on to the horse, she drew the animal forward to speak with the earl.

'I would like to go riding,' she said to him. 'Just for an hour or so, before we depart.'

His expression narrowed when he spied the bow and quiver upon the saddle, 'You cannot go alone.' There was a warning in his expression, as if he feared she would try to run away.

The truth was, she couldn't survive on her own if she wanted to. She knew nothing about how to find food or shelter and likely she'd die within a day if she tried.

'I promise I'll return.'

'Are you planning to search for *him*?' Penrith's expression remained neutral, though she saw the unrest in his eyes.

'He was taken four days ago,' she said. 'I'm not so foolish as to believe I could find him in an hour.'

'We'll board our ship soon,' he reminded her. He took her hand within his and his grip turned firm.

'Will you not give me the chance to grieve?' she responded. 'I—I need the time.' Even if she did nothing but wander through the trees or go to the loch where Callum had first taught her to swim, it would help her to close off the memories.

He stared at her, not at all understanding. 'There is much to do here, Marguerite, before we go. And I won't allow you to back out on our agreement. The Duc left MacKinloch alive. Now you must fulfil your part of the bargain by wedding me.'

Marguerite lowered her gaze to the ground. The energy to protest simply wasn't in her. She felt so lost, so unwilling to give herself to another, she didn't know what to do any more. Her gaze fixed upon the forest, remembering the days she'd spent with Callum and what it had been like to fall asleep in his arms.

The earl released a sigh, raising her hand to his lips. 'I am likely the greatest fool on this earth. Go, then, if it means so much to you. I'll see to it that you have an hour. But no longer.'

A smile broke free and she squeezed his hand in return. 'You're a good man, my lord.'

'Your dowry will help repair my estates,' was his pragmatic response. 'And your father has offered to pay me a great deal, for turning a blind eye towards your actions.' He crossed his arms and eyed her with distrust. 'But if you do not return—'

'I will,' she promised.

He accompanied her to the gate and within another few minutes, she was riding alone towards the forest. The trees surrounded her, blotting out the sunlight in filtered shadows. Marguerite turned her horse in the direction of the loch, letting her mind wander. As she continued deeper into the woods, she felt a sense of uneasiness, as though she were being watched. But there was no one at all, only imagined sounds.

When she reached the shores of the loch, she picked

up a handful of small stones and cast them into the water, watching the surface break.

God, let him be safe, she prayed. *Let him be alive.*

The vast loneliness closed over her, until she no longer knew how she would go through with this marriage. The idea of living each day with a man who did not desire her, or worse, having to endure his touch in order to conceive a child that he wanted, was like drowning. She didn't know if she could do it.

She returned to her mare and removed Callum's bow and quiver. The weight of the weapon was balanced and as her fingers curved across the wood, she could sense his presence and strength. When she tried to pull back the bowstring, it was so taut, she couldn't draw it further than a few inches. She fitted one of his arrows to the bowstring, wondering if she could manage a shot.

'Were you wanting a lesson?' came a deep voice from behind her.

The bow fell from her hands and she saw Callum standing a few paces away. Heedless of anything else, she flew into his arms, gripping him tight. Behind him were his brothers, who watched over them for a moment before retreating into the shadows.

'You're alive,' she breathed, lifting her mouth to his. The kiss of welcome was a merging of thankfulness, a sudden rush of joy mingled with tears.

'Are you well?' she asked, pulling back to look at him. His face looked as if he hadn't slept in the past few days, but there were no outward signs of suffering.

His hands threaded into her hair, lifting her face up. Touching his forehead to hers, he said, 'I came to take you back with me, Marguerite.'

She closed her eyes, filling up her senses with him.

The sound of his voice, so rare in the past, was dear to her. It had grown stronger, more fluent, in only a few days.

In his arms, she became whole again and the promises she'd made to the earl no longer held any weight. The desire to leave everything behind, to be with this man, was all she wanted.

'If I go,' she murmured, 'I'll never see my family again, will I?' She lifted her eyes to his and saw him nod. At one time, the knowledge had kept her from being with him, for she'd wanted both. She'd wanted to keep her father's love, remaining a beloved daughter in his eyes. And she'd wanted the man he would never approve of.

Now she knew the truth: there was only the choice of one or the other.

'Will you love me enough, since I won't have a family any more?' she whispered.

'Until the last breath leaves my body.' He gripped her so hard, she no longer knew where he ended and she began.

'Good.' She smiled and took his hand in hers. He picked up the fallen bow and slung the quiver over one shoulder. With her palm enveloped by his, she had no doubt that she had made the right decision. There could be no other.

He lifted her on to her horse and swung up behind her. His brothers joined them on either side and Marguerite greeted them. Although Bram and Alex were friendly enough, she sensed the tension.

Then Dougal came running towards them from the trees. Though the adolescent boy tried to put on a brave face, she saw the fear haunting his eyes. 'They're coming for her.'

At his words, dread sank within her veins. The earl had told her father. Or perhaps he'd sensed the truth and had brought his own men.

'Who?' Callum demanded, drawing an arrow from his quiver.

'Dozens of soldiers. If we don't let her go, they'll kill us all.'

In his arms, Callum could feel the sudden change in her. Her head lowered and her hands reached for his.

'I should have known,' she whispered. 'The earl wouldn't let me break the promise.'

Callum spurred the horse hard, riding north as fast as the animal would carry them. His brothers followed. Dougal hurrying to catch up. If there was an army, it was doubtful that they'd succeed in outrunning them—especially not with both Marguerite and him sharing a horse. But he had to try.

'I won't give you up,' he said against her ear. She leaned forward, holding tight to the horse, but he could feel her fear deepening.

When they cleared the forest, he started to change their direction east. Behind him, he heard the sound of horses approaching. Stealing a glance, he saw at least thirty men on horseback, riding hard.

His brother Alex came up beside him, raising his voice against the wind. 'Callum, they're going to overtake us.'

He ignored the words, trying to increase the pace of their horse, but Marguerite's mare was older, a gentle mount unaccustomed to such speed. She was struggling

o obey and he knew that it was only a matter of time
before they lost their lead.

Bram dropped back and Callum understood that his
brother was offering to grant him time. To fight the
men and do what he could to slow them down. But if he
chose this battle, it was far too grave a risk. He would
die in the effort, leaving behind his wife Nairna, who
was expecting a bairn.

Callum expelled a curse. When the horse reached the
hilly terrain, he pulled the mare to a stop. Her breathing
was laboured, her flanks slick with sweat.

Marguerite went so still and quiet that he sensed
what she was going to say. His arms closed around her
in an embrace that went beyond words. He needed her
to know that if they stood their ground, he would rather
die at her side than live thousands of days without her.

'I can't let your brothers die for you,' she said at last,
her voice hollow. Swinging her leg to the side, she rested
her cheek against his chest as the army closed in. 'You
gave me the greatest days of my life. I will never love
any man as much as I love you now.'

'Don't go,' he demanded. 'Stay with me and fight.'

She reached out to touch his cheek. 'I think I've always known that our paths could never be together.'
Her blue eyes welled up and a tear spilled over. 'I just
wanted to hope that, somehow, we would find a way.'

The pain of losing her was cutting his soul in half.
Callum held her in his arms, kissing her hard. He tasted
her tears and the bitterness of loss.

'Keep a part of me in your heart,' she whispered.
'You'll always live in mine.'

Then she dismounted from her horse and began the
solitary walk towards the soldiers waiting for her.

* * *

Her father and the earl stood with their men. Marguerite stopped walking, halfway between them. Lord Penrith raised his hand, signalling his men to hold back.

For a long moment, she held Callum's empty gaze with her own. His brothers spoke to him and he ordered them to go.

She could see in his eyes that he didn't want to leave her. He was waiting for any sign from her that she would stay with him. But if she tried, he and his brothers would die.

There was only one way to force him to go. She touched her fingertips to her lips and turned away, returning to the men who awaited her.

The force of her grief choked within her lungs. Then she moved towards one of the soldiers, recognising the horse he rode. It was Callum's stallion, Goliath. 'Give me your mount,' she ordered.

When he obeyed, she led the horse forward and guided the animal towards Callum, who was still waiting. He let out a sharp whistle, and the horse obeyed, returning to him. She watched him dismount and he adjusted her mare's saddle, returning her own horse to her.

Upon the saddle, he had wrapped the hair ribbon he'd taken so long ago. And when she saw it, she understood he would no longer keep it with him. He was letting her go.

She cast one look back at Callum and he disappeared over the hill.

The soldier helped her mount her horse and it was all Marguerite could do to keep from breaking down into sobs. Instead, she gripped the frayed bit of silk and led her horse a few paces in front of her father. She made it clear that he was not to send any of his men after the MacKinlochs. If necessary, she would stand between them.

The Duc's expression was grave, nor did he speak to her. When a few minutes had passed, Marguerite ordered, 'Send the soldiers back to Duncraig, Monsieur le Duc.' The word 'Father' was heavy upon her tongue and she found she could no longer call him that.

Guy de Montpierre studied her, then gave the order. The soldiers drew back and only when they were gone did she retreat. Lord Penrith drew his horse beside Marguerite, taking the reins of her mare and leading her toward the coast.

She went with him, fully aware of his anger. 'You brought my father here, didn't you?' He must have gathered the Duc's men, as soon as she'd departed. Or had he followed her?

He gave a nod. 'I knew MacKinloch would come back for you.'

She raised confused eyes to his. 'I didn't even know he was alive.'

'A man like Callum MacKinloch won't die easily. Especially when he has a woman like you to live for.'

Marguerite didn't know what to say, so she fell into silence as they rode the remaining distance to the shore line. A large ship awaited them just off the coast. Servants had loaded up smaller boats and were bringing supplies back and forth. Her own trunks were among them.

The earl helped her down from her horse and gave the mare over to a servant. 'You think I do not understand you,' he said. 'You think I can't possibly know what it is to love someone you cannot be with.' A stoic expression came over his face. 'But you would be wrong.'

In his eyes, she saw the frustration of loss. The earl was marrying her out of obligation, nothing more.

'We will not be happy, either of us,' she said.

'No,' he admitted. 'But you, at least, will not ask for more than I can give.' A twisted smile overtook his face. 'It would not be so bad, Marguerite.'

The earl took her hand and walked with her towards the boat. He never let go of her, and when they were on board, he ordered the men to row them to the larger ship.

Marguerite turned to look at the grey water, feeling as if pieces of herself were drifting away on the waves. When she raised her eyes to the hills, there was no sign of Callum or his brothers. They had gone.

The emptiness filled up every part of her, covering her with such desolation she could hardly breathe. Her hands were cold in the earl's palms when he guided her on board the larger ship. Marguerite left his side, walking to the bow. She rested her arms upon the wood, feeling the wind sweep past her face and hair.

All around her, the men continued loading the ship and her father boarded among the last of them. From her peripheral vision, it appeared that he wanted to speak with her. His expression looked tired, as if he'd aged a dozen years.

The afternoon had shifted into evening, and the Duc came to stand by her side. 'We'll sail south for a few hours and then drop anchor for the night,' he informed her.

Normally, they would not sail until the morning tide,

but she knew this was to put more distance between her and the MacKinloch men.

'Marguerite, did you hear what I said?' He touched her arm and she jerked back.

'I have nothing at all to say to you.'

'We let him go,' her father said. 'I kept my word to you and allowed him to live.'

Slowly, she faced him. He stood before her as the man she'd once adored, the man who had been the only parent she remembered.

'Why?' she asked softly. 'Why is it so important to you that I wed the earl and not Callum? My sisters have already made strong marriages. You don't need this alliance.'

'You are my last daughter. I want what is best for you.'

'You don't see what is best for me. I want to live with the man who will love me for the rest of my life. Other men see only my rich dowry. But Callum sees *me*.'

The wind grew colder against her skin and the ship began to move upon the water. 'None of that matters to you, does it?'

'Let him go, Marguerite. He's not good enough for you.'

She didn't bother wasting words, trying to convince a blind man to see the truth. Instead, she walked away from him, needing to distance herself from everyone and be alone with her thoughts.

Her mind was in turmoil, like the waves sloshing against the side of the ship. With each mile that passed, she saw her chance at happiness slipping away.

Not once had Callum ever given up. He'd travelled

countless days to find her. Even at the end, he'd been willing to fight to bring her away with him.

The icy water seemed to taunt her, pulling her away from the man she loved. The servants had set out a light meal for the others and they called out for her to join them. She ignored their summons, not at all hungry.

Behind her, she heard the sounds of the men eating and voices whispering about her. No doubt they were congratulating themselves for saving her from the MacKinlochs.

She hated them for it.

When darkness had spilled over the sky, overshadowing the sun, the earl returned to her again. He stood beside her, his hands resting upon the side of the boat. 'Are you well, Marguerite?'

'You know that I am not.' She let out a sigh, her hands twisting together.

'Words will not reassure you, will they?'

She shook her head. 'If the one you loved were standing on that shore, and you were in my place, what would you do?'

He grew very still, not answering for a long time. Then he admitted, 'I would leave the ship.'

Marguerite faced him and took both of his hands in hers. 'Both of us are behaving like cowards. You don't truly wish to wed me, for you love someone else.'

'It is different for me.'

'Is it? You're the Earl of Penrith. You own dozens of estates—there is no reason why you should not seize your own happiness.'

'Already I am treated as an outcast, because I have

his favour. Many men have sought to kill me for what I am. The Church believes—'

'Are you happy, living like this?' she interrupted.

The earl remained silent, staring out at the water. 'No. But I haven't a choice.'

'Is there no one else who could be your heir?'

He shook his head slowly. 'My brothers are dead. I am the last of my family, and if I do not have an heir, I forfeit my lands to the king.' A melancholy edged his face and he added, 'You see, you are not the only one with much to lose.'

His arm came around her shoulders and the gesture brought her a slight comfort. 'Marguerite, if I could find a way out for either of us, I would take it.'

She swallowed hard, feeling the fear overtake her. 'There is a way. But you won't like it.'

His hand tightened upon her shoulder. 'Tell me.'

'Let her go, Callum,' Alex advised. 'The Duc released us. If you seek her again, I doubt he'll let you live.'

'I'm riding to the coast,' he responded. 'To watch her go.'

His brother Bram rested his hand upon his shoulder. 'I'm sorry, Brother. We tried.'

'She did it to save us,' he said quietly. She'd sacrificed herself for all of them, granting them their lives.

'We'll set up camp here,' Alex said. 'Go to the shore, if that's your wish. We'll be here when you return.'

Callum gave them a nod and mounted Goliath, urging his horse towards the beach. The animal kept up a strong pace, but when they reached the place where the ship had departed, the memories overtook him.

Here, he'd taught Marguerite to swim, before warming her with a fire and joining with her. He remembered what it was to be inside her, watching her face flush with a shattering pleasure. And the night he'd been in chains, she had come to him, offering herself.

God above, but he loved her. He loved her quiet beauty and her courage. The way she'd taught him to write, offering him a way out of the suffocating silence. Letting her go was the hardest thing he'd ever had to do.

Even now, he found it impossible to turn his back on her.

Callum watched the ship sailing further out. Then he drew his horse south, riding parallel to its path until it grew too dark to see the white sails billowing in the wind.

Drawing Goliath to a halt, he watched the ship disappear into the mist. No other woman would ever mean as much to him as Marguerite. But she was gone from him now and he had no choice but to release her.

He lowered his head to his horse, closing his eyes against the pain of losing this woman. But there was nothing more he could have done.

Nothing at all.

'You cannot do this,' the earl insisted.

'My father will never let me go, unless he believes I'm dead,' Marguerite said. 'It's the only way.'

'And if you do die?'

'Then I won't have to suffer, living without Callum.'

'It's reckless and foolish.' The earl shook his head, denying it. 'I can't allow it.'

'Listen to me,' she whispered. She reached up and held his cheeks between her hands. 'I want both of us to be happy. Go back to England. Bring the one you love into your home and let me go.' She stood on tiptoe and pressed a kiss against his cheek. 'I want to do this, Lord Penrith.'

'Peter,' he corrected. Though he didn't smile, she saw regret upon his face. 'I'm going to lose your dowry, aren't I?'

'If I can ever find a way to repay you, I would give up every last jewel I possess.'

He let out a breath. 'I know I'll regret this.'

'Trust me,' she promised. 'All will be well.' He embraced her, but within his arms there was no hint of attraction between them. He might as well have been a close brother.

'I will pray for you,' he offered.

'And I for your own happiness.' Though inwardly the terror roiled against her stomach, it was time to put her fears aside and seize what she wanted. Even if it meant the greatest risk of all.

'There's just enough light,' she said. 'I have to go now.'

'You're certain?'

She nodded.

'Then take this with you.' He pulled a spare oar from the side of the boat. 'It may keep you from drowning.'

She rested it against the side of the boat and embraced him again. 'Help me with my outer garments, won't you? The weight will pull me under if I wear all of them.'

Lord Penrith leaned in and kissed her as a lover would, letting the others believe what they wanted. The kiss was warm and, though it did nothing to arouse her, it gave him the chance to unlace her surcoat, loosening it from her shoulders. When he pulled back, he blocked her from view and Marguerite lifted it away, dropping it upon the floor of the boat. Though she worried about the weight of her cote and chemise, she might need the warmth when she reached land later.

She took the oar in her hand and sent the earl a smile. 'Seek your own happiness, my lord. Just as I will.'

And with that, she stepped overboard, holding tightly to the wood as the frigid water closed over her head.

Chapter Fifteen

The water was so cold, it seemed to freeze her limbs in place. Marguerite struggled with the oar, but it wasn't helping her to float. A wave drenched her face and she fought to breathe.

Keep going, she urged herself. But she wasn't at all a strong swimmer and her feet could not touch the bottom.

Behind her, she heard the shouts of the men and another splash as someone came after her. The sound of them made her aware that if she didn't begin swimming as hard as she could, they would only bring her back again.

'Marguerite!' came the earl's voice. Seconds later, she heard him swimming towards her. Then a strong arm came around her waist, holding her above water. 'Little fool,' he whispered in her ear, 'you're not strong enough, are you?'

'I h-have to try,' she whispered back. 'Let me go.'

But instead of dragging her back to the ship, she realised he was swimming towards land, bringing her with him.

'I tossed your gown into the water, so they wouldn't see it,' he murmured, keeping her above the waves. When she was closer to shore, he asked, 'Can you touch the bottom?'

When she let go of him, the water was at the level of her mouth while she stood on tiptoe. 'Y-yes.' The freezing cold water made her limbs ache, but she could make the rest of the distance on her own.

'Hide yourself in the hills,' he said, letting her go. 'Godspeed, Marguerite.'

She heard him swimming back to the ship, and she whispered back, 'Godspeed.' That he had done this for her meant the world. She hoped that he would seek his own happiness with the one he loved. A man like the earl deserved no less.

Her body was leaden with fatigue, but she stumbled her way to the shore. Unable to see anything, she could only judge the distance by walking forward, the water growing more shallow. Each minute was endless, her body shivering violently.

When she reached the sand, she collapsed on her knees, unable to take another step. Behind her, the shouting continued and she heard her father's anguished voice.

Get up, she ordered herself. She had to keep going, no matter how difficult it became. Inside, she envisioned Callum's face, trying to gain strength from it. If somehow she could find him, all of this would be worth it. She wouldn't allow herself to think of how far they'd sailed or how impossible it might be to find him.

Time blurred and she climbed the hillside, not knowing where she was going or how she would ever reach

Callum. She didn't know the land and the sky gave no hint of light.

She walked, feeling the dizziness overtake her. The golden netting and barbette she'd worn seemed to weigh against her head and neck. She loosened them until they fell upon the ground.

Her thin gown was clammy against her skin, the wind making her shiver more. It was hard to breathe and she felt as if she were gasping for air.

How long had she been gone? Whether minutes or hours, she couldn't tell at all. Her hands were numb and when she tried to hold up the hem of her gown, she couldn't make her fingers work.

She kept moving, no longer aware of the direction. Was she going back towards her father's castle? Or further inland? Without warning, she lost her footing and stumbled hard, her body collapsing to the ground. The grass was soft beneath her, breaking the fall. How long was it until morning? Perhaps if she lay down to rest, she could see better when the sun came up.

Curled up upon the ground, she stared up at the night sky, wondering if she'd done the right thing. She didn't know if the earl would lie on her behalf or what he would say to her father.

Her heartbeat was racing in her chest, and she struggled to calm herself. She'd lost her shoes in the water, and her bare feet were so cold, she could no longer feel them.

Sleep, a voice inside her urged. *Don't fight it any longer.*

Callum woke before dawn, the nightmare pulling him out of sleep. Restlessness made him uneasy that something was wrong. He couldn't place the feeling, but he found himself packing up his tent and sleeping blankets with a sense of urgency.

He ate a bit of dried meat and an oat cake that he'd brought along as travelling food, then prepared Goliath for the journey home. Shielding his eyes against the sun, he stared below at the sandy beach and the glittering water. There was no sign of the ship. Marguerite was gone, as he'd expected.

He should rejoin his brothers and return home. But something held him here. Callum found himself riding along the coast again, searching for any sign of the ship, though it was useless.

They had already gone, taking her with them.

The grief and anger struck him so hard, he let Goliath ride at his fastest pace, letting the raw emotion out. With each mile, he raged against the injustice of being helpless to take Marguerite with him. He would miss her soft smile and the way she looked at him as if he were the only man who mattered.

There would never be another for him. Not like her.

He lowered his face against Goliath's mane, resting for a moment before he pulled on the reins to turn back. His brothers would be waiting for him.

Then he glimpsed something white upon the ground. He eased Goliath closer and when he saw it, his heart began pounding.

It was Marguerite's barbette and the golden net she'd worn in her hair. How had it come to be here?

His hunter's instincts heightened and he began tracking the bent grasses, leading his horse while he traced the path. It led away from the sea, the motion shifting in one direction, then another…as if she were disoriented.

He followed the path, unsure of what he would find. Trepidation coursed through him while he scrutinised every footprint, every hint that led him closer.

And when he reached an open clearing, he spied the fallen body of a woman lying motionless upon the ground.

Callum broke into a run, offering up a thousand prayers while his mind grew frozen with fear. When he reached the woman's side, he turned her over.

It was Marguerite.

Her skin was like ice and she didn't respond to his touch at all. Callum rested his hand over her heart and could barely detect it beating. God above, how had she come to be here?

She was only wearing a thin cote with no shoes and no head covering. He didn't know how long she'd been lying there, exposed to the elements.

Terror coursed through him with the thought that she might die. She'd tried to come back to him and her clothing was soaked from the sea. It was a miracle she'd made it this far, since she had only just learned to swim.

'Marguerite,' he said, touching her cool face. 'Look at me, Marguerite.'

She didn't respond and he had no way of knowing how to help her. He went to his horse and retrieved a woollen blanket, gathering it around her shoulders. When he lifted her into his arms, she seemed unaware of him.

Don't die, he prayed.

He mounted his horse, cradling her as he rode back to the place where he'd left his brothers. Not once did she open her eyes, but he tried to warm her along the way.

The ride was endless, with all of his concentration

focused upon her. The risk she'd taken was too grea
and he wasn't at all certain she would awaken. Her fac
was so pale, her breathing barely moving her chest.

Ahead, he spied the fire where his brothers wer
camped. When he reached them, he dismounted, bring
ing Marguerite with him. Bram and Alex stood up
while Dougal was still sleeping.

'I found her,' Callum told them. 'She tried…leave..
The words stumbled inside him, unable to form a clea
thought. All he could do was hold her as if his ver
touch could keep her with him.

Dougal had awakened and was staring at Margue
rite. 'Is she alive? She doesn't look it.'

'She is,' Bram said. 'Thus far.'

Words eluded Callum at this moment, the tormen
clawing into his consciousness at the thought of Mar
guerite dying. He couldn't let it happen. Not after ev
erything she'd endured in her attempt to escape.

Dougal wisely retreated. 'I'll look after your horse

'How long was she outside?' Alex asked.

Callum had no way of knowing and could only shak
his head. His brother exchanged a look at Bram. 'You'
have to warm her.' He ordered Bram to set up the ten
again and line the ground with blankets. 'Take the we
clothing off her and warm her skin to skin.'

Callum sent Alex a warning look. 'Don't…look.'

'Easy, Callum.' Alex's face held amusement. 'Both o
us are wedded men. Don't you think Laren and Nairn
would have our heads if we dared to look at anothe
naked woman?'

Their teasing diminished the tension somewha
and the words came easier to him. 'It doesn't mean..
I trust…'

While his brothers busied themselves with taking care of the fire and heating water for a tea, Callum carried Marguerite's body into the tent and laid her upon the furs. He closed the edges of the tent to give them privacy. With a hand upon her throat, he could barely feel her pulse.

You have to live, he prayed. With shaking hands, he lifted the wet gown away, then her chemise. Her skin was freezing cold and Callum cocooned her in the blankets.

When he exited the tent, he saw Alex with a wooden cup of steaming liquid. 'You might try to get her to drink this. It's not much, but it might help warm her from the inside.'

The drink was little more than heated water, but he took it from his brother. Before he entered the tent, Alex reminded him, 'Skin to skin, Callum. That will warm her the fastest.'

His brother Bram sent him a knowing look. 'And there's nothing wrong with enjoying some time with a beautiful naked woman.'

'Dougal will volunteer, if you're too shy,' Alex teased. 'He has no wife to take his head off.'

Their youngest brother's face blushed crimson and he hurried back to the horses, ignoring the remark.

Callum pointed toward the coast and ordered, 'Must…find the ship.'

'You're afraid the Duc will come after her,' Alex predicted.

He nodded. They would be searching, and he wasn't about to let them find her.

'They might believe she's dead,' Alex responded. 'Most women wouldn't survive what she did.'

The reminder only fuelled Callum's fear that sh
still might not live. She was so cold and unresponsiv
'Find them,' he repeated to his brothers and saw Bra
nodding his assent.

He trusted them to learn how close the soldiers we
while he tended to Marguerite. Hastily, he ducked bac
inside the tent and tried to raise her head.

'Open your eyes,' he pleaded. 'Marguerite, yo
must.'

When she remained unconscious, he gathered her i
his arms, supporting her. 'Drink,' he murmured, try
ing to lift the cup to her lips. The warm liquid dribble
down the side of her face and he realised he would hav
to try a different tactic.

Taking a small sip of the liquid, he drew his lips ove
hers, coaxing them open. Then he released the warm
water into her mouth with deliberate slowness. Whe
she didn't cough or sputter, he tried it again, transfe
ring the warm water until she had drunk half the cup
It was enough for now.

He stripped away his own clothing and pulled bac
her blanket. Her body was pale, but the sight of he
breasts and slim hips made him grit his teeth against th
memories of touching her, their bodies joined togethe

When he moved his body upon hers, rolling the
up in a blanket, he felt the extent of her cold skin. Sh
didn't move or give any reaction to him.

He drew her so close, her head was tucked beneat
his chin, her freezing skin against his. 'You're going
live, *a ghràidh*,' he swore. If the force of his will woul
keep her heart beating, he would do everything in h
power to make it so.

She slept against him, her soft skin gradually gettin

warmer. He spoke to her in a stream of words, telling her what she meant to him. How he would take care of her and love her for the rest of their days.

Hours passed, and his brothers left food just outside the tent. Callum tried to get Marguerite to eat, but she remained unresponsive. He covered her in blankets and dressed himself, before returning outside the tent to speak with his brothers. 'Where is the ship?'

'Still south of us,' Dougal answered. 'While you were with the lady, I rode down the coast with Bram. It looks as if they're still searching the water.'

'We need to take her back to Glen Arrin,' Alex warned, 'before anyone finds us here.'

Though Marguerite was no longer quite as cold, Callum wasn't certain it was wise to move her. But he knew her father would likely return and find her if they remained here.

'All right,' he agreed. 'We'll take her back.'

He studied his brothers and glanced at the tent. They had only a few hours to disappear into the hills, where the Duc and his men wouldn't find them.

He could only pray she'd survive the journey.

Callum held Marguerite throughout the gruelling ride. When she hadn't awakened on the third day, Alex had made the decision to hasten their pace for fear that she would die of starvation. The night before, Callum had tried to get her to drink more water, but though she took it, she remained motionless.

She was holding on to life by the barest thread. And he didn't know how to save her.

When they reached Glen Arrin that evening, relief

flooded through him. The other women knew more of healing than he did and he hoped that Nairna or Laren could help revive Marguerite.

As they rode closer, he welcomed the sight of the fortress. All spring and summer, they had continued rebuilding it larger than before and it was nearly completed. Limestone walls stretched around the fortress and the wooden tower was being lined with stone, to eventually convert it into a castle.

Yet the sight of his home didn't alleviate his fear. Marguerite's skin was burning hot and she'd slipped into a fever since yesterday. He didn't know what to do for her; never had he felt so defenceless. He could fight against any enemy, but this unseen foe might take her from him.

Nairna and Laren were there to greet them, but their smiles faded as soon as they saw Marguerite in his arms.

'Is she—?' Laren whispered. Her face looked desolate and she held on to her swollen pregnancy, as if to guard against the possibility.

'She's not dead.' Callum walked past them towards the fortress. But the fear of losing Marguerite had wound him up so tightly, he couldn't manage more than that.

Nairna, who was also heavily pregnant, struggled to catch up to him. 'Bring her inside. We'll move Adaira in with Laren and Alex.'

She led the way and Callum shifted Marguerite in his arms to get past the narrow winding staircase.

'It's good to hear you talking again, Callum,' Nairna said quietly. 'I always knew you would.' She opened the door leading to a tiny chamber with a single bed within.

t. A slight smile pulled at her mouth. 'If anyone could elp you, I always thought Marguerite would manage it.'

He cradled her in his arms and stared at his brother's vife. 'She can't die.' Gently, he laid Marguerite upon he bed, drawing a blanket over her. 'Is there anyone vho can heal her?'

'Your mother may have some remedies to help.' She ested against the wall, drawing her palm against her vomb. At his look of concern, she confessed, 'I get izzy sometimes. It passes.'

'But you and Laren are well?'

She nodded. 'Our children will come in the autumn.' lyeing Marguerite, she asked, 'Callum, does the Duc now she is here?'

'She threw herself off the ship. I think her father elieves she's dead.' He sat down beside Marguerite, ouching her hair. 'It was the only way he would ever et her go. She broke her betrothal to come back to me.'

Nairna's eyes filled up with tears. The chamber door pened slightly and Bram held out a tray with a bowl f a watery liquid. 'I have broth, if you think she can rink it.'

Callum pointed for his brother to set it down on a able. 'Send for our mother and I'll stay with her.'

'You're what she needs most right now, Callum.' Jairna touched his shoulder and returned to her hus-and, closing the door behind her.

When they were gone, he sat down again at Margue-ite's side. Though she had finally overcome the effects f being too cold, the fever worried him. Perspiration ampened her brow and she was so pale that he didn't now if he'd done enough to save her.

Months ago, she had come to him. She'd bathed him

and tended his wounds, letting him rest his head upon her lap. Her compassion had reached past his shadowed mind, granting him peace for the first time.

It felt awkward, speaking to her when she was unconscious, but Callum sensed that she was there, somehow. That she would hear him.

He moved beside her in the bed, pulling her close. She was so hot, he didn't think it was wise for her to be wearing so many heavy clothes. With the greatest care, he undressed her, easing the cote off until she wore only her chemise. The linen clung to her skin and he brought her head to rest upon his chest.

'I won't let you go, Marguerite. Not in life. Not in death.' He pressed his mouth against her temple, stroking her hair again. 'I've fought too hard for you.'

The weariness of the nights he'd spent keeping vigil were starting to press against his resolve. 'You're going to wed me, when you're better. I'll build you a house, anywhere you like.'

A seed of regret pulled inside him that he could never give her a castle like this one. 'It won't be very big, but it will do well enough for us.'

Around her neck, he spied the chain holding the glass pendant he'd given her. She'd worn it, even when she was leaving him.

He lifted up the chain, the slight weight resting in his palm. Formed of glass, it should have been fragile yet it remained strong. Like her.

Callum took a breath and began speaking again. He filled her ears with stories, talking to her until his voice grew hoarse. The memory of her had pulled him out of the greatest darkness, when he'd suffered beneath the ash. If his voice would somehow do the same for her, he'd speak for as long as he could.

When at last he was too tired to say another word, he stretched out beside her, holding her in his arms. As if he could bind her to him, forcing her to stay.

When his mother Grizel arrived the next morning, she brought a foul-smelling tea.

'They told me you're speaking again.' She eyed Calum with a curt nod, as if it mattered not at all to her. 'It's about time, isn't it?'

He ignored her brusque manner. His mother could never be accused of soft-heartedness. 'Can you save Marguerite?'

'I've a tea that will help bring down the fever. But you shouldn't have moved her. When a body grows too cold, it's better to warm her slowly. You might have killed her by journeying this far.'

Grizel's abrasive manner made him bristle. 'I was trying to save her.' He guided Marguerite to a seated position, supporting her in his arms.

His mother set down the tea and studied them both. 'How long has it been since she opened her eyes?'

'Four days.' He didn't miss the look of resignation in Grizel's face. She likely didn't believe Marguerite would live much longer. Even so, she continued her questioning.

'And how have you managed to give her food and water? I presume she can't drink on her own.'

Colour rose to his cheeks, but he admitted, 'I put my mouth upon hers and forced her to drink.'

Grizel lifted the tea to him, her expression discerning. 'Keep doing the same, to make her drink the tea And if she awakens, send for me.'

If. Not when. The worry gnawed at his composure but he forced himself to nod.

His mother's gaze moved from him back to Marguerite. 'She was always too fine for a man like you, bu I'll grant that she had courage.'

He had no reply for her framed insult, for it was true He could only hope that if Marguerite regained her strength, his poverty wouldn't matter to her.

Before Grizel closed the door, she added, 'I am glad you returned, Callum.' With a faltering smile, she departed.

He rested his cheek against Marguerite's, apologising for his mother, in case she had overheard any of it As time passed, he fed her the foul-smelling tea, his lips upon hers to ensure that she drank it.

He continued talking, all through the day and into the night, telling her about the years he'd spent imprisoned. Of how he'd regained his skill with a bow and arrows, and the nights he'd dreamed of her.

'If I could fight this battle for you, I would,' he swore She'd done everything in her power to come back to him. The thought of losing her now was like a dull knife within him. He held her feverish body close, feeling the desolation wash over him. Her heartbeat was so frail her breathing laboured.

She might not live to see the morning. The though was worse than any torture. He'd faced his own death time and again, until it no longer held any threat over him. Death was inevitable for every man. But nothing frightened him more than losing Marguerite.

'You're everything to me,' he told her. 'Don't let go.'

And when at last he could stay awake no longer, he lept with her cradled against his heart.

Chapter Sixteen

Her eyes wouldn't open. Marguerite felt a man's body against hers and she snuggled instinctively into hi' warm skin. Inside, her stomach was aching from lac' of food, but she had not the strength to speak.

She'd glimpsed the peaceful Heaven that awaited he' and the temptation to leave behind the pain and suffer ing was strong. But a man kept talking to her, tellin' her stories about his boyhood. The familiar voice wa' chaining her to him, pulling her away from Death' arms.

'Marguerite.' The voice of Callum broke through he' reverie, reaching towards her. She felt his lips agains' hers and a cool liquid entered her mouth. Was it water' She tried to taste it and when she moved her lips, sh' heard his encouragement.

'Drink,' he urged. 'That's it.'

The sweetness of the water reminded her of the wa terfalls from the mountains. Clear and pure, it quenche' her thirst. Though she couldn't yet open her eyes, th' touch of Callum's mouth captivated her.

Something else moved against her mouth and sh'

asted a broth. This time, she drank too fast and choked. She coughed to clear her throat and he rubbed her back, trying to help.

At last she opened her eyes and saw him holding her. Callum's face held weariness and his long black hair hung against his shoulders.

'You look terrible,' she managed. As if he'd been imprisoned once more, his face was gaunt, the sleeplessness etched in the shadows beneath his eyes. 'You ought to bathe.'

The thankfulness eased across his face in a relieved smile. 'I'll let you bathe me, when you've regained your strength.'

With that, he gathered her in his arms and held her tight. In his embrace, she felt the fierce love and she tried to lift her arms around his neck. 'I'm sorry to have been so much trouble,' she said. 'I don't remember what happened after I jumped from the ship.'

'You spent hours without shelter,' he told her. 'I didn't find you until morning and you nearly died.'

'I remember…how cold I was.' The exertion of speaking was starting to hurt and she rested her head against him.

'You're safe now. We brought you back to Glen Arrin.' There was a gruffness in his voice and a moment later, he sat up, tucking her into the bed. 'When you've recovered, you're going to wed me.'

'I am?' Her voice was weak, but his proclamation amused her. 'You're not going to ask me?'

'No.' He rested both hands on her shoulders. 'If I have to chain you to my side, I'll be wedding you. You won't have a choice in this, Marguerite.' His expression

had darkened, and she saw the suffering he'd endure
over the past few days.

'I love you,' he said. The words washed over her, fill
ing her with light that pushed away the shadows of the
past. Callum's eyes held the look of a man who woul
worship her for the rest of her life. And it was enough

Lifting her hands to his face, she drew him dow
to kiss her. It was a kiss of welcome, of a promise t
stay with him.

'I will marry you,' she promised. 'Nothing woul
give me greater happiness.'

The wedding was delayed by the early birth of Lar
en's twins. Marguerite was enchanted by the tiny in
fants, but when Alex handed her his newborn daughte
to hold, she felt awkward and clumsy.

The girl's head was no larger than her palm. Whe
she tucked the sleeping infant beneath her chin, sh
marvelled at the soft skin. Callum came up behind he
and drew his arms around her waist. 'She's a wee one
isn't she?'

'She's beautiful. I'm half-afraid I'll drop her.'

'If you're wanting me to, I could give you one o
those,' he offered against her ear. 'Tonight, after w
wed.'

At the reminder, Marguerite's face flushed. It ha
been some time since she'd lain with him and she sense
that he would be insatiable once they were togethe
again. She kissed the babe upon her forehead and passe
her back to Laren.

To Callum, she murmured, 'I wouldn't mind havin
a child.' Standing on tiptoe, she whispered in his ear, '
cannot wait until this night.'

She deliberately let her lips graze against his ear and Callum took her hand, starting to lead her away. Marguerite laughed at his eagerness. 'Not now,' she protested. 'I want to go and visit with Nairna.'

'She can wait.' Callum continued walking, ignoring his brother and Laren. A flush came over Marguerite's face, for she'd only just regained her strength a few days ago. He wasn't planning to…seduce her, was he? In spite of her attempt to remain calm, she wanted to feel his hands upon her, to surrender her body beneath his.

'Where are we going?' she asked, trying to sound more dispassionate than she felt.

'To see the house I built for you.' Callum led her outside the fortress, into the hills. The sun was shining, and it would only be hours until the visiting priest arrived and they could marry and enjoy feasting with the rest of the clan.

He led her past the small gathering of huts, toward the pathway that went into the forest. About a mile into the woods, she saw a small clearing with a newly finished thatched house. The smell of fresh wood shavings made her smile, and he led her inside, showing her the hearth and the bed against the far wall.

'When we have children, we'll make it larger,' he promised. 'But for now…' In his expression, she saw the shadow of regret, as if he'd wanted to give her more.

'It's perfect,' she said, moving into his arms. And it was. She didn't care that it was nothing but a simple home with four walls and a roof. Within the forest, it reminded her of the forbidden days they'd spent together. She could be happy here, with him.

But though she drew her arms around Callum to kiss him, she couldn't let go of the sense of unrest. She'd fought hard to love this man and to share her life with him, yet the shadow of fear lurked within her.

His mouth came over her lips in a fierce kiss, his hands moving down her spine. 'Tonight you won't sleep, Marguerite. For I'll be inside you, showing you all the ways I love you.'

She couldn't catch her breath as his tongue invaded, stroking hers with sensual promise. Her body seemed to melt into his, wanting more.

'I'm going to touch you all the ways I've been dreaming about, these past few weeks,' he swore.

He rose hard against her, pressing at the juncture of her thighs. She lifted her leg against him, her heart pounding faster as his hand moved under her skirts, feeling for the bare flesh. His rough palms moved over her bottom and when he reached between her legs, she felt two of his fingers pushing inside her.

A ragged curse came from him as he rubbed her intimately. 'You're wet for me, Marguerite. God above, I could sheathe myself in you right now.'

In answer, she reached for his trews, stroking the thick heat of him through the wool. He withdrew and entered his fingers in a slow rhythm, making her close her eyes as the sweet torment claimed her.

'Look at me,' he commanded. 'Look into my eyes while I touch you. I want to see you come apart.'

She clung to his shoulders for balance, a sigh escaping as her body strained against his touch. Over and over, he moved his hand, his fingers caressing deep within. The ecstasy was making her tremble, her breathing coming in short pants as he thrust again and again.

She moved against him, seeking the pleasure he was trying to give, until finally, his hand moved in a faster rhythm, shattering her apart. Her release was a shimmering ecstasy that convulsed within her. She reached for him, wanting desperately to give him the same fulfilment.

'Callum!' came a shout.

The dangerous look in her lover's eyes made her lower her leg. 'I may have to murder my younger brother, sweet. Stay here while I go and kill him for interrupting us.'

Marguerite straightened her skirts and sat down on the bed, hardly able to stand. 'Quickly, then,' she answered with a smile. Inside, her body was molten, aching for him. She tried to calm herself when she heard the voices outside, wondering what this was about. A moment later, Callum returned to her and retrieved his bow and a quiver of arrows.

The look upon his face was harsh and unforgiving. The foreboding within her stomach took root and swelled. 'What is it?' she whispered.

'Soldiers gathering from the west.'

Her heart sank and the tremulous fear rose up so hard, she couldn't stop her hands from shaking. 'English?' she ventured.

He shook his head slowly. 'It's your father's men, come to invade Glen Arrin. Stay here, Marguerite. Whatever happens, don't leave this house.'

Callum rode out with his brothers, cold rage cloaking his mood. He didn't know what had prompted the Duc to make this journey, but he intended to face down the man and make him leave.

Better if he believed Marguerite was dead. No doubt he'd come to make sure of it.

He joined with Alex and Bram, while Dougal stayed with the women. The other clansmen armed themselves, positioned on every side of the fortress. There had been time to evacuate the rest of the women and children to Bram's house at the top of the hillside.

'Do they know she's here?' Alex asked.

Callum could only shake his head. 'Let them believe that she's dead. It's her only hope of gaining her freedom.'

'Where is Marguerite now?'

'She's hidden in the forest, in our house.' He drew his horse forward, riding toward the army of men. It infuriated him that the Duc would come this night, the night they were meant to marry. Was there no way the man would ever let them be?

'Steady your temper, Brother,' Alex warned.

Bram came along the opposite side, his expression grim. 'The priest is with them.'

Callum let out a curse. If they'd found the priest, then the man might have confessed the truth, that Marguerite was here and they would marry tonight.

'Somehow, I don't believe the Duc came to witness our marriage,' he said. More likely to prevent it.

But still he kept moving forward until the army spread out. He reached into his quiver for a black-feathered arrow and nocked it to his bowstring. Let them come, if they would.

'What do you want to do?' Alex asked.

'Allow them to make the first move.' Callum kept the arrow fitted, waiting for the Duc to make his decision. 'We'll make no assumptions until we know why they're here.'

The soldiers behind him were dressed for a battle.

They wore chainmail armour and all had spears, bows and other weapons. A second row of horsemen stood, prepared for a fight.

Neither army moved and time slowed as they stared at one another. Callum realised that the Duc would not believe him if he claimed Marguerite was not here. He would turn over every stone, searching every house until they found her.

He didn't want to kill Marguerite's father, or be placed in a position where he had no choice but to take the Duc's life. The silence weighed upon both sides, but a quarter of an hour later, movement attracted their attention.

Callum saw a group of women walking in the space between the two sides. Nairna had changed into a loose-fitting gown of silk, struggling to walk with her swollen belly. Her hair was braided back, with flowers woven into the strands. Beside her walked Laren, carrying both babies. Though Alex's wife had her arms full, she, too, was clad in wedding finery. Behind them, he could see nothing but the glint of golden hair.

And his heart sank, not knowing why Marguerite had ignored his command.

She walked slowly, each step filled with purpose. Nairna and Laren had helped her prepare herself, and Marguerite wore her hair down around her shoulders. They had combed it for her, crowning her with a wreath of heather and gorse. Around her throat she wore the blue pendant and her gown was the same shade of sapphire. A golden girdle hung against her hips and her feet were barefoot on the summer grass.

She'd told Nairna and Laren of her plan and despite

the risk, it was all she had. Something had to be done before fighting broke out. And though she had made her decision to stay with Callum, no matter what happened, she would do everything in her power to prevent bloodshed.

'They look as if they're going to kill each other,' Laren murmured, clutching her children tightly to her breast.

'They won't dare attack, with us between them,' Marguerite said.

When her father caught sight of her, his visage transformed. There was immense relief, followed by anger and renewed determination.

She continued walking until she stood before his horse. Then she held out her hands as if to greet him. 'Will you come and accept my kiss of welcome, Father?'

Her father did not dismount. Instead, he stared at her. 'I thought you were dead.'

'I almost died,' she agreed. 'Callum found me and brought me back here.' She turned her attention to the priest, who was approaching. 'I hope that you have come to join in our wedding celebration.'

'I will not celebrate your marriage to a common Scot.'

Callum rode up at that moment. The look of vengeance that passed between him and her father made her uneasy, so she offered, 'Will you accept our hospitality and continue our discussion in private?'

The Duc said nothing and his silence stood as a refusal. Marguerite wondered if she would ever break through to him. She reached up and took Callum's hand. When her father still did not speak, she added, 'Your men may wish to refresh themselves in the castle. If

hat is agreeable to you, Laren?' she asked the Lady
of Glen Arrin.

Alex's wife held on to her babies and nodded. 'So
ong as they leave their weapons behind.'

Her father looked as if he wanted to openly attack
he fortress, but Callum met his unspoken threat with
a promise of his own.

'I will speak to you, Marguerite,' the Duc agreed at
ast. 'But not with *him*.'

'You will speak to both of us. Or not at all,' she
countered.

They were at an impasse and her father looked as if
he'd rather give the command to attack.

'I was willing to face death rather than live without Callum,' she said quietly. 'If need be, I will face
it again.'

Her father's hardened expression held disbelief. He
stared at her, as if trying to guess whether she would
follow through with her threat. Callum dismounted and
brought his hand around her waist. At his side she faced
the Duc, waiting for his response.

'Please,' she asked gently. 'If you love me at all.'

There was no expression on her father's face, but
eventually, he drew his horse forward in a walk, refusing to lower himself. She led him into the fortress, not
at all knowing what she would say to him.

Nairna busied herself with getting the Duc wine and
food, while Laren began changing the orders for the
feast. Marguerite held on to Callum's hand, but in his
grasp she felt the tension. He wasn't about to negotiate
with the Duc—he was well past that point. She had to
intercede before they killed each other.

When they reached the Hall, the Duc refused to sit.

He stood and faced her. With a discreet signal, Callum ordered the others out. He stood at her side and waited.

Marguerite squared her shoulders and faced her father.

'You let me believe you were dead,' he raged. 'Do you have any idea what that felt like?'

She saw the pain in his eyes and the anger that went deeper into his heart. 'I am sorry it had to be this way. But you never listened to me. You dismissed my feelings and behaved as if I didn't matter.

'And when you made me drink that potion, I realised that you were never going to hear what I had to say. You wanted what *you* believed was best for me. Never what I wanted.'

She let go of Callum's hand and said, 'When you are ready to see that I am happy here, that I am loved by this man, you are welcome to join in our celebration.' With a step towards the Duc, she said, 'For this night, you could be my father again. Not my enemy.'

The Duc studied her, his face intent. 'And what have you to say, MacKinloch? I presume you can still speak.'

'Thanks to Marguerite, yes.' He came forward and rested his hands upon her shoulders. 'You and I may never come to an agreement. But I would slay a thousand enemies to protect your daughter. I would give my life for hers and I swear I will make her happy.'

His words filled her with such joy that Marguerite stepped back into his embrace, bringing his arms around her. 'Let me go, Father.'

The Duc said nothing, watching her. In the space of a few moments, he seemed to age, his expression holding bitterness. 'I always wanted the best for you.'

'I've found my own happiness. And if you would only bend your convictions, you'd see that.'

'You would truly turn your back on your birthright?' he asked. 'On all the wealth you would have possessed?'

She reached up and touched the flowers in her hair. These will be my jewels now. Will you not put aside your anger?' She closed the space between them, reaching up to touch her father's cheeks. 'For this night, simply be happy for me.'

'And what of the earl? A betrothal cannot be so easily broken, Marguerite.'

'He helped me to the shore,' she admitted. 'I let him go, just as he released me.' At his doubt, she added, 'He knows, Father.'

The Duc reached out and took her hand. In that moment, he looked so weary that she didn't know what to believe. 'I suppose he must have. Someone pulled up the anchor and the ship drifted for miles before we realised it.' He squeezed her palm and reached out to touch her hair. 'You look so much like your mother, *ma petite.*'

She sent him a blinding smile, understanding the apology he had not spoken.

Chapter Seventeen

Callum stood before Marguerite, still in disbelief that her father was witnessing their marriage. The priest spoke a blessing in Latin, joining their hands together while Marguerite smiled at him. Her blue eyes were filled with joy, while he'd hardly managed to speak the vows that now married them.

He leaned in to kiss her and his kinsmen cheered. The dark look in the Duc's eyes wasn't entirely pleased, but he'd agreed to a reluctant peace between them. Though he didn't like letting his daughter go, his capitulation had done a great deal to heal the distance between them.

Callum met the man's gaze, offering the silent promise to always make her happy.

Laren and Nairna had created a feast that was nothing short of miraculous. Several of the soldiers had spent the afternoon fishing, and they ate cold mutton, roasted fowl and salmon, as well as oat cakes and bowls of summer berries. There was music and dancing all around them, and later, the Duc agreed to dance with Marguerite. Her face shone with love, and when she looked back at him, Callum returned the same silent message of love.

'What happened to Aunt Beatrice?' she asked her father.

'I sent her back to France. She was causing more trouble and I heard tales from my men that you were right.' He shrugged. 'It was her idea about the herbs.' Touching her cheek, he said, 'I never should have agreed to it. I ask your forgiveness.'

She nodded, recognising the sincerity in his voice. He'd allowed his anger to blind him. 'I'm glad she's gone.' Resting her head upon his shoulder, she added, 'I still owe you the prize from the day I let you win our race.'

When he said nothing, she raised her head to look at him. 'Do you remember? I promised to visit you.'

There was a small hint of emotion in his face. 'I would like that very much.' His arms tightened around her and in his arms, she sensed his love.

The night continued with more feasting and music. The Duc expressed interest in the stained-glass window within the fortress he'd spied earlier. After he'd drunk a few more cups of ale, he spoke with Laren about commissioning a glass window for his château in France.

Though he sat with Marguerite and forced himself to eat, Callum wasn't at all interested in food. She caught his gaze and her smile faded into the look of understanding.

She extended her hand to him and he followed her away from the celebration, to the woods that beckoned. They had just entered the trees when, abruptly, Marguerite stopped walking and leaned against one of the tall oaks. Reaching up to him, she pulled him into a deep kiss.

He took her mouth with his, claiming her with a husband's right. She met the kiss with her own passion, winding her arms around his neck and offering everything of herself.

When she withdrew, her breathing was staggered, her mouth swollen. 'I couldn't wait any longer.'

'If you hadn't led me here, I might have carried you off,' he answered. The need to feel her bare skin against his, to show her how much he loved her, was so strong that he lifted her into his arms.

'Then again, perhaps I will.'

She laughed against his shoulder as he took her into the forest, the sunset gleaming red and gold upon the horizon. He carried her into their house, closing the door behind them. Then he lowered her on to their bed.

Marguerite reached for him and Callum worked to free her from her gown while she worked to help him from his own clothing. She reached to lift away the crown of flowers upon her hair, but he took it from her. 'Wait.'

He settled back to look at her. With her hair unbound and her beautiful body revealed to him, it stole his senses to think that she was now his wife. He broke off a spring of purple heather from the wreath and brought it to her body. With the rough sprig in his hands, he traced patterns upon her skin.

'What are you doing?' she whispered, gasping when he drew the blossom over her erect nipple.

'You taught me to write,' he answered. 'I thought I should practise.' Swirling the blossom around her breast, he added, 'The letter S was always hard.'

'I know something else that is hard,' she answered, reaching for him.

When her palm closed over his shaft, he inhaled sharply and let the heather fall to the linen sheets. Lowering his mouth to her skin, he began to kiss her, over her shoulders and up to the sensitive place upon her throat. She wanted him. He could sense it in the way her pulse pounded beneath his lips.

He kissed the column of her throat and brought his hand lower. She tightened her grasp upon him and he wanted her so badly, he fought to control his lust.

'Slow down, sweet.'

'Perhaps I don't want to.' Her thumb moved over the crest of his erection, and she sent him a wicked smile. 'I was abducted this night by a Scottish warrior. I hope to be ravished by him.'

He removed his clothing, sitting beside her on the bed. 'If that is your wish.'

He took her breast in his mouth, suckling hard against the taut nipple. A shocked breath escaped her, along with a sigh of pleasure. Marguerite's face transformed with need, colour rising in her cheeks. She rolled to her side, whispering against his mouth, 'You're a temptation I never could resist, Callum.' She ran her fingers over his back. 'Let me touch you for a moment.'

He stilled, letting her do as she pleased. She guided him to rest upon his stomach and she straddled him, her damp womanhood touching his lower spine. With her hands, she touched the scars of his past, trailing her fingers across his back.

'I remember the day I found you. I was so afraid you might die.' She bent and touched her mouth to his scars and the motion grazed her breasts against him. It was torment, having to remain still and not touch her, while she caressed him. 'I think, somehow, I knew we would be together.'

'I thought you were an angel of mercy,' he admitted. 'Perhaps you were. Because I swear, on my life, this is my heaven.'

He rolled her over, needing to pleasure her, to worship every part of her skin. He filled his palms with her breasts while, below the waist, he nudged himself between her legs. Marguerite raised her knees up, welcoming him. She gasped as he rubbed against her cleft while his fingers coaxed and fondled her breasts.

'Tell me how you want to be touched.'

Her breath caught in her lungs when he warmed her skin, awaiting her response. She guided the head of him into her moist passage and he pressed forward within her slick flesh, filling her up.

He tasted her, nibbling the curve beneath her breast. Her nipple hardened, showing him that she liked his kiss. 'Tell me, Marguerite.'

She moved against him, pulling him deeper inside, murmuring in French as she tried to make him move.

'I don't speak French, *a ghràidh*.' But he acted on instinct, thrusting within her until she cried out with shivered ecstasy. Slowly, he moved her hips to the edge of the bed and he stood, still sheathed inside her. With her legs around his waist, he drove inside her, penetrating from a higher angle.

Her fingers dug into the bed, her eyes wild as she submitted to his thrusts, arching hard. Her walls clenched his shaft and she trembled at the force of his lovemaking.

'I love you, my wife,' he said, filling her again.

'Je t'aime,' she responded, reaching for his hips. Callum ground himself against her and saw the renewed look of arousal in her eyes. The intense contact made her shudder. When he began to plunge with a rhythm, pressing his body harder against her centre, she began speaking words of encouragement.

'There,' she pleaded, telling him how much she loved the touch of him deep inside her.

The exquisite pleasure of watching her reach for release, her body trembling with need, was making him grow harder within her. She was so wet, so eager, he couldn't stop the shout that roared from him when her legs tightened around his waist, grasping him with all her strength as the release flooded through her.

He kept up the pulsing rhythm until his own satisfaction came hard and fast. And when he lay down on top of her, their bodies were merged together as one. Callum held her close, his heart beating so fast, he couldn't believe she now belonged to him.

'You were mine since the moment I saw you,' he murmured against her hair.

She smiled up at him and in her blue eyes he saw the unspoken promise of every tomorrow they would spend together.

No other words were needed.

Epilogue

Four years later...

A group of messengers rode into Glen Arrin, wearing the insignia representing Edward of Caernarfon, the King of England. When Marguerite saw them, she clutched her young infant daughter protectively. From the serious manner of the men, she could not imagine that they bore good news.

'Stay back,' Callum warned, transferring his bow into his left hand. His three-year-old son Ailric gripped the child-sized bow in his own hand, mirroring his actions.

'Do you want me to take the children away?' Marguerite asked, unsure of whom the messenger had come to see.

'Not yet. They didn't come to fight.' Callum nodded behind him. 'But keep your distance. Go with your mother,' he warned Ailric.

'I help,' Ailric offered, raising his miniature bow. Callum ruffled the boy's hair, pushing him back to Marguerite.

'Do as I say, son.'

The men remained outside the gates and Callum walked closer to them. Marguerite held the baby and gripped Ailric's hand, her heart pounding with fear. Though they had done nothing wrong, she couldn't guess why the king's men would be here.

A few moments later, the men entered the fortress, led by Dougal. The young adolescent had grown into a handsome young man and Marguerite hoped that one day he would find a good woman to wed. He spent far too much time tending the animals instead of sharing time with people.

'Why have you come?' Callum asked, still keeping his bow in one hand.

'We wish to speak with Lady Marguerite de Mont-pierre, daughter of the Duc D'Avignois, wife of Callum MacKinloch,' the first man said.

Marguerite stepped forward. 'I am she.'

Callum remained in front of her, and she didn't miss the subtle tension in his stance. If needed, he could re-lease half-a-dozen arrows, defending them.

'And you were once betrothed to Peter Warrington, the Earl of Penrith?'

She nodded. 'Has something happened?' Fear rose in her stomach. Lord Penrith had been a good man, one she'd been fond of, even if she could never wed him. After her marriage to Callum, he had written to her from time to time and seemed especially pleased that she'd birthed a son so shortly after she'd wed.

The messenger came forward and inclined his head, acknowledging Marguerite. 'The Earl of Penrith is a good *friend* of His Majesty's.'

A blush coloured her cheeks, for she now under-

stood who it was that Lord Penrith had been fond o
And it was no wonder he could not share in the lif
he'd wanted.

'What does this have to do with me?'

'His Majesty wished to bestow more estates upo
the earl, as gifts. There are lands here that were seize
by the king. It is his Royal Wish that peace be restore
in Scotland.'

Marguerite waited, still not understanding what th
messengers were speaking of. 'But why—?'

'His Majesty, out of favour and love for Lord Per
rith, has agreed to grant the earl's request. The land i
Scotland will be given to your firstborn son.'

Shock rendered her speechless and she could thin
of no reply. The earl had wealth enough of his own an
needed nothing further. That he had passed the land o
to her son was a gift she had never expected.

The messenger's gaze fell upon Ailric and he adde
'The King has honoured the bequest. You and your hus
band shall guard the land until your son comes of age

Marguerite dug her fingers into Callum's arm, hop
ing he would understand what this meant. He exchange
a look with her and nodded. Covering her hand with hi
own, he asked the messenger, 'Should we plan a visit t
court, in order to offer our thanks to the king?'

The messenger inclined his head. 'That would b
most wise. And Lady Marguerite may wish to spen
time with Her Majesty, Queen Isabella, since they shar
the same homeland.'

The man began speaking of land rights, but befor
he could go on, Callum interrupted. 'Where is this lan
that will be granted to our son?'

'It is a few days' journey from here.' He shrugge

The keep burned to the ground, I fear, and it isn't a large fortress, by any means.'

A strange premonition sank within her blood and Marguerite suspected where this was leading. 'Who owned the land before?'

'The Earl of Cairnross,' the messenger admitted. 'You may have heard of him.'

Marguerite nearly choked at the mention of the man who had killed her maid and caused torment to so many prisoners. To own the land, rebuilding a fortress upon the blood of so many men, seemed like a cruel jest.

Callum gripped her hand to keep her calm. In his eyes, she saw the reassurance.

'Come inside and you may take shelter with us before you return to England,' he offered to the messenger. To his younger brother Dougal, he instructed, 'See to it that Laren finds a place for these men.'

The messenger withdrew a gold ring and handed it to Marguerite. 'This ring is to be given to your son. It belongs to the earl and is a sign of the king's favour.'

She smiled and thanked him, concealing the ring in her palm. Her daughter began to fuss and Marguerite handed the infant over to Callum, where she calmed instantly.

The men followed Dougal back to the fortress. When they had gone, she turned back to Callum. 'Will it be painful for you to return to Cairnross?'

He shook his head. 'The memories of that place will never be gone from me. But we'll rebuild it and make new ones.' Leaning in, he stole a kiss from her. 'I always wanted to give you land and a castle. I suppose I finally can, thanks to the earl.'

With their children between them, she rested her

forehead against his. 'I never needed them, Callum
Smiling at their son and daughter, she added, 'Fo
you've already given me treasures beyond price.'

* * * * *